THE DUKE
GETS DESPERATE

His gaze dropped to her mouth. "This attraction between us is a curse."

Raya sucked in a breath. Putting words to the connection, saying it aloud, made the inexplicable pull between them terrifyingly real. "I don't know what you're talking about."

"Liar."

She licked her lips. "The very idea is repulsive."

His pupils dilated as he watched the movement of her tongue. "Nauseating."

"We should keep as far away from each other as possible."

"An ocean would not be far enough away," he growled, "to relieve myself of the affliction of you."

Also by Diana Quincy

DIANA QUINCY

THE DUKE GETS DESPERATE

Sirens in Silk

AVON

An Imprint of HarperCollinsPublishers

THE DUKE GETS DESPERATE. Copyright © 2023 by Dora Mekouar. All rights reserved. Printed in the United States of America. No part of this book may be used or reproduced in any manner whatsoever without written permission except in the case of brief quotations embodied in critical articles and reviews. For information, address HarperCollins Publishers, 195 Broadway, New York, NY 10007.

First Avon Books mass market printing: September 2023

Print Edition ISBN: 978-0-06-324749-9
Digital Edition ISBN: 978-0-06-324751-2

Cover design by Amy Halperin
Cover illustration by Victor Gadino
Cover images © Dreamstime.com; © Shutterstock

Avon, Avon & logo, and Avon Books & logo are registered trademarks of HarperCollins Publishers in the United States of America and other countries.

HarperCollins is a registered trademark of HarperCollins Publishers in the United States of America and other countries.

FIRST EDITION

23 24 25 26 27   BVGM   10 9 8 7 6 5 4 3 2 1

To Taoufiq, for painting our lives
with your love for us

THE DUKE GETS DESPERATE

CHAPTER ONE

Yorkshire, England
1886

As far as funerals went, this was one of the more aggravating.

Standing by the graveside as the vicar droned on, Anthony Carey, Duke of Strickland, resisted the urge to swat a fly that buzzed past his nose. He felt like a fraud presiding over the entombment of a woman he detested. But there was no one else to bury his stepmother. The late Duchess of Strickland had no children and her blood relatives were an ocean away. Deena Darwish Carey was proving a nuisance in both life and death.

"This turnout is pathetic," murmured the Honorable Mr. Guy Vaughan. "I do hope more than a dozen people show up when they put me in the ground."

"You should probably try to be nicer to people," advised Basil Trevelyn, Earl of Hawksworth. The three men, close friends since university, stood shoulder to shoulder. They were joined by a handful of servants and villagers who came to attend the duchess one final time.

To Strick's surprise, he experienced a pang of sympathy for Deena. He'd never wondered whether the flamboyant American ever felt lonely in England with no family or close friends. Strick assumed she'd take a string of lovers after losing her much older husband, but Deena led a surprisingly quiet life after being widowed two years earlier.

"At least Strick finally gets his castle back." Guy spoke quietly. "Assuming Deena kept her word and left Tremayne to you."

"It should have been mine all along," Strick muttered. The bitterness of losing his childhood home to a foreign interloper lingered. As did the shock of discovering his late father had deliberately allowed the entail on the castle to lapse so he could leave the property to his wife, rather than his son and heir to his title.

"Who else would the late duchess leave the castle to? She has no relations in England." Hawk waved a hand in front of his face. "Damn flies."

"True," Guy put in. "And Deena did say, on more than one occasion, that the late duke wanted the castle to stay in the family."

Hawk shooed another fly away. "Let's hope she obliged him."

Anticipation shot through Strick's veins. The reading of the will was scheduled for immediately after the funeral. Castle Tremayne, home to eight generations of Careys, was in Strick's blood.

He knew every turret, each battlement and every inch of the bailey by heart.

He and his sisters had played attack on the castle countless times as children, defending Tremayne against imaginary invaders, only to have Father surrender the castle to one very real transgressor. Hopefully, the Deena disaster could finally be put into the past, a tiny blip in the long history of Castle Tremayne and the Dukes of Strickland.

Strick surveyed the familiar faces assembled in the churchyard—some somber, others obviously bored. The mourners included Tremayne's butler and housekeeper, the local seamstress and her husband, who ran the village tavern, and Elton Foley, the local railroad factor who wanted to lay tracks through Strick's property. An offer Strick repeatedly rebuffed.

A loud sniffle cut through the air. Strick looked in the direction of the noise, his gaze landing on the lone unfamiliar face in the small crowd, an elegant, well-dressed woman draped in black lace. He had the fleeting impression of enormous dark eyes before she looked down, obscuring her face. She dabbed a snowy kerchief against her cheeks. Was she *crying*?

"Finally," Guy muttered. "I need a drink."

Strick belatedly realized the vicar had stopped talking. The gravediggers approached with shovels in hand. People scattered, returning to the business of the day. Life went on.

"Good luck with the will," Hawk said before

going off with Guy. "Join us at the tavern after?"

Strick nodded. He watched for a moment as the gravediggers shoveled dirt onto Deena's coffin. When they were almost done, he thanked the vicar and prepared to depart. He paused, glancing around for the mysterious woman. But she was gone.

Putting her out of his mind, Strick strode out of the churchyard to reclaim his castle.

"MY STEPMOTHER DID *what*?" Outrage slammed through Strick. That witch saved the very best for last, delivering one final wallop from the grave. He should have known. What a fool he was to hope.

"Her Grace left the castle to a Miss Raya Darwish of New York City." Combs, his late father's solicitor, looked suitably sympathetic as he repeated the terms of the late Duchess of Strickland's will. "But, naturally, you retain all of the land, including the tenant houses and—"

"Those are already mine," he snapped. "Father left them to me." The late duke's will gave Strick most of the land while Deena got the castle, the gardens and a small adjacent meadow. His head felt as if it was about to explode. Losing Tremayne once was bad enough. But twice? It was a serrated dagger straight through the heart. "Who the devil is Raya Darwish?"

"That would be me," a smoky, American-accented feminine voice said from behind him.

Strick pivoted in his chair. It was *her*. On the threshold to the library stood the woman in black lace from the funeral. "And who the devil are you?"

Huge, almond-shaped eyes with uptilted corners met his. "Who is asking?"

Few people, and even fewer women, looked him straight in the eye. Most were intimidated by his title. "I am the Duke of Strickland."

She did not cower. Far from it. "Is that your actual name?" She pronounced her letters softly, the words much less crisp than the King's English. "Or do you have a name like the rest of us mere mortals?"

"Anthony Carey, at your service."

She lifted a dark brow. "Somehow I doubt that." Miss Darwish focused on the solicitor. "Do forgive me for being tardy, Mr. Combs. I had to settle my aunt at the inn. She isn't feeling well."

Combs stood. "Not at all. It's only a few minutes past the hour. His Grace was eager to begin."

"Begin?" she asked politely.

Strick reluctantly came to his feet. A gentleman did not sit in the presence of a lady. "How did you know Deena?"

"What business is that of yours?" She shot him a cool glance. "Are all dukes rude, or is it just you?"

Strick gritted his teeth. Few people dismissed a duke with such casual disregard. He was accustomed to being treated with deference. But this woman was American. What did he expect?

Combs's face reddened. "The contents of the will have proven upsetting to His Grace."

"Who's Grace?"

"No, no." Combs smiled, obviously dazzled by the woman. She wasn't a standard beauty, but those dusky luminous eyes, sharp-cut cheekbones and smooth olive-toned skin drew a man's notice. "'His Grace' is how one refers to a duke."

She looked bored. Ignoring Strick, Miss Darwish focused on the solicitor. "I do not mean to be rude but why have you asked to see me? I really should return to my aunt."

Strick stared at her. "Is it possible that you don't know?"

She closed her eyes and exhaled slowly before tipping that arresting gaze to meet his. "I do not believe I was speaking to you."

Strick rolled his tongue in his cheek, struggling to keep his temper in check. "You expect us to believe that Deena just sprang this on you?"

She looked at Combs. "To what is Grace referring?"

Combs pressed his lips inward. "The Duke of Strickland is referred to as *His* Grace, not Grace. And *His* Grace is referring to the fact that the late Duchess of Strickland has left her castle to you."

Her plush mouth dropped open. "She *what*?"

"Left. Her. Castle. To. You." Strick emphasized

each word like he would for someone with hearing problems. Or for an imbecile.

"This great big pile of rocks?" Surprise lit her face, adding a luminous quality to her skin. She shook her head. "Impossible."

"On that, we agree." Disbelief pumped through Strick. "What was your relationship to Deena?"

She blinked. "She is . . . she was my father's cousin."

"Well, she bloody well never mentioned you," Strick snapped. "What a convenient time for Deena's mysterious relations to finally make an appearance."

"My aunt and I journeyed here from New York," she told him, still obviously dazed. "We departed America shortly after Cousin Deena invited us to visit."

"New York? I am acquainted with a family that lives on Fifth Avenue, the Van Ackers. They're of Dutch origin, I believe." Maybe she'd go running back to her New York life as soon as she realized how far in debt the castle was. "Perhaps you are acquainted with them?"

"That is doubtful." She shook her head, as if still trying to fully comprehend her sudden change in circumstances. "We do not keep company with the sort of people who live on Fifth Avenue. And our people are Arab, not Dutch."

"Is that so?" Deena never mentioned having Levantine origins. But it made sense given her gently bronzed skin, and the dark hair and eyes shared with the woman before him. He wasn't surprised Deena lied about her background. He'd pegged her for a fraud the moment she arrived on his father's arm. "Deena said her family had a home on Fifth Avenue and a country seat in New Jersey at Fairlawn, near Paterson, New Jersey."

"My uncle lives in Paterson and he owns a shop." She regarded him through narrowed eyes. "There are many Arab businesses in Paterson, but I've never heard of any of the Darwishes owning a country estate. We are a merchant family."

"I see." Confirmation that Deena was a fraud wasn't as satisfying as Strick might expect. Especially not now. "And what sort of work does your father engage in, if you don't mind my asking?"

She lifted her chin, the light in her eyes burning so brightly that he almost blinked. "Darwish and Company manufactures and distributes the finest silk embroidered table linens along the entire eastern coast and possibly in the west as well."

"You're a factory worker."

"Hardly." Disdain punctuated each word. "My family *owns* the enterprise. We employ thirty-six workers."

"I see." Deena had handed his castle over to the daughter of an American merchant. "And when did you last see your cousin?"

"Never."

"Never?" he repeated.

"We corresponded regularly and were supposed to meet for the first time this week. But I arrived too late." She swallowed, her eyes watering. "And now, I will never have the opportunity to know my cousin."

Deena gave his castle away to some girl she'd never even met? He stared at Raya Darwish. "Perhaps she invited you here to tell you that she intended to leave *my* castle to you."

"If it's your castle, how could Deena leave it to me?"

"Well, technically . . . What I meant . . . It's—" He allowed the words to die on his tongue. Frustrated disappointment ripped through him. He had to escape. Strick stormed out of the library. He'd entered just minutes earlier, hopeful that this was his library. That the halls leading to it all finally belonged to him.

Not that Tremayne belonged to any duke. If anything, the dukes belonged to the castle. Like the eight dukes before him, all the way back to his Cornish ancestor who built the castle centuries ago after wedding the daughter of a local lord, Strick was supposed to be a caretaker. His responsibility was to hold the castle and all of its valuables in trust for future generations. He owed it to Tremayne's past inhabitants. And to the ones yet to be born.

But restoring and protecting Tremayne was out of his hands now. First Father, and now Deena, had seen to that, carelessly giving away a treasure neither of them earned. All it took to thwart four hundred years of history was one debauched duke and his grasping American wife.

Miss Raya Darwish, a Yank with no understanding or apparent appreciation for English customs and conventions, who'd never set eyes on Castle Tremayne until a few minutes ago, was free to do whatever she wanted with the treasure that had been home to generations of Careys.

And there wasn't a damn thing he could do about it.

RAYA TIGHTENED HER mantle around her as the duke stomped out the door. He was well-built and not unhandsome, with a structured jaw and pale brown eyes hooded by a heavy brow bone. His tawny hair was neatly combed except for a cowlick that sprang from the back of his head. But any physical appeal he might have was negated by his boorish behavior.

"Well," she remarked to the solicitor after the duke made a slammed-door exit, "his manners leave something to be desired." Not that she expected any better. She'd recently learned to anticipate the worst from men.

"His Grace is understandably upset," Mr. Combs said soothingly. "This is the second time he's been disinherited."

"If what I just witnessed is his usual graceless behavior, then it is no wonder." She was practically disinherited herself when her brother tossed her out of the family business after Baba died. But she hadn't behaved like a spoiled brat and lashed out at everyone.

"You may take possession of the castle immediately," Mr. Combs was saying. "Would you like the staff to remove your things from the inn?"

"Oh . . . I think my aunt and I can manage on our own." Raya couldn't believe she was expected to take possession of a dilapidated old castle. She shivered at the thought of moving into the drafty fortress. Strolling barefoot in a New York blizzard sounded more appealing. "May I ask, how did Deena die?"

"Her Grace fell from the ruins of an old abbey on the property. It's quite the tragedy."

Unease rippled through Raya. "Are you certain she left the castle to me?" she asked, half hoping it was a terrible mistake. "There isn't some error?"

"Quite sure. You may see for yourself." He handed a document to her. Deena's will. Feeling light-headed, Raya lowered herself onto the nearest seat, a worn, cracked leather chair. Inhaling the cool stale air, she tried to digest the words before her.

"As you can see," the solicitor said, "all is in order. You are the new owner of Castle Tremayne. You are a very fortunate young lady."

She didn't feel lucky. The musty stone walls seemed to be closing in on her. "And I can move in immediately?"

"Of course. The castle is yours. You must treat it as such."

"But . . . Where will the duke live?"

"He owns a comfortable house on the property."

"I see." Taking up residence in a decaying mausoleum was the very last thing Raya wanted to do. Especially without Deena. But her funds were running low and staying at the inn was costly. Renewed anger toward her brother burned behind her collarbone.

The company is no place for a girl, Salem had said. *You should marry.* But they both knew the true reason he pushed her out of Darwish and Company. Raya understood more about running a business than Salem ever could and her brother didn't care to be shown up by a woman.

It was Raya's idea to expand from tablecloths to include matching napkins and towel sets. She alone thought to hire the local Arab women on Washington Street to embroider the goods, using traditional Palestinian stitchery to make Darwish linens stand apart. Raya convinced the uptown shops to carry their products and, once the society ladies discovered Darwish's unique silk embroidered goods, company profits more than doubled. Thanks to Raya's initiative, Darwish and Company's embroidered linens could now be found in some of the finest homes on Fifth Avenue.

But none of those accomplishments mattered now. With no income and meager savings, Raya was reduced to depending on Salem's largesse for her daily expenses. Visiting Deena was supposed to be a respite from all that. And now this.

It was altogether too much to process at once. But Raya resolved to tackle the problem in her usual way.

"Thank you, Mr. Combs." Rising, she shook out her skirts, the floorboards groaning beneath her half boots. "This has all been a terrible shock, but I suppose we must get on with it."

CHAPTER TWO

A castle?" Aunt Majida repeated in Arabic when Raya returned to the inn to find her snuggled in bed with her *tatreez*. Majida didn't look up as she stitched neat silk thread patterns into the linen fabric. "What is it like?"

Raya grimaced. "Old and smelly. And the walls make strange noises. *Wallah*, I swear it sounds like there is something alive in there."

"Why would Deena leave her castle to you and not the son? Boys are supposed to inherit."

"I have no idea." Raya plopped into the nearest chair. "And why shouldn't girls be allowed to have anything of their own?"

"A girl has a husband to support her." She looked up from her *tatreez* just long enough to throw Raya a pointed look. "Unless the girl is too stubborn. But a boy, he has the responsibility of taking care of his family. That's why your Baba, *Allah yerhamo*—may God have mercy on his soul—left the business to Salem."

"Men cannot be trusted," Raya retorted. "I put all of my faith in Salem and look where that got me."

Auntie's mouth twisted. "Salem takes care

of you, Naila and your mother. He pays for the house and the food and takes care of your Baba's business. He's a good boy. You should be ashamed to talk bad about him."

"We shall see how well Salem manages the business on his own." Her brother was affable and charismatic, but lacked the drive and acumen required to make a business thrive.

"If your head wasn't so hard, you'd already be married. Boys don't like girls who are too strong-willed. Or too smart."

Raya's brother was certainly proof of that. They'd worked well together for the longest time. Raya thought they were close, but then Baba died and everything turned upside down. "I'm not going to pretend I'm a *habila* to make a man feel better about himself."

The windows rattled as wind whistled through them. Rain spattered against the panes.

"Curse the devil," Auntie Majida grumbled, setting her needlework aside to pull the stiff bed linens up to her neck. "The weather here is so cold and damp."

"You did not have to accompany me." Once Raya announced her intention to travel to England against her mother's wishes, her late father's widowed sister insisted on chaperoning.

"Of course I did. A young girl cannot travel alone. Although," Auntie amended, "you are not so young anymore."

"Exactly. I am twenty-six, far past marriageable

age and, therefore, well past requiring a chaperone."

"If you acted shy and quiet when eligible boys came to meet you, you'd be married by now."

"I refuse to behave like someone I am not." She had this same conversation with Mama dozens of times. "I have a brain."

"Then use it!" Auntie shook her head. "Both you and your sister Naila are not clever enough to get married. Nadine is *shatra*." Nadine, their eldest sister, was married with children. Naila, the middle sister, remained unwed at the age of twenty-eight.

"I don't see what is so clever about getting married. Women take a terrible risk when they depend on a man to guarantee their future."

"*Hakki fathee.* Stop with the empty talk. A girl is meant to get married."

Raya fell back on her usual argument. "What can I do? It's not my fault that my *naseeb* hasn't shown up." Arabs believed in fated mates, which meant that destiny would deliver your life partner at the right time.

Majida ignored that comment. "I cannot believe Deena left her house to you. You never even met."

"We knew each other through our letters." She and Cousin Deena had exchanged weekly missives for the past year. "When Baba died, she wrote to Mama to express her condolences. She also sent me a very kind note and we corresponded regularly after that. Deena told me Baba always said I was like her."

"God forbid! She was *dashra*. Deena did whatever she wanted without thinking about how it would hurt our family name."

A knot formed in Raya's throat. "I looked forward to her letters and came to value her advice."

Majida's lips turned downward. "The last thing any respectable young girl should do is listen to that *dashra*."

Deena's letters were full of amusing anecdotes and observations about life in England. Even though they'd never met, the two women bonded through their letters. "I wrote to Deena about Salem making me leave the company. She knew how much it upset me and was very kind and consoling."

Auntie blew out her lips, making a derisive sound. "Only women whose families need money should work. We are not poor. You working makes the entire family look bad."

Raya resisted the urge to lash out. Baba had expected Raya and Salem to continue working together after his death. She and her brother were once close. Raya focused on the nuts and bolts of business operations while Salem, with his warm charisma, was the salesman and face of the business. That's how Baba had set things up but, on paper, her father left the business to his son.

But right after Baba died, Mama pushed Salem

to banish Raya from the business. *Maybe now she'll stop being hardheaded and find a husband to marry.* Salem laughed it off at first but changed his tune after he and Raya butted heads over business matters in the weeks after Baba died. Her brother's betrayal stunned Raya. She'd never forgive him.

"And now Deena is dead." Auntie sighed. "What a *mushkila*. A big problem. What are we supposed to do now?"

"We are going to get on with it."

"How do we do that?"

"We start by packing our bags and moving into my new castle."

"A FACTORY WORKER?" Guy exclaimed when Strick joined his friends at the tavern. "Your evil-but-glorious stepmama left your castle to an American factory worker?"

Strick reached for his tankard. "Deena was far from glorious."

Guy sipped his ale. "Given the chance, I would have bedded her in an instant."

"There's no accounting for taste." Many men found Deena alluring. Strick was not one of them. He drew deeply on his hand-rolled cigarette, an expense he might not be able to afford for much longer, given the sorry state of his financial affairs. The rents and meager crop yield barely covered servants' wages and minimal castle upkeep.

Guy sighed. "Pity she isn't an heiress. One could more easily overlook her common roots if Miss Darwish possessed a substantial fortune like all of these American heiresses wedding into the nobility."

"*Buying* into English society," Hawk corrected. The earl was a bachelor with a dim view of love and marriage. "Purchasing an aristocratic husband as if they were shopping on Bond Street."

"Bartering a title for wealth is hardly a new concept." Strick's father wed his mother, a viscount's daughter of considerable wealth, for her dowry. It was an unhappy match, one Strick had no intention of emulating. "I am personally against marrying for money. I saw firsthand how miserable it made my parents."

But Strick could understand the temptation. The noblemen needed the cash infusion for their crumbling estates. Agriculture had sustained noble families like Strick's for generations but lower crop prices and rents were making modern life difficult. England once led the world in grain production, but now the Americans were growing the crop on their endless prairies. Many tenant farmers were abandoning the countryside for employment in the city.

"Do not tell me you intend to marry for love?" Guy said to Strick.

"God forbid," Hawk interjected with a mirthless laugh. "Love is a sham. It is far wiser to approach marriage as a business transaction."

Guy studied him. "One day you will tell us what happened to you in America."

"No," Hawk responded, "I will not."

Strick knew better than to question Hawk about his long-ago visit to Philadelphia. Whatever occurred during Hawk's three months in America transformed him. A far more cynical person returned from abroad—the light within him visibly dimmed—than the agreeable man with a ready laugh who'd departed.

"I don't know about wedding for love," Strick said. "But I do hope to at least like and respect my wife. I delayed marriage until I could put Tremayne to rights . . . but that is no longer my role." His stomach burned, rioting against the reality that Castle Tremayne was truly lost.

"I hear Viscount Hamilton is selling the family seat in Wiltshire," Hawk said. "He can't keep up with the costs."

Guy lifted his glass in the duke's direction. "Strick could sell his metalwork collection."

"I fully intended to once the castle was mine." Strick's responsibility to his home took precedence over his treasured antiquities. "Unfortunately, two of my most valuable pieces, a couple of goblets, disappeared a few months before Deena's demise." He wouldn't put it past his stepmama to sell his relics to fund her opulent lifestyle, but she adamantly denied touching them.

"You could always dig up a few more." Guy twisted his lips. "Although how you can stand to muck around in the dirt, I will never comprehend."

"There is nothing that fascinates me more." Strick didn't expect Guy to understand his interest in artifacts from a civilization that existed several hundred years ago. "In fact, I am off tomorrow to visit an excavation site in Northamptonshire." It was an important dig, but going away also meant that he wouldn't have to watch Miss Darwish take possession of his home.

"Maybe you'll find some new shiny baubles," Guy said. "Although I fail to see the point of collecting old things if you don't intend to make a profit. You've never sold anything."

"My interest is in decoding the hidden meaning etched into these ornamental objects." Over the years, Strick had become so expert in the language of Anglo-Saxon art that both collectors and academics sought his opinion. "If I hadn't been born a duke, I would happily spend my life going from one dig to the next."

Guy grimaced. "That sounds rather dusty to me. I'll stick to gaming dens. Hell, I'll even take a ballroom with giggling debutantes over muddying my boots."

"These pieces tell us so much about the lives of the people who made them," Strick explained, despite knowing his words fell on deaf ears.

"There are times when you are truly boring." Guy made a show of yawning. "Let us return to the far more interesting subject of Miss Darwish.

She actually *admitted* to you that she works in a factory?"

"It's hardly a crime to work for your livelihood. Miss Darwish *claims* her family owns the enterprise. But maybe mendacity runs in the family. Deena certainly lied about her origins."

"As Miss Darwish should. Why reveal one's background if it is less than glorious?"

"What do you think she'll do with the castle?" Hawk asked.

"I've no idea." The reality of Deena's duplicity slammed into Strick again. "Drive it into the ground more so than it already is?"

The three friends sat in somber silence contemplating Strick's immeasurable loss. Guy owned his home outright, a gift from his viscount father to his second son. Hawk might face various financial challenges related to his various estates, but he'd never expected to inherit at all. His cousin, the late Earl of Hawksworth, perished in a carriage accident along with his three young sons, leaving no direct male heirs. So the title fell to Hawk, the next eldest male relative.

Strick took a long pull on his cigarette. It wasn't the physical loss of his home that cut the deepest, it was his inability to pick up the mantle, as he'd been groomed to do practically since birth, and carry the legacy forward to the next generation. The silence broke when Elton Foley, the railroad man, approached them.

"May I offer my deepest condolences, Your Grace?"

"Foley," Strick said in greeting.

"I wonder if you have reconsidered my proposal."

"I have not. I will not allow a loud, smoky railroad to despoil the natural beauty of my land." Strick stared the man down. "Now, if you will excuse us, I am having a drink with my friends."

"Of course, of course." Foley dipped his chin and vanished into the tavern crowd.

"What is she like?" Guy asked once Foley was gone.

"Who? Miss Darwish?" Strick pulled on his cigarette. "She's a termagant."

"Is she at all like the late duchess?" Hawk inquired.

"Only in that both are thoroughly disagreeable." Strick exhaled. "And they share the same coloring—dark hair and dark eyes." Deena, small and trim, had been the life of the party, given to laughter, dancing, singing off-key or otherwise causing a commotion. Miss Darwish seemed quite the opposite. She was of average height and curvaceous, contained and reserved. A steely ice queen with a barbed tongue.

Hawk bottomed out his drink. "Were they close? Your stepmother and the merchant girl?"

"No." Acid burned in Strick's stomach. "Miss Darwish says they never met."

"What?" Astonishment stamped Guy's face. "Then why did Stepmama leave the castle to her?"

"Probably to twist the knife in the chest wound caused when Father left the castle to her."

Hawk frowned. "I thought Deena intended to leave the castle to you, or your heir, so that Tremayne would remain in the family."

Strick lifted his glass in mock salute. "It's no surprise Deena wasn't a woman of her word. She and the cousin probably cooked up this scheme together."

"An American merchant inheriting an English castle," Guy said. "The girl must feel like a princess in a storybook."

Strick poured the ale down his throat. "Just wait until she has a look at the estate ledgers." He set the empty tankard down with a clank. "She's about to discover that life at Castle Tremayne is no fairy tale."

CHAPTER THREE

The sun cut across Raya's face. She stretched, taking care not to disturb Auntie Majida snoring beside her. They'd fallen asleep almost immediately after arriving at the castle the previous evening. A nice tenant farmer from the nearby village, Mr. Price, gave them a ride from the inn.

Raya snuggled into the soft feather mattress and luxurious bed linens. Cousin Deena clearly had an appreciation for life's finer things. Her rooms in the family wing were a bright spot in the otherwise dreary castle. Everything else Raya had seen so far was tired, faded and in desperate need of refurbishment, but the duchess's generous rooms were the opposite.

They were fresh and clean, the mint velvet bed linens of the latest fashion. A matching sofa and pair of chairs faced the marbled hearth. The chamber felt like a shiny, new trespasser in the moldy castle. Raya yawned, burrowing into the warmth of the massive four-poster bed, happy to keep the rest of the castle at bay for just a little bit longer. Closing her eyes, she must have dozed off. When she blinked her eyes open again, a sharp, red-tinged gaze stared back at her.

Raya yelped and shot up to a sitting position. Then she recognized Mrs. Shaw, the humorless housekeeper they'd met last night.

"Good morning, Miss Darwish."

Beside Raya, Majida jerked awake. "*Shoo*? What! What is it?"

"Good morning, Mrs. Kassab," Mrs. Shaw said.

"It *was*, until I saw you," Majida mumbled in Arabic, her voice scratchy with sleep. "Why is this female donkey waking us up?"

The housekeeper's cold gaze moved from Raya to Majida and back again. "At Castle Tremayne, the morning meal is served at nine a.m."

What time was it? Raya rarely slept late. And how had the housekeeper gotten in? Raya was positive she'd bolted the chamber door before going to sleep. "Could you have the tray brought up?" They'd enjoyed tea and sandwiches in Deena's chambers the previous evening.

The housekeeper pursed her lips. "Unmarried young ladies take their breakfast in the morning room. Only wedded ladies are allowed the morning meal in their rooms. Would Mrs. Kassab care to breakfast here?"

"We'll both eat in the morning room," Raya said.

"Very well. I've brought in warm water. Your bags have been unpacked and your clothes ironed."

Majida continued speaking in Arabic. "Hopefully, they didn't steal anything."

"Thank you, Mrs. Shaw," Raya said. "We shall be down for breakfast as soon as we're dressed."

"Very good, Miss Darwish." The housekeeper remained planted in place.

"Why is she standing there like a donkey?" Majida rattled off in Arabic. An uneasy silence descended, broken only by Majida coughing.

Mrs. Shaw wore an expectant expression. "There is no lady's maid at present. I shall help you dress."

Majida scowled. "*Hill 'an teezi.* Now she wants to see a show?"

"What is she saying?" Mrs. Shaw regarded the other woman with suspicion. "I am afraid I do not understand Mrs. Kassab."

Raya wasn't about to tell the housekeeper that Majida had just told Mrs. Shaw to get away from her arsehole. "Thank you, but we do not require assistance."

Mrs. Shaw closed her eyes and took a long breath. "It is the custom of the ladies of the house to be dressed and bathed by a lady's maid."

Raya didn't have a personal lady's maid back home. The upstairs maid attended to her and Naila when they needed help getting ready. "As I said," she spoke firmly, "we shall be fine on our own."

Mrs. Shaw didn't appear to think much of Raya's plan, but she assented. "As you like." The housekeeper departed, her nose firmly in the air. Once they were dressed, Raya and her aunt emerged from the duchess's warm rooms. They were met by a whoosh of chilly air and a young man with red, curling hair.

"Miss Darwish and Mrs. Kassab." He bowed. "I am Otis, the footman. I will show you to breakfast."

"What does a footman do?" Raya asked as they followed him.

Otis grinned. "Anything he's asked. But mostly we serve at table, answer the door, wash the dishes after meals, shine shoes and boots as needed, light the lamps in the evening and extinguish them when the family adjourns for the evening."

"Have you worked here long?" Raya asked.

"Coming up on five years. This way."

"I suppose that means that you attended to the duchess."

"I did. It's very sad what happened to her."

"What was she like?"

"She was kind to me. Her Grace liked to laugh."

They descended the spiral staircase and followed Otis down several battered corridors with creaking stone walls. Their destination was a faded room with cracked wallpaper and old-fashioned furniture. Huge silver candelabras dominated a long dark dining table that could easily seat twenty.

They were greeted by the butler. "Good morning." Philips was tall and thin with bulging eyes that reminded Raya of a grasshopper. He stood at attention with his hands clasped behind his back. "Otis will serve you."

The breakfast laid out on the sideboard was in a series of silver platters with domed covers that surely contained far more food than Raya and Auntie Majida could ever consume. Raya preferred to fill her own plate as she did at home. How would Otis know what she liked? But she allowed the butler to seat her at the head of the enormous table.

Majida took the seat beside her and they feasted on eggs, steak, bread, fish and cheese. Breakfast at home was a much lighter affair with eggs, boiled cheese, za'atar with olive oil, labneh, olives and homemade bread.

"The bread isn't as good as mine but the steak is *zaki*, delicious," Majida declared as she polished off her second plate of food. Her words were punctuated by a deep cough.

Raya studied her aunt's worn face. "I hope you are not getting sick."

"The weather here is so cold and damp. I've been touched by the chill."

"Maybe you should rest."

Philips cleared his throat. "I thought I would give you a tour of the castle after breakfast, if Mrs. Kassab is up to it."

"*Yalla.*" Majida pushed heavily to her feet. "Let's go see what Deena gave you."

The tour began in the Great Room, an immense chamber with high rafters, generous arched windows and a hearth so massive Raya could easily stand inside of it. She envisioned how magnificent this sulky place must have once been. What had these walls witnessed? The parties, the powerful lords, the intrigue. It wasn't hard to imagine Tremayne as a working castle, alive and thriving, bustling with activity. How sad to find it reduced to a shadowy shell, its past luster stripped away.

Their footfalls echoed as they left the Great Room, passing a wall mural featuring the disembodied faces of people floating along various landscapes. Raya was no art expert, but the mural was terrible.

"What is this?" she asked. "It seems out of place."

"The late duke was an amateur painter," Philips informed them. "He worked with an art teacher, an accomplished artist from the village."

"I hope the teacher didn't get paid," Majida said in Arabic. "That looks like *khara*."

The mural did look like dung but Raya kept that opinion to herself. The butler guided them from room to room until Raya's head was spinning. The castle was an enormous maze, a kaleidoscope of dingy unused rooms, chipped plaster ceilings, dull marble fireplaces and imposing columns with peeling paint. Dusty paintings and artifacts covered most of the walls.

Raya's mood brightened when they reached a delightful round-shaped chamber with arched alcoves and fashionable furnishings. Like the duchess's chambers in the family wing, the morning room stood out among the bleak surroundings like a shiny coin in a puddle of mud. "Oh, this is lovely," Raya said.

"The morning room is where the duchess spent most of her time," Philips informed them. "She had the chamber refurbished."

"That sounds like Deena," Majida murmured in Arabic. "She was a spender."

"And now, perhaps you'd like to see the roof," Philips said.

Raya's throat closed up. "Maybe another time. My aunt is still tired from our journey and she'd like to rest."

Auntie Majida rolled her eyes. *"Khayifa."*

Raya didn't care if her aunt called her a fraidy-cat. No amount of jeering could get Raya on any roof. Not after what happened with her cousin Farouk when she was eleven.

"As you like." The butler led them back to the duchess's rooms, which they would have never been able to find on their own. Majida immediately climbed back into bed and was gently snoring within minutes.

By that evening, Auntie's cough turned into a fever, leaving Majida bedridden for the next few days. Raya stayed with her aunt, sleeping on the sofa and tending to Majida's needs. By the fourth day, Auntie's fever broke and she was back to working on her *tatreez*, cross-stitching wine-red silk thread on a white background. The intricately embroidered panel would one day adorn the bodice of a traditional Palestinian *thobe* dress.

Raya grew restless enough to want to explore the castle. Leaving Auntie happily engrossed in her needlework, she ventured off on her own, roaming the dim corridors, exploring several bedchambers and other spaces whose purpose wasn't entirely clear to her.

The Darwishes lived in a handsome four-story brownstone on Henry Street in Brooklyn, where all of New York's prosperous Arabs lived. But none of the homes in Raya's flourishing New York neighborhood compared to the astonishing scale of the castle.

Turning down a long corridor, Raya spied a spiral staircase and realized she'd reached one of the two castle towers. Philips's tour that first morning hadn't included either tower. Curious about the highest part of the castle, she mounted the staircase, each step grunting beneath her slippers, and came to a closed door.

Finding it unlocked, she pushed it open and ventured inside. The appealing scents of smoke, books and a hint of masculine cologne washed over her. She paused, feeling like an interloper. But then reminded herself that she owned the place.

She forged ahead into rooms furnished with dark woods and worn leather. Books and other artifacts littered the surfaces. The marble hearth was cold and unlit, cleaned free of ashes. Yet the rooms were cozy and inviting, as if the castle had embraced the inhabitant. Had the old duke spent time here? Did the butler or someone else on the property frequent this space?

She wandered into an adjoining room, a study with a desk and shelves full of books and glass-fronted cabinets, a full-length mirror in one corner. As she drew closer, Raya's eyes widened. The cases were full of the most exquisite jewels she'd ever laid eyes on. Her attention went to an intricately carved gold brooch etched with designs that looked like animal limbs. Next to it, a necklace with detailed swirling designs resembling snakes caught the light. A patterned gold-and-garnet bracelet took her breath away. Riveted, she tried to open the case only to find it locked.

"What in Hades do you think you are doing?" a male voice bellowed behind her.

Startled, Raya whipped around, stumbling back against the case. She stared into an angry angled face with a dark stubbled jaw and un-tamed tawny hair. It took her a moment to recognize the Duke of Strickland, looking nothing like the polished, clean-faced nobleman she met at the reading of the will.

This unkempt version of the duke brought to mind a fierce medieval knight, especially against the backdrop of the castle's ancient stone walls. Instead of armor, he wore clothing suited for the outdoors, a loose wool coat that didn't reach his knees and well-worn trousers tucked into the muddy boots.

"Oh," she replied as coolly as she could manage, "it's you."

"Move away from my things," he barked.

"*Your* things?"

"Yes, *my* things." He was an unmovable slab of muscle and roiling anger. "You might have inherited the castle but you don't get to barge into my rooms and help yourself to my relics."

His rooms? "Mr. Combs said you have a house on the property."

"These are . . . were . . . my apartments."

"I didn't realize."

"Well, now you do." He undid the buttons at the neck of his double-breasted coat, baring the strong cords of his throat. She'd never really noticed a man's neck before but glimpsing the tender bare skin felt strangely intimate.

"What are you doing in here?" he growled. "Didn't Philips tell you that these rooms are off-limits?"

"No, he did not." Anger crept in behind the surprise. She straightened to her full height. "And I do not appreciate being accused of snooping."

"Then maybe you should refrain from sneaking into people's rooms and rummaging through their possessions."

He advanced on her, coming near enough for her to realize how strongly built he was, and to note the tiny lines framing his golden-brown gaze. She guessed him to be a few years older than her. Maybe in his midthirties. He also wasn't as tall as he'd first seemed, but with his brawny body and commanding voice, he was an overwhelming presence.

"Surely," he continued, "once you let yourself into my apartments, you realized that someone actually lives here."

Refusing to be intimidated by a bully, Raya resisted the urge to retreat. "Since I now own this castle," she retorted, taking a step forward, "I assumed I have entry to every room."

His heated gaze ran over her. "Are you accustomed to entering a bachelor's accommodations?"

That's when it struck Raya that she was alone with a man in his private rooms. Which had never happened before. It was scandalous. Her Arab relatives would be in fits of shock. Even though society's rules were ridiculous and she was doing nothing wrong, Raya suddenly felt self-conscious. The duke was close enough for his scent to reach her—notes of the outdoor chill, of exertion and tobacco, of shaving soap and male skin.

"I most certainly am not. Not that it is any of your concern." The back of her neck tingled. "As I said, I did not know that you lived here."

"I spend my time between the castle and my cottage on the estate. Storing my artifacts takes a great deal of space. The more valuable pieces are safer here."

Her curiosity overcame her irritation. "What kind of artifacts?" The pieces in the case were breathtaking.

"Anglo-Saxon." The anger lines in his face smoothed a little. "The Saxons inhabited England until the Norman conquest."

"And you collect these things?"

"I do. I became intrigued with archaeology after watching the demolition of a medieval structure whilst at university," he told her. "Shortly afterward, I attended my first excavation. That sparked my academic interest in Saxon artifacts."

"You actually go to dig sites?" She found it hard to envision the spoiled aristocrat she'd first met mucking around in the mud. "I would have thought a man like you wouldn't want to dirty your boots."

He speared her with a cutting look. "Maybe you should not make assumptions about people you know nothing about. I acquired most of these pieces from excavations of known Saxon settlements. In fact, I've just returned from a dig."

That explained his rugged appearance and crusty boots. And made him marginally more interesting than the petulant overgrown brat from their first meeting. "Well," she said, "I have no objection if you wish to keep these rooms for your relics."

Anger flashed in his eyes. Had he misunderstood her? She was trying to be generous.

"You are welcome to stay as my guest," she clarified.

CHAPTER FOUR

Dusty and fatigued, the last thing Strick needed after returning from a dig was to find the American rifling through his things. But what sent him over the edge was her giving him permission to enter his own family home.

"How very magnanimous of you to allow me to keep a room in the home that has belonged to my family for centuries," he fumed.

Her expression hardened. He'd never stood close enough to see the tiny mole above her left eyebrow. She smelled of lemons, a bright, warm scent that did not suit such a cold-natured woman. "I am *trying* to show you a kindness."

To be beholden to a stranger who had no true right to Tremayne infuriated him. "If it were not for your deceitful cousin, I would require no favors from you."

She flattened her lips. "In our tradition, it is inappropriate to speak ill of the dead."

"Which tradition do you speak of? American? Arab? America confuses me. Almost everyone in your country came from somewhere else."

"I assume it is wrong to speak ill of the dead in any country or culture."

Unfortunately, the interloper wasn't wrong. Strick summoned whatever gentlemanly courtesy he could muster. "Please accept my belated condolences on the loss of your cousin," he said through gritted teeth.

"Thank you." She paused, her curiosity seeming to overcome her disdain. "Why did I receive the castle if Deena's duke had children to leave it to?"

"That is a question I've asked myself every day since the will was read."

"And what answer did you come up with?"

"There were many things about our way of life that your late cousin didn't comprehend. She had no appreciation for duty or tradition."

"What about your father?"

"What about him?"

"Did he also have no appreciation for duty or tradition?"

"My father was far more interested in carousing with your cousin than he was in securing the dukedom for future generations. You wouldn't understand."

That icy facade melted a little. "I understand more than you can know." To his surprise, compassion shone in her face. "I know what it is to be robbed of something that feels vital to who you are as a person."

"I cannot imagine you and I could have much of anything in common." An English duke and the American daughter of Arab merchants couldn't come from more dissimilar circumstances.

She stiffened. "What you are overlooking," she informed him, "is that thanks to my cousin Deena, we now have a very large, very old castle in common."

The unfairness of it waved over him. "I have not forgotten what Father and Deena robbed me of. And I never will." The loss of his castle, his safe place, was a festering wound constantly being picked at. "Now, if I am *allowed* to keep these rooms, perhaps you will also grant me a modicum of privacy by vacating them posthaste."

"With great pleasure," she said cuttingly, striding out of his apartments with her head held high.

Leaving the scent of lemons and warm woman trailing in her wake.

THE SUN SHONE the following day so Raya seized the opportunity to get outside and explore the property. As she walked, she replayed her encounter with the duke the previous afternoon. She'd never met anyone so thoroughly unpleasant and ungracious. She almost regretted letting him keep his rooms and prayed their paths would rarely cross. The castle was certainly mammoth enough to keep out of each other's way.

Tremayne's grounds were breathtaking. Although shabby and overgrown in some places, the sunlit gardens and meadows were a refreshing change from the gloomy castle. She trekked through a charming deer park and over a field of bright pink wildflowers. Surprised to find bright flowers so late into the fall, Raya couldn't resist the urge to lie down with her arms flung out by her sides. Cushioned by the grass beneath her, she stared up at the blue sky, enveloped in the warmth of the sun and the sweet strong smell of the flowers. Relieved to be free of the stagnant castle, she inhaled the fresh outdoor scents. New York City air was never so sweet.

A pang went through her at the thought of America. Would the ancient pile of stones she inherited ever feel like home? She missed Mama and her sister Naila and even her eldest married sister, Nadine, who could be quite tiresome. But Raya did not miss her brother. She was still too angry.

Closing her eyes, Raya almost dozed off, but then she thought of Auntie Majida, who might be awake and missing her. She reluctantly sat up.

"Oh, I didn't see you there."

She turned in the direction of the male voice. It was a young man, his soft brown curls illuminated by the sun behind him. She lifted her hand to shade her eyes, getting a better look at him. He was very handsome; he looked like a male angel. "Hello."

"It's fortunate I didn't step on you." There was laughter in his voice. "I am Alfred Price."

"Price?" She came to her feet. "I have met your father, I think."

"Have you?"

"He was kind enough to give me and my aunt a ride from the inn to Castle Tremayne a few days ago."

"Ah, yes." Curiosity lit his eyes. "You must be the new castle owner."

"You have found me out. I am Raya Darwish."

"A pleasure to know you, Miss Darwish. May I accompany you part of the way home?"

She should probably decline. Her aunt would definitely not approve. But Majida didn't need to know. "If you'd like."

"I most assuredly would." He fell in step beside her. "How do you like your new home?"

"To be honest, it's all a bit overwhelming."

"I can imagine. It's not every day that one inherits a castle."

"That is for certain. We don't have castles in America."

"I suppose your United States are too young for that."

"There are wealthy men in America building enormous mansions in New York but nothing as old as Tremayne."

"Have you met Strickland?"

"The duke? Yes, of course."

His friendly tone dropped away. "Have a care with him."

"With the duke?" She was put off by the sudden change in his demeanor. "Why?"

"Oh." He paused. "Forgive me."

"For what?"

"I naturally assumed you would have heard," he hedged.

"I have only been here a few days."

He halted, a shadow coming over his face. "I don't mean to overstep but you are an innocent who is new to our quaint little village." He released a breath, running a hand over the top of his head. "You should be forewarned."

"About?"

"Strickland."

"What of him? I already know he is rather . . . disagreeable."

Mr. Price paused. "I suppose you have not heard the rumors about how your cousin died."

"I try not to pay attention to rumors, Mr. Price." Gossip and backbiting ran rampant at home in Brooklyn and Raya ignored it there, too.

"Strickland hated her."

"If you are referring to Cousin Deena, I already gathered that there was no love lost between them."

"Strickland believes she took advantage of his father. That she pressured the old man to write a will giving her the castle when he was in his cups."

"The duke is entitled to his opinion."

"The duchess didn't fall."

She halted. "I beg your pardon?"

A muscle twitched high in his cheek. "She was pushed from the top of the ruins."

Raya's neck tingled. "I understood her death was an accident."

"That's what Strickland wants everyone to believe. This is not America, Miss Darwish," he said tightly. "There are certain people, such as our nobility, who can do as they please. They are never held to account."

The banked intensity behind the man's words made her uneasy. "Thank you for accompanying me this far, Mr. Price, but I think I should continue on alone."

"Are you certain?"

"Quite certain." She walked on ahead. "Good day. Please give my regards to your father."

"I did not mean to upset you. I just thought you should know," he called out after her, "that Deena's death was no accident."

Raya quickened her pace. She did not look back until she reached the bustling back courtyard of the castle, which was called the outer bailey. A quick glance over her shoulder confirmed Mr. Price hadn't followed her. She exhaled. The man had practically accused the duke of murder. Strickland might be ill-tempered and self-absorbed, but a killer?

She pondered Mr. Price's words as she made her way past several small sandstone structures with thatched roofs. A few people moved about while a handful of goats trotted along the dirt path. Raya would have liked to greet some of the people but, as with the servants in the castle, everyone cast their eyes downward whenever she passed. Very few people at Castle Tremayne spoke to her and those who did, primarily the butler and housekeeper, barely managed to contain their disapproval.

She spotted Otis emerging from one of the small outer buildings. He grinned. "Good day, Miss Darwish."

Her eyes went to his basket. "What do you have there?"

"Cheese from the dairy. Cook sent me to fetch it."

"May I ask you something?"

"You are my employer. You may ask me anything you like."

"How did the Duchess of Strickland die?"

His smile faded. "She fell from the old abbey. Everyone was surprised that Her Grace went out to the ruins on the day she died."

"Why? Wouldn't it have been natural for her to want to explore them?" Raya would never be caught near the top floor of anything, but she'd love to see an old abbey from the ground level.

"Her Grace preferred indoor pursuits."

"I see." She bit her lip, then decided to ask the question at the top of her mind. "Did the duchess fall? Or was she pushed?"

Otis reddened. "The magistrate said that Her Grace's death was an accident."

"Do people believe that?" she pressed. "Do *you* take the magistrate at his word?"

"Servants are not supposed to have opinions." He avoided her gaze. "If you will excuse me?

Cook will have my hide if I'm not back with her cheese soon."

"Yes, of course."

Relief etched his freckled face. "Thank you, miss."

She watched him scurry back to the castle. Why was Otis reluctant to speak about Deena's death? Did he share Mr. Price's opinion?

A sudden blast of torrid heat jolted Raya from her thoughts. Clanking sounds of pounding metal came through the open double doors of the small courtyard building.

This must be the forge. As she moved closer, a great roaring firepot came into view. Raya's eyes widened. The blacksmith wasn't wearing a shirt. She'd never seen a man's bare chest before. Baba and Salem always wore their undershirts around Raya and her sisters.

The man's skin glistened with perspiration. Rivulets of moisture trickled down a sculpted chest and well-defined stomach. The pronounced muscles in his thick arms contracted as he pounded a slab of metal into submission. The overt display of primal masculine strength made Raya hot all over, as if someone had dumped her into a vat of boiling oil.

The blacksmith's weighty metal hammer froze in midair. Raya forced her eyes up from the man's glorious chest and found herself staring into a soft brown gaze shot through with gold.

CHAPTER FIVE

The Duke of Strickland flung the hammer down with a loud clank.

"What the devil are you doing here?" he barked. Perspiration dampened his disheveled dark golden hair. Most people would look a mess in his place, but his current state gave the duke a disconcerting raw appeal.

She snatched her gaze away, staring into the firepot, then at the dings on the old iron anvil, anywhere but the duke's angry expression . . . or his magnificent athletic form. "I apologize." Her cheeks burned even hotter, which shouldn't be possible. "I didn't mean to intrude."

Out of the corner of her eye, she watched the duke snatch up a white shirt and drag it over his head, covering himself. "And yet, once again I find you where you shouldn't be."

How dare he admonish her as if she were a child? "Is it *I* who should not be here?" she retorted. "Or is it *you*?"

His neck flushed, matching the color of his heat-reddened face. "The forge is still mine."

She belatedly realized there was another man at work near the blazing fire. He'd also relinquished his shirt. He had a fine form, but his bare skin had no effect on her, except to provoke embarrassment for intruding on half-dressed men.

"You shouldn't be here." The duke came around from the workbench. "I will see you back to the castle."

"That will not be necessary." She drew herself up. "I can find my own way back."

"Derek," he called to the other man, "I shall see you later to finish up."

The man's curious gaze cut from the duke to Raya. "Very good, Your Grace."

Feeling like she had no other choice, Raya fell in step beside the duke. Heat seemed to radiate off him.

"I do not know how it is in America," he said brusquely, "but in England it is unseemly for unmarried young women to be in company with gentlemen in various states of undress."

"It is the same in America," she said, her voice as dry as sand. It was even more inappropriate among the Arabs. "We are not barbarians. I hardly make a habit of ogling half-dressed men."

The fortress hovered over them, two massive stone towers flanking the three-story structure like soldiers standing sentry. Raya craned her neck to take it all in.

"I cannot believe this is a family home."

"Fortifications such as Tremayne aren't meant to be private abodes. They were built as a demonstration of power and wealth, and to entertain visitors who would then be in awe of the wealth and power on display."

"The builders certainly succeeded in making the castle intimidating." Were they actually having a civilized conversation? "How many rooms does it have?"

"One hundred and ninety-seven."

She sucked in a breath. The enormity of the property was hard to grasp. Just the Great Room alone was bigger than most decent-sized houses in Brooklyn.

"And what are your plans?" he asked, abruptly changing the subject. The sun slanted against his hair, making it look like spun gold. "To stay here in England indefinitely, separated from your family?"

"To be frank, I am not sure. I came for a visit. I didn't expect to inherit a castle." She scanned the structures around them. "What are all these buildings?"

"Some, like the old malt house, are vacant." He pointed around them. "That's the barn, as you probably surmised."

Raya knew what a barn was. "And those are used to shelter animals?"

He nodded. "And their feed and other supplies." He pointed to the other outer buildings, his manner brusque but not unpleasant. "Those are the stables, that's the brewery, the bake house, sawmill, the dairy and, of course, you are familiar with the forge."

"What happens in the sawmill and the dairy?" She'd already witnessed firsthand what work went on in the forge.

He explained the functions of each structure and even escorted her inside for a look. The workers treated the duke with great deference while seeming confused about how to respond to her.

The dairy had rows of milk bowls laid out in various states of making cream and cheese. In the sawmill, workers stripped bark from logs and cut wood into various sizes. She was surprised to learn that one structure was devoted to weaving. Inside, a lone older woman worked a loom in the deserted-looking space.

"The castle has its own weavers?" she asked as they stepped back out into the sunshine.

"It used to be a much more robust operation," he replied. "Now it is just Betsy. There is little for her to do."

"Why do you keep her on?"

"Betsy has been with the Carey family since she was a little girl. Her father was the master loomer before her. I cannot turn Betsy out. She would not be able to find work elsewhere."

"It's like a small village all on its own," Raya said. "Tremayne is very impressive."

"We've had to be self-sufficient in order to survive. In the event of a siege, the castle had to hold for months. There needed to be enough stores to see the castle through." His pride for the place of his birth shone with every word.

"Tremayne has never fallen. Not once in four hundred years."

"You love it here." It wasn't a question. The duke's affection for the decrepit property was palpable. But then why didn't he take better care of it? Why hadn't he repaired and refurbished the inside? The walled garden was lovely but untended and overgrown. Why had he allowed the place he treasured to fall into disrepair?

"Of course, I treasure my home," the duke answered. "Tremayne has been in my family for centuries. This place is in my blood."

And yet Deena left the castle to Raya, a complete stranger. Guilt waved over her. Yes, Tremayne was legally hers, but what right did Raya really have to take this man's home. She couldn't blame Strickland for resenting her. In a way, hadn't Salem done something similar to Raya?

Mr. Price's insinuations rolled around in her head. "Did Deena hate you?"

Surprise lit his eyes. "You are very direct," he said gruffly. "It would be fair to say that we did not get on."

"Is that why she left everything to me, someone she'd never met? To get back at you?"

A muscle ticked in his left cheek. "We shall never be able to ask Deena why she did what she did." He paused. "And she didn't leave it all to you."

"What do you mean?"

"She left the castle to you. That includes the gardens and a small meadow beyond the formal gardens. However, all of the surrounding land and properties, including all of these outer buildings and the houses rented to our tenant farmers, are mine. My father left them to me."

Raya gaped at him. "But why would he do that? Even I can see that the castle cannot exist without what the land provides for it."

"Exactly." The duke wore a grim expression. "And Deena knew that as well. She's left us in a situation in which neither of us can exist without the other."

THE FOLLOWING MORNING, Strick made an appearance at breakfast, his first since the Americans' arrival. He turned up at Miss Darwish's request. The chit had no notion that few, with the exception of royalty, dared to summon a duke.

Miss Darwish's invitation, like the lady herself, was direct and to the point.

> *Please join us for breakfast tomorrow.*
> *I'd like to talk to you about*
> *the future of Castle Tremayne.*
>
> *Sincerely,*
> *Raya Darwish*

Strick was curious despite himself. What did she have in mind for his castle? But then, bitterness sliced through him. *Her castle.* Tremayne wasn't his.

He arrived to find Miss Darwish sitting at the burr walnut dining table sipping a cup of coffee, appearing completely at home. She looked surprisingly appealing in an emerald-green dress with long fitted sleeves worn over a high-necked white lace blouse. A double-stranded thick gold chain adorned her neck.

"Good morning, Duke."

The butler stiffened. "The Duke of Strickland is to be referred to as His Grace."

Miss Darwish appeared to resist the urge to roll her eyes. "Your Grace then," she said in a pleasant tone. "Thank you for coming."

"I could not resist. It is not often that someone summons me."

Philips made a strangled sound. Otis, standing by the sideboard, struggled to maintain a neutral expression but the flicker of amusement in his eyes gave him away. Strick took the chair Philips pulled out for him at the opposite end from where the lady sat.

Miss Darwish frowned as she regarded him across the long length of the table. "You are very far away." She picked up her plate. "I shall move closer to you so we can better discuss our business."

Philips flushed a bright red at the unheard-of etiquette breach, while Otis pressed his lips inward.

Philips stepped forward. "Miss Darwish—" He appeared poised to physically intercept her.

But Miss Darwish was already up and coming toward Strick with her plate in one hand and cup of coffee in the other. She wore several thin gold bangles on her wrist that clinked when she moved. "Don't bother," she said, assuming the butler intended to be of assistance. "I don't need any help."

Strick gave a subtle wave of his hand, signaling for the butler to stand down. Miss Darwish settled herself to Strick's right.

"There. This is so much better." Dark luminous eyes met his. "Don't you agree?"

"Immeasurably better." A nod to Otis sent the footman to the sideboard to fill a plate for him.

She sipped her coffee. "Why is it inappropriate for me to call you Duke?"

"Among the English, addressing a duke too informally is considered a massive faux pas."

Curiosity lit her face. "Why?"

"Only people of my station, or of a similar rank, should take the liberty of addressing me as 'Duke.'" Otis set a filled plate before him.

"I see." She considered this as she buttered her toast.

"But you may feel free to call me Duke or Strickland." He picked up his fork. "Is your aunt not joining us?"

"No, I had hoped she would be feeling well enough to come down but she is still feeling poorly."

"*Still?*" This was the first he'd heard that the aunt was ill. "What is the matter with her?"

"She had a fever that broke but a deep cough has persisted."

He set his fork down. "And how long has this been going on?"

"Almost five days now."

"What did Dr. Michaels say?"

She looked surprised. "Is there a doctor nearby?"

Strick suppressed a groan. All he needed was for another Darwish to perish under his roof. Well, technically not his roof. He turned a cold stare to his butler. "Why has the village doctor not been summoned?"

Philips stepped forward. "Miss Darwish has not asked for the doctor."

"*I* am asking," he said sharply. "I want Miss Darwish's aunt attended to without delay."

"Very good, Your Grace. I shall see to it immediately."

A becoming flush enlivened Miss Darwish's face, emphasizing the precise angle of her cheekbones. It struck him that she truly was an attractive woman—when she wasn't addressing him in a cutting manner. "That is very kind of you."

"We cannot have your aunt falling seriously ill." For his own sake as well as the aunt's. The last thing Strick needed was another complication. And more rumors. "Dr. Michaels is very capable."

"I've been worried about her," she said. "Thank you."

"You must ask for what you need," he said gruffly. After all, she did own the place, a thought that still prompted acid to flare in his gut.

"I suppose you are wondering why I asked you to join me this morning."

He sliced a piece of beef. "I trust you will not keep me in suspense."

"I think you should have the castle."

His fork stopped halfway to his mouth. "I beg your pardon?"

"It's rightfully yours. I think we can both agree on that."

Strick motioned for the staff to leave them. He waited until they were alone before resuming the conversation. "I am afraid I don't take your meaning."

"Auntie Majida and I don't belong here any more than you belong in New York. After our talk yesterday, I couldn't stop thinking about how unfair it is that I own this castle when it rightfully belongs in your family."

He didn't know what to make of her. Did she truly intend to hand the castle over? Maybe she'd finally grasped the full extent of Tremayne's debts. "That is most generous." *Unbelievably so.*

"So," she continued, "I don't know how to sign it back over to you but I'd like to do that."

He eyed her suspiciously. She could not be serious. "You are certain?"

She gave a firm nod. "Absolutely."

"This is . . . most unexpected."

"You don't believe me."

"It is hard to believe."

"I used to help my father run the family business. I am very good at what I do. My initiatives doubled our profits. However, after my father died, my brother Salem banned me from the business. So"—she paused to take a deep breath—"I know what it is to lose something central to one's life. Especially at the hand of a family member I once trusted. You could say that Darwish and Company was my castle."

He easily envisioned her as an able businesswoman. Except that it was profoundly bad business to give away an asset as valuable as Castle Tremayne. "If you are serious, I shall direct my solicitor to draw up the papers."

"Wonderful," she said crisply. "All we have to do is negotiate a price."

"Excel—" Strick's thoughts stumbled. "I beg your pardon?"

"Do not worry, I'm not greedy." Her tone became very brisk and to the point. "Let us say fair market price, minus a twenty-five percent good faith discount."

"Fair market value," he repeated.

"Minus twenty-five percent." She focused intently on him, exuding the air of a woman accustomed to negotiating . . . and succeeding. "I don't need a castle, just enough to start my own business in America. And some extra funds to help stock and support the enterprise until it becomes profitable."

"You expect me to set you up in business in New York?"

"You speak as if I am asking for special favors, which I most certainly am not. It is a reasonable offer."

Even if his goblets, two of his most valuable relics, hadn't vanished several months back, Strick still couldn't afford the price of the castle minus twenty-five percent.

She misread Strick's hesitation. "I see you intend to strike a hard bargain. I might be willing to go up to thirty percent. You would pay me the price of the castle minus thirty percent."

The full depth of the absurdity of Strick's situation assailed him. Here he was, a peer of the realm, negotiating the future of his family home with the daughter of an Arab-American merchant. It was so farcical that he couldn't contain himself.

He burst out laughing.

CHAPTER SIX

The duke's guffaws startled Raya. The uproarious gusty laughter was oceans away from the wry rumble she expected from such a surly man.

Her stomach hardened. He was laughing at her. "I fail to see what is so amusing." She spoke in a cool tone. "It is a perfectly fair offer. The castle is worth far more than I'm asking for."

She'd come up with the plan the previous evening and was so excited she barely slept. She'd found a way to turn her depressing inheritance to her benefit. The idea of returning home to build her own enterprise from the ground up, of assuring her own future, exhilarated her. She would never again be at the mercy of any man.

"Forgive me." He slowly got ahold of himself. "You are perfectly correct. There is nothing humorous about our situation."

"Precisely," she said in a tight voice.

"It is the irony of the situation that amuses me."

"I don't understand."

"I realize you just arrived, but look around you."

Raya surveyed the room, the faded cushions on the dining chairs, the worn wood.

"What do you see?" he asked.

"A dining room that has seen better days."

"Exactly, and why do you think that is?"

She bristled. "I am not a student who needs to be quizzed." Raya did not appreciate being treated like a child. "If you have a point to make, kindly make it."

"Why do you think the castle is so run-down?"

"I did wonder why you don't do a better job of looking after the property. I don't mean to insult your castle management skills, but you did ask."

"The reason the castle has seen better days is because there is no money."

"I'm willing to set up a payment plan. I am not asking for a fortune."

"Which is a good thing. Because it doesn't exist."

"How is that possible?" She gaped at him. "You own all of the land, the tenant homes and farms."

"Times are changing. Many farmers are moving to the city. People like me cannot live off the land as we used to. The rents and farm yields barely cover castle expenses." Contempt laced his next words. "And it did not help that your cousin spent lavishly, wasting what little money we did have."

The Cousin Deena he described did not sound like a very nice person, and was nothing like the compassionate, vibrant woman Raya came to know through her letters.

"So, you see, I cannot buy you out." He sat back in his chair and crossed his arms over his chest. "But you are welcome to leave."

"Leave?" She scoffed. "I cannot go back empty-handed. Auntie Majida and I barely have sufficient money for the voyage back to New York."

"I can provide the funds for your passage."

She shook her head. "Only a fool would return home with nothing after inheriting a castle. And I am not an imbecile." She realized the duke was studying her face. Raya was accustomed to being the object of a man's scrutiny. She was equally used to men's gazes sliding away once she began talking about matters that truly interested her, such as sales figures and product distribution.

"Well," the duke said, "you shall have time to think on it while I am away."

"Are you going somewhere?" Disappointment weighted her limbs. They had a deal to conclude. The man hadn't even made a counteroffer. There had to be something at Tremayne that he could leverage.

"I'm off to London to arrange a showing of my Anglo-Saxon metalwork. I will be gone for a few days."

"What sort of showing?"

"I contract with a gallery, or other space, to exhibit my pieces. I've amassed one of the most extensive collections of Saxon metalwork in all of England."

"And people pay an entrance fee to see your collection?"

"They do."

"Do you pay the gallery to exhibit your pieces?"

"Yes, why do you ask?"

"No reason in particular." She came to her feet. "Well, if you can't buy me out, I guess Auntie Majida and I are here to stay, at least for the foreseeable future."

Surprise stamped his aristocratic face. "Did you not hear me? There is no money. There's barely enough to maintain the household as it is. And there are fewer funds coming in each month. The situation will only become more dire."

She set her shoulders. "We'll have to find a way."

"A way to what?"

"To make money, of course. We can't sit by and do nothing while the funds dwindle away."

"What exactly do you know about running a castle?"

"I've worked practically my entire life. I learned everything there was to know about Darwish and Company and the linens industry and I made a great success of it. And I'll do the same with Tremayne."

His lip curled. "While your earnestness and naivete are truly charming, successfully running a castle is far different than selling a few table linens."

Raya didn't care for the way he talked down

to her. Yet another man discounting her abilities. Her resolve hardened. She'd show him. And her brother. "We'll just have to see about that, won't we?"

"THANK YOU, MR. WARD," Raya said after meeting with the castle's steward later that day. "Our meeting was very informative."

And depressing. A heavy weight settled over her after seeing firsthand just how little money was coming in. She was stuck. Both of her viable options, staying at the cash-strapped castle or returning home to be at Salem's mercy, were terrible choices.

"My pleasure, Miss Darwish." Mr. Ward was a kindly elderly man, one of the few friendly faces at the castle. He knew everything about the estate. A steward, Raya learned, kept all of the accounts, managed contracts and maintained the estate's relationship with the tenant farmers.

"Thank you for agreeing to stay on for a little longer until I have a better grasp of the castle's inner workings." Unfortunately, she wouldn't have Mr. Ward's expertise to draw on for much longer. He was retiring to spend more time with his daughter's family in the Lake District.

"Of course," he answered. "I am deeply sorry I wasn't able to deliver better news."

"As am I."

He walked her out of the bleak room on the ground floor that he used as an office. They reached the circular stairwell in the front hall. Raya was about to go up to be with Auntie Majida when Mrs. Shaw appeared at the top of the stairs. The housekeeper descended, trailed by three strangers in overcoats. The older couple and a young lady smiled at Raya and murmured, "Good day." Mrs. Shaw barely acknowledged Raya as she led the visitors outside.

Raya watched after them. "Who are they?"

"Tourists, most likely." Mr. Ward answered as if the sight of strangers roaming the castle was a normal occurrence.

"Tourists? What are they doing here?"

"When the master is away, it is not unusual for people to tour the castle."

Raya moved to look out the window just in time to witness the male visitor discreetly press money into Mrs. Shaw's palm. "Do they pay an entrance fee?"

"No," he scoffed gently, "it would be unseemly to charge for a tour."

She frowned. "Let me see if I understand this correctly. Strangers visit the castle and can appear at the front door at any time, unannounced?"

"That is correct. And Mrs. Shaw usually accommodates them. Tremayne is one of the oldest properties in this part of England that is still a fully functioning residence. This tour is quite popular because, in all of her four hundred years, Tremayne has never fallen."

Raya had been so busy plotting her escape that it

never occurred to her that anyone would want to tour the fusty old castle. "And Tremayne's history captures the public's imagination?"

He nodded. "Visitors enjoy seeing the parapets, the drawbridge and the tower."

"They visit the tower?"

"The unoccupied tower," he clarified. "Not the tower His Grace occupies."

"How often do people visit?"

"I would say at least once a week someone who happens to be passing through will stop in and request a tour."

Raya found this all very curious. "Are they are permitted to go abovestairs?"

"Only to some of the unused guest chambers. Certainly not His Grace's private apartments. Nor the family wing where you and your aunt are staying. And the morning room is off-limits."

Thank goodness. The morning room and the duchess's chambers, the two spaces Deena refurbished, were the only spots in the castle where Raya felt at ease. "Does Mrs. Shaw always give the tours?"

"Showing visitors around the castle is generally considered the housekeeper's purview."

She recalled seeing the visitor press money into the housekeeper's palm. "I imagine the tourists pay Mrs. Shaw for the privilege."

"They might leave a tip for her trouble, but that is rarely discussed."

"And why is that?" How much money was

Mrs. Shaw earning on the side? "Let me guess. It is unseemly to discuss money?"

He nodded. "Precisely."

"I see." That made no sense at all. While Tremayne was hurting for funds, the housekeeper was pocketing tips from visitors? "Mr. Ward?"

"Yes, miss?"

"Before you leave us for good, I would like to take a complete look at all of the accounts and contracts."

His overgrown, salt-and-pepper brows rose. "Are you familiar with such things?"

"I am. My family owns a business in America. I worked quite closely with my father."

"I see. I shall have them delivered to you."

"Thank you."

Asking to see the accounts made Raya feel like she was overstepping. The butler and housekeeper certainly behaved as if the duke still owned the castle. But Tremayne belonged to her and it was time Raya acted like it.

She'd start by putting her skills to use. That began with gaining a thorough understanding of Tremayne's finances. "Please have them sent to the morning room."

THE DAMN GOATS were getting into everything again.

Strick shooed the tiresome creatures away from the forge as he strode back to the castle, welcoming the cool rush of air after the oppressive heat of the forge. He spotted Miss Darwish coming out of a vacant building, looking to be in surprisingly good spirits. Before he could duck out of the way to avoid her, she caught sight of him and their eyes met.

Any good cheer drained from her face, leaving her customary peevish expression. "You've returned," she remarked with the enthusiasm of someone facing a tooth extraction.

"There's nothing like stating the obvious," he replied. "Did you save the castle from impoverishment while I was away?"

"Not yet." She shot him an acidic look. "But I will."

Strick gritted his teeth. This virago brought out his worst impulses. Imagine possessing the gall to think she could run Tremayne better than him. He raked his perspiration-dampened hair back from his forehead. His white linen shirt clung to his skin. He was in no condition to greet a young lady, but he didn't care what this shrew thought of him.

Her midnight gaze briefly dipped to his chest before darting back to his face. "Did you find a place to show your collection?"

"I did," he said curtly. It could very well be his last exhibition for a while. Each year it grew more costly to rent a display space for his metalwork. "May I ask after your aunt?" He didn't need this one hounding him if the old lady's health went downhill.

"Aunt Majida is doing much better. Thank you for sending the doctor." The words were conciliatory. Her attention caught on the belt buckle Strick held in his hand. "Were you working in the forge again?"

"Indeed."

"Did you make that?"

"Yes." He relished working with his hands, shaping metals to create things of use. "I did."

"May I see it?"

He paused, braced for more criticism. But then she audaciously held her hand out, leaving him no choice but to place the buckle in her open palm.

She studied the metal, turning it over. Her hands were not delicate. They moved with purpose and efficiency. Her nails were short and clean. "It's beautiful."

He enjoyed her compliment more than he should. "Must you act so surprised?"

"Do you make other things?"

"I do. I forged a few pots that are now utilized in the kitchen. Some of my tools are used around the castle. But the jewelry, such as belt buckles and rings, doesn't have any practical use."

"What do you do with them?"

"Mostly toss them into a basket in my apartments where they collect dust. The pieces aren't worth anything. It's just a hobby. I'm not a skilled metalsmith by any means."

"You waste the metal?"

Was she calling him a spendthrift? "If you'll excuse me, I have to be anywhere but here."

"Look out!" she exclaimed.

Too late he realized that one of his father's damn goats was tucked up behind his legs. He stumbled, his arms flailing as he struggled to regain his balance. Miss Darwish reacted. She leapt forward and grabbed his forearm with a firm hand, helping him get his bearings so he didn't land on his arse. Reflexively, his own fingers tightened around her wrist to steady himself.

Sensation tore up his arm. He raised his astonished gaze to meet hers. Lustrous dark eyes stared back at him. A shocking physical craving for Miss Darwish as a woman sliced straight through to his cock.

Stunned, Strick dropped her wrist. "I beg your pardon." He avoided looking at her. "I really should get rid of these creatures. They're nothing but a nuisance."

"What?" she asked, a hazy expression on her face.

"The goats. I should rid myself of them."

"Oh. Are they valuable?"

"I see you never fail to get to the financial heart of any matter." He spoke in a mocking tone, anything to distract from the new, wordless attraction between them.

"It is past time someone at Castle Tremayne did," she shot back.

Strick breathed a sigh of relief. They were back to sparring. Bickering was infinitely more manageable than being physically attracted to a woman whose acid tongue should deflate any man's cock.

"I am told the goat skin is valuable," he said, adding an edge of derision to his tone. "For parchment and the like."

She petted the animal, her cool distant manner fully restored. "I see."

He followed the slow, hypnotic movements of her hand. "My father acquired an entire herd of these animals because he was taken with them. Not for any practical reason."

She ran her fingers over the creature, examining the matted, stringy fur. "Is this an Angora goat?"

"I've no idea." He rarely paid attention to his father's many useless impulse purchases. Besides, he was oddly mesmerized by the movements of her fingers. She might not be beautiful, but Raya Darwish had an unfortunate appeal. And his idiot cock took note.

"Mr. Habib, who lives down the road from us on Henry Street in New York, uses the fleece from goats to make shawls and scarves."

He shot her an incredulous look. "From *that* shaggy hair?" The animal looked knotty, dirty and not at all soft.

"I am friends with his daughters Janan and Samira. They say the younger animals have softer, finer hair that is good for scarves. They gave me one for my birthday last year." She continued petting the creature. "Thicker, coarser hair can be used for coats or rugs."

"Aren't you a font of information?" Most young women of his acquaintance had neither the knowledge nor the desire to learn anything beyond how to wed a title.

She narrowed her eyes at him. "I am simply saying the goats are more valuable alive than dead." Her voice was stiff. "Their skin is a one-time use. The hair regrows. Their fleece is a valuable commodity."

"If you are so interested in the nuisances, you are welcome to take charge of them."

Her arched brows lifted. "I can do whatever I like with the herd?"

"Absolutely."

Her face brightened. Strick pretended not to notice or care. Just like he also ignored the sparks firing off deep in his groin.

CHAPTER SEVEN

Raya slammed the ledger shut. The castle finances were every bit as bad as Mr. Ward indicated. If she didn't find a source of significant income soon, there was no way to keep the castle afloat.

She looked around Cousin Deena's well-appointed sitting room. It was warm and comfortable, but she couldn't help wondering how much it cost to keep the fire running. The furniture was newly upholstered, the decor fresh and updated. Was Deena a complete spendthrift? Raya stood and stretched, her shoulders stiff from studying the books for hours. She needed some fresh air. Maybe a walk would help drive thoughts of the duke from her mind.

They hadn't come face-to-face since yesterday when his touch literally electrified her. He'd departed about an hour ago. Raya watched from the window as the duke mounted his enormous stallion, his posture erect, his bearing proud, strong thighs hugging the animal's body.

Objectively, she could not deny that he was a handsome man. Had he felt the charge between them? Raya hoped she'd imagined it. No logical person could be attracted to that ogre.

As she emerged from the castle to take her walk, Raya encountered an attractive young couple on their way in.

"Oh, hello there." The man's eyes twinkled. "You must be Miss Darwish. I have been hoping to meet you. How are you settling in?"

"Really, Guy," the woman admonished, tapping his arm. They were clearly related, sharing the same green eyes, pale complexion and deep auburn hair. "Do not overwhelm Miss Darwish before we've even been properly introduced."

"Quite right," the man, a near replica of his companion, said good-naturedly. "Please do excuse me. Allow me to make the introductions. We are your neighbors. I am Guy Vaughan and this is my sister, Miss Frances Vaughan."

"How do you do?" Raya ran a self-conscious hand over her skirt. She'd dressed comfortably to look over the estate ledgers. She would have preferred to meet the neighbors in one of her finer gowns, rather than a simple white button-up shirt, dark unadorned skirt and brown leather belt. Especially since the handsome Vaughan siblings were a study in fashionable elegance.

She pulled her shoulders back. Raya wouldn't allow herself to be intimidated by the Vaughans or anyone else. She might be a stranger in a strange land, but she was also the legal owner of this old fortress. "Welcome to Castle Tremayne."

Miss Vaughan's delicate brows rose almost imperceptibly as she exchanged a quick look with her brother.

"Thank you," he answered for them both. "My sister and I are very fond of the place."

"Do you visit often?"

"Strick and I are longtime friends," he explained with obvious warmth in his voice.

"Strick?"

"Strickland, the duke."

"Ah, yes, of course." The surly man actually had friends. "If you are here to visit the duke, I am sorry to tell you that he is not at home."

"Oh?" Surprise lit Miss Vaughan's face. "I wasn't aware that His Grace was going away."

Did Strickland make a habit of keeping his neighbor's sister apprised of his comings and goings? Raya supposed a woman as polished and elegant as Miss Vaughan would be a suitable match for a duke.

"Where did he go?" Guy asked.

"I have no idea."

"Well, we already know the duke." Miss Vaughan favored Raya with a friendly smile. "This visit will give us a chance to become acquainted with the new mistress of Castle Tremayne."

The visitors left her no choice but to invite them in. Raya didn't know how things were done in

England, but Mama would have her head if she didn't offer her guests something to eat and drink. Arabs forced hospitality on people whether they liked it or not.

"Please do come in." Raya led them inside, where the butler stood waiting. "Mr. Philips, will you bring some refreshments?"

Philips's stoic expression eased. There was even a hint of a smile when he greeted the Vaughans. He obviously had a fondness for the neighbors that was absent in his dealings with the new mistress of the house. "Of course, Miss Darwish. I shall bring the tea tray in posthaste."

Raya wasn't sure which room to escort her guests to. "Where do you normally serve tea?" she asked the butler.

"In the drawing room, if that is acceptable."

Raya couldn't remember which room that was. Guy sensed her confusion and came to the rescue. "Shall we?" He offered one arm to his sister and the other to Raya and proceeded through the castle's mazelike twists and turns. Raya allowed herself to be led, while Miss Vaughan glided through the dark corridors with the confidence of someone who knew the place well. The housekeeper seemed to appear out of nowhere.

"Why hello, Mrs. Shaw," Guy said genially. "Still putting the fear of God into the young housemaids?"

The older woman beamed. "Mr. Vaughan. Miss Vaughan." The dour housekeeper *was* capable of smiling. "May I say how good it is to see you again?"

"You may, of course," Miss Vaughan said. "I trust you are well."

"Well enough." The housekeeper didn't spare a glance for Raya. "The recent changes have been . . . difficult."

Raya's cheeks burned at the obvious barb. She would never allow any worker at Darwish and Company to treat her with such disrespect. But she needed the housekeeper until she learned all there was to know about how Tremayne operated.

"All change is difficult," Guy said smoothly, "but times move on and we must all adjust. Don't you agree?"

Raya wanted to hug the man. His loyalty might be to the duke, but Guy skillfully quelled the housekeeper's transparent attempt to malign her new mistress.

"Yes, of course," Mrs. Shaw said with a strained smile. Guy promptly guided them away from the housekeeper and into a moldy formal room with worn velvet curtains that allowed little sunlight.

They settled in, Miss Vaughan perching on the edge of her rickety chair, her spine perfectly erect. It was hard to tell Miss Vaughan's age, but she was probably in her early twenties. The three of them spoke politely on a number of mundane topics including the weather and Raya's journey from America. Before long, Otis appeared carrying a tea tray laden with pretty little sandwiches and tasty-looking desserts. Raya couldn't help but wonder how much the abundant spread cost.

"Do you miss America?" Miss Vaughan inquired as she sipped her tea.

"I miss my sisters and mother."

"Is that all?" Guy asked.

Raya bit into a wafer. It was delicious. Everything that came from the kitchen was beyond compare. "To be honest, I miss working."

"Working?" Miss Vaughan repeated.

"As in a job?" her brother added.

"Yes, my family owns a factory in New York."

"Your family is in trade?" Miss Vaughan asked.

"I told you that," Mr. Vaughan said to his sister.

"I do not think so," she replied in a moderate tone. "I would have remembered."

"We mostly produce aprons, tablecloths and other linens," Raya told them.

"I see." Miss Vaughan maintained a politely neutral expression.

"What sets our goods apart is the hand embroidery done by the Arab women who live on Washington Street in New York."

"The Arab women," Miss Vaughan echoed.

"Precisely. They were sitting at home in need of work and I provided a respectable way for them to earn an income for their families."

"How industrious of you," Mr. Vaughan remarked.

"I took it upon myself to make certain that our products are stocked by the finest shops on Sixth

Avenue." Once Raya started talking about her passion for Darwish and Company, it was hard to stop. "That is why our pieces are in the finest homes on Fifth Avenue."

"I see." Miss Vaughan looked slightly dazed. "Coming here must be quite a change for you."

"Oh yes," Raya agreed. The pain of losing her place in the company, of her brother's betrayal, waved through her again. "Very much so."

"Becoming the mistress of a castle at such a tender age when one is all alone must present a significant challenge," Guy put in.

"I am not alone. My aunt accompanied me."

"Will we have the pleasure of meeting your aunt?" Miss Vaughan asked.

"Not today, unfortunately. I am sorry to say that she is indisposed." Auntie Majida was feeling much better but still kept mostly to the duchess's chambers. "Have you and the duke been neighbors for a long time?"

"Since boyhood, actually," Guy told her. "Our families lived next to each other in London. It was a stroke of luck that an appealing property became available for purchase near Tremayne so we are neighbors still."

Had they known Deena? Raya didn't know if it was appropriate to ask, but she couldn't resist. "Were you acquainted with my late cousin?"

"The duchess?" Guy's eyes twinkled. "We were. She was a singular woman."

Raya wasn't sure what he meant by that but

the amusement in the man's gaze suggested he hadn't hated Deena.

"I fear we've been remiss in offering our condolences," Guy said.

"Thank you," Raya answered. "Unfortunately, I never met Deena. Do you mind my asking what she was like?"

"She was a force unto herself." He smiled at the memory. "A woman of great magnetism. She was the center of attention the moment she entered a room."

"It is so sad," Raya ventured to say. "The way she died, I mean." The horror of Deena being pushed to her death shivered through her.

"I cannot imagine why she was out at the ruins so near to dark," Miss Vaughan said. "It is not safe to visit the abbey at night."

"But Deena was never one to follow the rules," Guy said. "She did as she pleased."

"She must have lost her footing in the dark." Miss Vaughan set her tea down. "They say that is why she fell."

"They?" Raya asked.

"The magistrate," Guy answered. "There was an inquest. Her fall was deemed an accident."

Raya exhaled. Of course Deena's death was an accident. Taking up residence in a desolate castle alongside a resentful duke, coupled with the strange encounter with Mr. Price, had sent her imagination running wild.

After about thirty minutes, the Vaughans rose

to take their leave. As Raya saw them out, they came across Mrs. Shaw leading another group of tourists up the stairs.

"It is such an odd practice," Raya remarked, "to have strangers touring the house."

"It is quite common in great homes like Castle Tremayne," Guy told her as they said their goodbyes. "Some houses attract so many tourists that the owners appoint certain days to open the home to visitors."

"That seems like a sensible way to handle things," Raya said.

"There is royal precedent. Queen Victoria opened Hampton Court to paying visitors decades ago."

"What is Hampton Court?"

"One of the royal palaces. She has many others."

"How interesting." Raya's mind swirled as she waved goodbye to the Vaughans' departing carriage.

An audacious plan started to percolate in her head.

STRICK STRODE OUT of his tower apartments the following morning and almost collided with the American.

"What the devil are you doing here?" he barked. "An unmarried young lady should not be in the vicinity of a bachelor's apartments." Particularly not one who looked as appealing as Raya Darwish. Her rose-colored button-up gown illuminated her skin and its fitted silhouette emphasized abundant curves that made a man wonder how quickly he could unfasten her buttons.

"I need to speak with you."

"Why didn't you send a note?"

"I wanted to have a private conversation."

To his ire, he still sensed the pull between them. An unspoken conversation now continuously simmered beneath all of their interactions. "We can speak in private somewhere other than my apartments," he said brusquely. "Philips can arrange a meeting in one of the more public areas of the castle."

"That's just it. I am not comfortable with people knowing who I am talking to and when. And frankly, it's none of their business."

"If this is about me buying the castle from you, there is nothing further to say on the matter. My financial situation has not changed."

"I do want to talk about finances, but what I need to discuss with you has nothing to do with your buying the castle."

"Do you need money?" She'd mentioned running low on funds. "Mr. Ward can assist you with obtaining spending money. What little there is," he amended.

"No." She licked her lips. "It's not about that either."

Strick followed the movement of her tongue. What would it be like to kiss her? Cursing to himself, he forced his attention away from her mouth. "Are you going to enlighten me anytime soon," he said sharply, "or am I expected to stand in the corridor all afternoon?"

"Queen Victoria opens Hampton Palace to paying visitors," she blurted out.

"It's called Hampton Court. Do you want to visit the palace?"

"No." The cords of her throat worked. "I want to do the same thing here."

"I am afraid I don't take your meaning," he said impatiently, quashing the urge to pull the she-dragon flush against his body and find out how her lips tasted.

"I want to open Castle Tremayne to paying visitors."

His mind blanked. "What?"

"I said"—she forced the words out loudly and clearly—"that I want to open Castle Tremayne to paying visitors."

His neck flushed fire-hot. "You cannot be serious."

"I am. Very." She lifted her chin. "The housekeeper conducts tours all of the time. And the visitors pay her."

"I am aware of Mrs. Shaw's actions. It is all very discreet," he explained tersely. "It is customary for grand houses to allow guests to tour the premises from time to time. And if any fee is ever collected, those monies go to charity."

"Have you ever heard the saying that 'charity begins at home'? Castle Tremayne needs the money."

"Good God!" He gawked at her. "You're serious."

"I am resolved. And I have a great many other ideas—"

He cut her off. "If they are as daft as this one, I have absolutely no interest in hearing them."

"Daft?" Her ears turned a bright red. "It is not a silly idea."

"Who told you about Hampton Court?"

"Mr. Vaughan. He and his sister visited yesterday while you were out."

"Do not tell me that Guy put this idea into your head?" It would be just like his friend to create mischief. Nobody appreciated a good joke more than Guy.

"No, I thought of it on my own."

"Well, put it out of your head because it isn't happening."

She crossed her arms. "Why not?"

"I will not allow you to turn my home, the distinguished country seat of generations of dukes of Strickland, into a crass American business enterprise. Not under my watch."

She gasped. "Crass?"

His heart skipped a beat. An angry Raya Darwish, with those enormous flashing eyes and rosy cheeks, was a sight to behold. "It is unseemly, Miss Darwish. I forbid it."

"You *forbid* it?"

"Absolutely. I could never sanction something so vulgar."

"We would be celebrating the castle and its history," she retorted. "The tours would honor this place, not denigrate it."

"Forgive my directness, but your view on this matter does not interest me." He spoke forcefully so she would immediately banish the outrageous idea from her mind. "Nothing will make me change my mind."

"What do you suggest? I suppose you could sell off some of the land."

"Absolutely not. Less land makes the running of the castle even less viable."

"What then? Are we supposed to sit around and do nothing while the castle collapses around us? At least my plan would help refill the castle coffers."

Strick gritted his teeth. This woman had been here all of three weeks and had the audacity to think she could save them all? "We have survived for hundreds of years. And we will continue to do so while keeping our dignity and respect for family history intact."

"Dignity and respect won't pay the bills."

"The answer is to cut expenses and find ways to make the farms more profitable. Better investments and careful money management are what is required to address this situation. Desecrating the glorious history of Tremayne by throwing its doors open to paying strangers is not the solution."

"I am sorry but—"

"There is no need to apologize," he interrupted. "We'll put this silly idea behind us and forget you ever mentioned it."

"No, you don't understand. I am not apologizing."

"You aren't?"

"Absolutely not. I was not *asking* you if I could open the castle to paying visitors." Her solemn gaze met his. "I am telling you."

"I beg your pardon?" he barked.

"As a courtesy."

"You intend to proceed with whatever fantastic notion that strikes your fancy because Deena left the castle to you." Outrage burned in his lungs. "Without any regard for my opinion."

"I will do what it takes to make certain the castle survives into the next century. I plan to save your home even if you won't."

"Listen to me, you little upstart—" But she was already walking away. *Where the devil was she going?* No one dismissed a duke. "Now, wait one moment."

"I will not stay here to be insulted. You should thank me."

"Thank you?" he repeated incredulously. "For *what?"*

"For being willing to do what you cannot."

"And what is that?"

"Whatever it takes to save your home," she shot back. "It's unfortunate that you cannot say the same!"

She stormed down the corridor leaving a seething, speechless Strick behind.

CHAPTER EIGHT

Raya summoned the housekeeper and butler immediately after leaving the duke, her heart still pumping frantically.

She'd expected Strickland to object to her plan but the full force of his anger, the way his powerful body tensed and quivered with fury, unnerved her.

Guilt flared in Raya's belly but she immediately extinguished it. It wasn't as if her plans were totally alien. Castle Tremayne already allowed strangers to gallivant through its public rooms. The only difference going forward would be who they paid and how much. Strickland was overreacting. He'd calm down once the profits started flowing in. She learned long ago that money had a way of smoothing out almost everything.

Mrs. Shaw appeared in the morning room first. "You summoned?" she said dryly.

"I did."

"Isn't Miss Vaughan lovely?" the housekeeper said. "His Grace is so very fond of Miss Vaughan. We all assume he will one day make her his duchess."

"She is lovely." Raya ignored the stab in her

chest. What was that? Could it be jealousy? *No.* That was ridiculous. She refocused. "I summoned you because I'd like to know which rooms you include on your tours."

The older woman stiffened. "I have done nothing wrong."

"Of course not," Raya said soothingly. "I would just love to know which rooms visitors enjoy the most."

She expected little assistance from the housekeeper once the woman learned Raya was opening the fortress to paying visitors. But, in order to plan the best tour possible, she needed to know which parts of the castle appealed to visitors. No one was in a better position to answer that than the housekeeper.

"May I ask why?" Mrs. Shaw asked warily.

None of your business. Raya forced a pleasant expression. "My cousin is coming to visit." It wasn't a complete lie. At some point one of her many cousins might visit. "I would like to know which parts of Tremayne to show her."

The housekeeper relented. "The tower is popular. The turrets, of course. The Great Room always awes visitors. The gallery. Several of the bedchambers with the oldest furnishings. The rooftop. The undercroft."

"Undercroft? What is that?"

"It is the closest Tremayne has to a dungeon."

Raya shivered. "Those really exist?"

"They do."

The butler joined them in the morning room. "You summoned, Miss Darwish?"

"I did." She waved him forward. "Please come in."

He and the housekeeper exchanged glances. "Am I late? I do apologize."

"Not at all," Raya assured him. "There is something I'd like to tell you both."

She proceeded to outline her plan to open the castle to paying visitors. The butler and housekeeper stared at Raya as if they couldn't quite believe what they were hearing.

"And so," Raya concluded, "this naturally means that you, Mrs. Shaw, will no longer be able to conduct private tours for tourists—"

"But—" the housekeeper interjected.

Raya kept talking. "That must stop immediately. From here forward, any and all funds from tourists must go toward castle upkeep."

The housekeeper sucked in her cheeks. "Clearly, Miss Darwish, you are unfamiliar with how things are done at Castle Tremayne. Providing discreet tours to visitors falls under my rights and duties."

Philips interjected. "May I ask what His Grace has to say about this?"

Raya straightened, refusing to be intimidated. "I am the new mistress here and I alone make any final determinations."

Mrs. Shaw sniffed. "In other words," she said not quite under her breath, "he disapproves."

Raya possessed enough experience with belligerent employees to know how to manage them.

"If the changes are too distasteful to you, I will understand."

A satisfied smile curved the housekeeper's lips.

"And," Raya continued, "you are welcome to find yourself another position."

The butler's eyes widened. Mrs. Shaw's lips flattened and then she smiled, but it did not reach her gaze. "As you wish, Miss Darwish. We will, of course, do as you ask."

"Very good," Raya said. "Thank you."

But in the days that followed nobody did as she asked.

Everyone pretended to, but they moved so slowly that by the third day of trying to ready the chambers for visitors, Raya realized what was happening. The servants were purposely working at a snail's pace. It dawned on her when it took Milly, one of the maids, almost an entire day to clean a single window in the Great Room.

"Do you think you could clean the windows a little more quickly?" Raya asked the young maid.

Milly looked downward, avoiding Raya's gaze. "I'll try, miss. I am under strict orders from Mrs. Shaw to clean very, very thoroughly."

"I am sure you can do an excellent job while working more quickly."

"Yes, miss. I will try. When I start back up tomorrow."

"Why tomorrow? It's only three o'clock in the afternoon."

"Yes, miss, you understand I have other chores. Mrs. Shaw will have a cross word for me if I do not finish my work." The girl scurried away.

"Never mind that I am your actual employer," Raya mumbled after the girl. She eyed the portable pair of steps and cleaning supplies, buckets and sponges the maid left behind. She rolled up her sleeves. "I can do it faster myself."

She moved the steps and cleaning supplies over to the next window and got to work. She dipped the sponge in water and climbed the steps, stretching as high as she could to reach the top of the window.

The perch gave Raya her first opportunity to study the pointed-arch casements in detail. She hadn't taken much notice of the stained-glass accents before now, unable to see past the grimy ancient windows and murky view. Now, as she cleaned the muck away, the panes cleared and began to sparkle, allowing the artistry of the colored glass designs to reemerge. The glinting sun illuminated a whimsical kaleidoscope of colors. Enchanted, Raya took extra care with each stroke, until the window shone as brightly as it must have during its heyday—one of the brilliant jewels in the castle's crown.

"What are you doing up there?" The booming male voice startled Raya. She jerked in his direction, losing her balance on the top stair.

"Arghh!" Tumbling off the steps, she braced for a hard fall. But instead of hitting the floor, she collapsed into strong, muscled arms and was promptly nestled against a firm, warm chest.

"Damnation!" the Duke of Strickland said irritably. "Are you trying to break your neck?"

Her ears burned at being admonished like a child. "Are you trying to *make* me break my neck?"

"I saved you from falling," he said stiffly. "One would expect a thank-you."

"I wouldn't have fallen if you hadn't bellowed at me."

"I do *not* bellow."

"If you hadn't sneaked up and startled me, I wouldn't have fallen. Thus, I did not need rescuing."

Annoyance smoldered in his eyes. "I did not *sneak* up on you."

Raya had never seen his eyes up close. They were the softest brown shot through with gold. She belatedly remembered that she was pressed up against his chest. He was practically caressing her. She watched, fascinated, as his gaze dropped to her lips. And then came back up to meet her eyes. The air between them crackled.

Raya swallowed. "Kindly unhand me."

He jolted out of whatever momentary spell gripped them. And practically dropped her. The sudden loss of support prompted Raya to reflexively wrap her arms around his neck. The scent of him—warm man, shaving soap and unbridled masculinity—swept through her.

She was so light-headed that her brain may as well have fallen out of her skull. She leaned into the hard surface of his body. One of his arms remained wrapped around her upper back, steadying her. Raya's skin tingled, her breasts felt very sensitive. It was the most intimate embrace she'd ever experienced. Why couldn't she feel her legs? If she lost her grip on the duke, she risked sliding to the floor.

He brought a hand up to cup her jaw. His touch was gentle but certain. "Are you well?"

"Hmm?" Her cheek warmed under his touch. "Oh yes"—she stared into that amber-shot gaze—"I am fine."

"You seem unsteady."

She blinked. What was happening? How could such a disagreeable man have this kind of effect on her?

"Maybe that's why you fell," he added.

That snapped her back to her senses. "No." She dropped her arms away from him. Her legs held up just fine. "I fell because you startled me."

Exasperation rippled over the defined planes of his face. He withdrew his hands and stepped back, putting space between them. "Let's not rehash that tiresome topic."

"That suits me."

"Excellent," he retorted. "I shall leave you to whatever it is that you were doing."

"Before you go, I have a question to ask."

He looked past her to the cleaning supplies. "I do not wash windows."

"Very amusing." She led him to the ugly mural just outside the Great Room. The castle tour would go directly past the eyesore. "I wanted to ask you about your father's artwork."

He surveyed the wall painting. "This atrocity can hardly be considered art."

"Well," she said hesitantly, "it is . . ."

"An abomination? A monstrosity?"

"I gather you do not have a sentimental attachment to it? I thought you might since it is your father's work."

"Work?" He barked a laugh. "Folly is a better word for this travesty. I planned to get rid of it at the first opportunity."

"And do what with this wall?"

"Anything at all would be better than this. These are the faces of Father's supposed friends. The men who gamed and drank with him. Ne'er-do-wells of no fortune who were happy to spend Father's money."

She studied the wall. "What would you replace it with?"

"I intended to hire my father's art teacher to do a mural, perhaps a vignette of different scenes here at Tremayne."

She made a face. "Your father's art teacher?"

"Do not hold my father's work against him. He's actually quite accomplished. I prefer to engage the services of someone from our village when possible. And his work is very good."

"I shall have to take your word for it. Now, if you will excuse me"—she turned to head back to the Great Room—"I have some windows to clean."

He followed her. "I know I shall probably regret asking, but why are you cleaning windows? You do have a staff."

"Do I?" she mumbled mostly to herself.

"Why aren't the maids doing this?"

"They are, but it took one of the maids almost an entire day to do *one* window. It's a miracle anything ever gets done around here because they work very, very slowly."

He frowned. "Truly?" But then comprehension lit his face. "Ah. I see."

"And I know what they are doing." Frustration poured out of her. "They pretend they are following my instructions, but they're not."

He tried to suppress a smile. "I daresay you are correct."

"You're obviously enjoying this." She narrowed her eyes at him. "Maybe you told them not to listen to me."

"I did no such thing." He turned to go. "I shall leave you to it."

"Are you sure?" She spoke to his back. "You've made it clear that you are against opening the house to paying visitors."

He paused to look back at her. "I do think your scheme is ill-advised. And not just because it is unseemly. There are only so many visitors this far out from London."

"What do you mean? Lots of people would love to see the inside of a castle."

"We're a train fare and half-day's carriage ride from Town. When you factor in transportation costs, plus the expense of staying at an inn— either here in the village or in Leeds—visiting Tremayne becomes a very costly prospect indeed."

"Oh." Her lungs felt heavy. "I hadn't thought of that." In her mind, Raya envisioned streams of visitors pouring into the castle. But if she couldn't attract enough tourists, she'd have to think of other ways—besides the tour itself—to make money from the people who did have the time and funds to visit.

"At present, you are the mistress of Castle Tremayne and, unfortunately, may do as you wish. Until, that is, I gather enough funds to buy you out."

She snapped to attention. "You intend to buy the castle back from me? I thought you didn't have the money."

"I don't. *Yet*. But hearing your plans for Castle Tremayne has forced me to consider doing whatever is necessary to buy my home back."

"Oh." If he succeeded, Raya could return to New York and start her own business. She should be thrilled, yet she was oddly disappointed at the idea of not staying long enough to set Castle Tremayne on the road to profitability. "I see."

"Assuming that your offer still stands," he said cuttingly. "One never knows. Your late cousin indicated that she would leave the castle to me. Obviously she did not keep her word. The question is, will you?"

She exhaled loudly through her nostrils. "If you manage to come up with the money, Tremayne is yours," she ground out. "I cannot wait to be rid of both you and your dilapidated old castle."

"We are finally in agreement on something because the feeling is most definitely mutual." He spoke with an exaggerated courtesy that made her want to gnash her teeth.

Maybe he'd come up with the money, maybe he wouldn't. Until she saw the cold, hard cash, Raya intended to push forward with her plan. And that started with showing both the duke and the servants that she wasn't a woman to be trifled with.

RAYA WAS ALREADY in the Great Room late the following morning when Milly arrived to continue cleaning the windows.

Her eyes rounded when she realized that Raya wasn't alone. "Who are these people?" the maid asked, staring at the half-dozen people busily cleaning the windows and polishing the floors.

"They are workers I engaged to ready the castle

to receive visitors," Raya answered cheerfully. Otis had proven very enterprising when she asked him to secure some daily hires from the village. In return, she tipped him handsomely and promised not to reveal his role in bringing in extra help.

Milly's forehead puckered. "Does Mrs. Shaw know about this?"

"I've no idea." But she was certain that word would reach her quickly.

As she waited for the housekeeper to make her inevitable outraged appearance, Raya surveyed the progress they'd made. The windows and walls shone, the musty scent banished, replaced by notes of the linseed oil and beeswax used to shine the square oak paneling.

It did not take long for the housekeeper to turn up. Fury lit her face as she took in the activity in the chamber. "What is the meaning of this?"

"You seem unable to inspire your staff to complete tasks in a timely manner," Raya told her. "I took it upon myself to engage daily workers who can get the job done."

"In all great houses, the cleaning staff is under the housekeeper's direction."

"Housekeeperrr?" Auntie Majida spoke from the threshold. "*Intee* . . . you . . . is the housekeeperrr? Then why them don't finish nothing on the time?"

"Good morning, Mrs. Kassab," Mrs. Shaw said with icy courtesy. "I hope you are feeling better."

"*Ah* . . . Yeah, I doin' good," Majida replied in heavily accented, broken English, which was often sprinkled with a smattering of Arabic words. "Now I'm helpin' Raya."

Raya blinked. "You are?"

The housekeeper spoke at the same time. "Help her with what?"

"Her sayin' maybe she needin' a new housekeeberrr. Maybe I'm doin' it."

"You?" Mrs. Shaw said to her. "A housekeeper?"

"I'm workin' before in a big mansion on the avenue in New York City."

"Fifth Avenue," Raya supplied. Even though it was a lie. Auntie Majida had never been a housekeeper to anyone on Fifth Avenue or anywhere else. In fact, she employed a housekeeper back in Brooklyn.

"I'm bromisin' Raya I helping her. If her needin' a new housekeeberrr."

Alarm shadowed the housekeeper's face. For the first time since Raya met her, Mrs. Shaw appeared shaken. She apparently had no trouble believing Auntie was a servant rather than someone who employed domestic help.

"What you say?" Auntie Majida continued, laying it on a bit too thick. "I'm being the new housekeeberrr?"

Raya bit her lip to keep from smiling. "I'm sure that won't be necessary, Auntie. I believe Mrs. Shaw and I understand each other now." She turned to Mrs. Shaw. "Do we not?"

"Yes." The housekeeper's answering smile was more like a grimace. "I believe we do."

"I do hope you'll lead the tours," Raya added. "And if the tourists wish to show you some gratitude *after* paying the entrance fee, you are most welcome to keep whatever tips you earn."

Mrs. Shaw's face brightened, but she maintained an unsmiling expression. "If you insist on opening the castle to paying visitors, and you bid me to conduct the tours, then I shall do as you ask. After all, you are mistress here."

"Thank you, Mrs. Shaw. I shall leave you to oversee the workers while I escort my aunt to her room."

"*Hamara*. What a donkey," Majida said in Arabic as they departed. "She's a servant but she thinks she's better than us? Why? Because her skin is lighter than ours?"

"And we're foreigners. They probably don't even consider us real Americans since our ancestors are Arab and not Dutch." Raya looped her arm through her aunt's. "But I think she finally understands that I am mistress of Castle Tremayne."

CHAPTER NINE

"*ourists?*" Guy exclaimed. "Miss Darwish is opening Castle Tremayne to paying visitors?"

Strick sliced into a cut of veal on his porcelain plate. He'd joined Guy and Frances for luncheon at Trentham House. "She believes the extra funds will be sufficient to keep the castle running."

Frances signaled for the footman to refill Strick's wineglass. "Is there anything you can do to stop her?"

"Nothing except find the funds to buy the castle back."

Guy and Frances exchanged a quick glance before Guy said, "You're not going to marry for money, are you? I thought you were against the practice."

"I am more inclined to allow Foley to cut a railway across my land than be forced to wed a woman with whom I have nothing in common."

Frances smiled. "A wise point of view."

Guy reached for his wine. "I suppose that means you're not marrying the American in order to get your castle back."

Frances scoffed. "Don't be silly," she admonished

her brother. "Miss Darwish may be agreeable, but she is not of Strickland's class."

"Frances," her brother laughed, "you truly are a snob."

"It is possible," Strick said, "that the situation might very well take care of itself."

"How so?" Guy asked.

"It won't be long before the chit realizes her scheme won't amass nearly enough to keep Tremayne running. There are only so many visitors who will travel this far to tour a castle."

"But Tremayne is so very beautiful," Frances said on a sigh. "I would travel far and wide to visit."

"You are biased." Strick spoke fondly to her, in the manner he addressed any of his three sisters. "You practically grew up at the castle." Frances and Strick's youngest sister, Helena, had been great friends growing up. His sisters were all married now and living far from Tremayne.

She smiled. "Guilty as charged. However, even the impartial will find Tremayne breathtakingly beautiful."

"Still, Strick has the right of it," her brother interposed. "We are quite a long way from London."

"Miss Darwish does seem awfully clever." Frances turned to Strick. "Don't you think so?"

"I think she is a nuisance." *A nuisance who heated his blood*. He'd actually had the impulse to kiss the harridan when she landed in his arms.

He couldn't get the sensation of those warm generous curves pressed up against him out of his mind. He realized that Frances was addressing him. Something about the veal.

"The meal is excellent, Frances," he responded. "My compliments to the chef."

"Mrs. Williams shall be very happy to hear it." Frances acted as mistress of her bachelor brother's household. "You know how much she enjoys feeding you."

"Ever since Guy and I started stealing her gooseberry pies when we were eleven."

Guy snorted. "I'm rather certain she made extras whenever she made gooseberry pie after that."

Strick rose. "I should be on my way."

"So soon?" Frances didn't hide her disappointment. "Do stay for dessert."

"I cannot. I must go and oversee a delivery at Orchard Cottage."

Guy's brows went up. "Are you still storing your antiquities at the cottage?"

"Some of the larger pieces." He'd taken to stowing some of his more valuable artifacts at the cottage after two important objects, part of a three-piece set of goblets, went missing from the castle shortly before Father died. Deena was known to sell off family treasures—paintings, sculptures, vases—to fund her opulent lifestyle. But she'd vehemently denied taking the glasses. "The smaller pieces are under lock and key at the castle."

"One hopes that isn't necessary," Guy said, "unless Miss Darwish has sticky fingers as you believe her cousin did."

Strick quashed an immediate urge to defend Miss Darwish. While she possessed many unpleasant qualities, the American did not strike him as a thief.

But all he said was "One never knows."

RAYA STARED UP at the stately stone manor she'd come across on her walk. The three-story home was spacious and comfortable-looking, far more inviting than the castle.

"Coveting my cottage, too?" asked a familiar voice.

Stiffening, she turned to see the duke approaching. "This is your house?"

His usual frown was in place. "My cottage, yes."

"Only in England is a huge house with three levels called a *cottage*."

He went past her toward the front door. "My father gifted it to me on my twenty-first birthday."

She whistled. "Imagine receiving a beautiful house like this for your birthday. I suppose the son of a duke is used to being handed everything."

"Says the woman who was given a castle for no reason at all," he shot back. "Were you about to let yourself in to rummage through my things?"

She surveyed the stone facade and thatched

roof. "If you keep apartments at the castle, why not rent this property out? Maintaining both is a waste of money."

A muscle ticked in his jaw. "Most noblemen have several homes. This is my sole abode. Besides, this is where I do most of my work."

"What kind of work exactly?"

"Not that it is any of your business." He unlocked the front door. "But you might as well come in and find out."

"How much does the circus charge in London?" she asked, following him inside.

He blinked. "I suppose about three shillings for a box and two for a seat in the pit. Why do you ask?"

Because circus rates seemed like a good place to start when deciding how much to charge castle visitors. But she kept that to herself. "I was curious if the price differed from America."

"And does it?"

She had no idea. "I suppose."

The inside of Orchard Cottage was as inviting as the outside, far more so than most of the chambers at the castle. The rooms were comfortable and lived-in. The scent of tobacco, books and old things filled the air. But what made the decor truly special were the antiquities adorning the tables and shelves. Intricately decorated masks and helmets hung on one wall, a collection of gold-colored shields graced another. It felt as if she'd entered the duke's inner sanctum, a glimpse into the more private side of him. She ran a hand over a carved box on an oak side table.

"That's made of whalebone," Strickland informed her. "These, like the pieces in my display case at the castle, are all Anglo-Saxon pieces."

"It's all so . . . special." Raya was unable to find the right words to convey her feelings. She knew nothing about art or artifacts, but these pieces moved her in a way she could not explain. "The intricacy of the carvings is astonishing."

He shot her a wondering look. "I would not have thought you would have an appreciation for artistry."

A not-so-veiled insult. "And why is that? Do you assume Americans are too crass to enjoy art? Or maybe you think Arabs are heathens with no appreciation for fine arts. Even though we come from the very cradle of civilization."

He shrugged. "I am making assumptions solely about you, not entire groups of people. You, Miss Darwish, seem far more moved by money than beauty."

"I do appreciate money and I am not ashamed to admit it. Money is a source of independence, especially for women." If she'd taken a salary, or her fair share of the profits, from Darwish and Company, she wouldn't be in her current penniless predicament. "It means our lives are not dependent on the whims of undependable men."

"You do know that some men can actually be trusted to do the right thing?"

"Like my brother? Or your father?"

He gave her a wry smile. "Point taken."

"I am not skilled at separating the trustworthy men from the fickle ones so I must rely on myself."

He considered her words. "Sometimes it can be difficult to tell. It took years for me to develop the experience and skill to separate a genuine artifact from a fake."

She surveyed the chamber. "I would guess that these pieces have both artistic and monetary value."

"Their real worth lies in what they reveal about the past. Every Anglo-Saxon piece tells a story." The amber in his eyes shone. "That box for example tells the story of Æthelflæd, one of the great Anglo-Saxon queens."

"I'm shocked the men of her time allowed a woman to rule."

"Would you like to see more?"

He was civil, almost pleasant. Maybe his love of artifacts overcame his disdain for her. "I would. Very much."

He led her through adjoining rooms and down corridors, pointing out objects of interest, explaining their provenance. He answered her questions patiently, thoroughly, dropping his characteristic terseness. He kept his voice low and respectful as if they were in a house of worship. Or a museum.

Discussing his artifacts transformed Strickland's demeanor. He became animated, his eyes alive with passion. His voice deepened and warmed, like a cozy blanket on a winter night.

Upstairs were two chambers full of books, notebooks and piles of paper. "And this," he said, "is where I do the work."

"What sort of work?" she asked, slightly dazed by the warm intimacy between them. "I assumed collecting artifacts is more of a hobby."

"This is where I try to uncover the meaning of the patterns, carving and engraving on the artifacts," he explained, "to decode the language of Anglo-Saxon treasures."

"They have hidden meanings?"

He reached for a brooch covered with dense geometric carvings. "What do you see?" His hands were large and capable, the back of his right marred by an angry puckered pink scar.

"It's nothing," the duke reassured her when he saw the mark had caught her attention. "Just an old burn injury from working in the forge. What do you see when you look at the brooch?"

"A series of lines and shapes."

"At first glance, yes." He moved nearer so she could see the object more clearly. Near enough for his masculine scent to coat her nostrils. "But if you look more closely"—he lowered his chin so that their bent heads were almost touching—"what do you see?"

It was hard to concentrate with his potent male energy in such close proximity, but Raya applied herself to the task. At first, she couldn't make out the shapes. Until . . . "Are those snakes?"

"Precisely." He pointed to another curve. "How about this?"

"Birds' heads?"

"Exactly. The bird heads could be a tribute to Odin, a powerful Germanic God." His shoulder brushed hers. "The snakes can confer authority."

Raya's stomach fluttered at the contact. She swallowed. "I never realized."

"The Saxons loved riddles and puzzles and they put it in their metalwork. I spend a great deal of time attempting to decipher them for people."

"You do?" She'd assumed Strickland collected historic objects as an indulgence for his own amusement. "What people?"

"Scholars, collectors, museums, what have you, will ask me to look at pieces in their collections. There is more to these objects than meets the eye."

"Just as there is more to you than meets the eye." She looked up from the brooch, still acutely aware of his closeness, attuned to the rhythm of his breathing.

The gold in his eyes twinkled. "I think perhaps you are a riddle."

Raya frowned. "How so?" She prided herself in being a straightforward person.

"You admire these pieces."

"Very much so." The beauty and significance, the history, of these objects filled her with awe. And made her feel very connected to Strickland. Their gazes caught and, to her surprise, she registered his admiration. Her skin tingled. What was wrong with her? She moved away, putting distance between them. "I should return to the castle."

"Before you leave, there is one more piece I think you will appreciate." He led her to the dining room.

"Oh, it's magnificent," she breathed once he brought out an embellished green drinking glass ornamented with an anguished man whose limbs were entwined in vines.

"It's one of a set of three. They depict the death of King Lycurgus," the duke said softly in her ear, the words vibrating through her. "Unfortunately, two of them have vanished. Hold it up to the light."

"I don't want to break it."

"I trust that you won't."

Mesmerized, not just by the goblet but also by the magical cocoon that seemed to envelop them, she did as he asked. The goblet transformed from shades of green and gold to reds and pinks. "It's breathtaking."

His lips were close to her ear. "As are you," he said, his breath warm and humid against her skin.

"What?" she asked, turning her face toward his. She must have misheard him. That's when she realized they were just inches apart. The gold in his eyes seemed deeper, more saturated. Raya's heart slammed against her ribs as they stared into each other's eyes. She did not back away. Instead, her gaze dipped to his parted lips and she moved toward him.

In one swift motion, he swept her up in his arms and melded his lips to hers. He expertly toyed with her mouth, applying light pressure with soft-firm lips that made her blood roar in her ears. He intensified the kiss, the pressure enlivening every cell in her body. She closed her eyes, losing herself in him.

Abdullah, the grocer's son back on Washington Street, had stolen a kiss back behind the store when Raya was nineteen. But that clumsy, slobbery attempt was nothing like the confident, seductive movements of the duke's mouth.

He cradled her head in his large hands, positioning her perfectly to receive him, his knowing lips fused to hers. The tip of his tongue briefly slipped between her parted lips and touched hers. He nipped gently at her mouth, exploring, becoming intimately acquainted through touch and sensation. Raya sighed, giving herself completely over to the dance.

Her legs almost collapsed under her when he trailed kisses along her jawline and up to her ear.

He nibbled on her earlobe, overwhelming all of her senses.

She moaned.

STRICK HADN'T MEANT to kiss her.

It was the furthest thing from his mind when he greeted her outside the cottage. But the sheer delight Miss Darwish took in his collection changed everything. Witnessing how the artifacts moved her, how completely in sync they were as she absorbed the wondrousness of his objects, the way her breathing dipped when the goblet changed colors, entranced him. He was seduced by the obvious emotion that welled up within her when she examined the relics. He delighted in answering her questions, quietly conscious of the rhythm between them, a throbbing living thing that astounded. And aroused.

And so, he kissed her.

And what a kiss. She responded enchantingly, following his lead and at times taking control from him. He allowed her to take command, eager to see where she would take them—until she pressed her supple curves against his all-too-willing body. He fought the urge to pull her down to the carpet and make love to her right there, with the glare of the sun on the ancient drinking glass glinting down on them, anointing their joining.

Then she moaned.

Strick's eyes shot open. *What the hell was he*

doing? He reluctantly broke away and stepped apart from her.

"Oh." She blinked, her beguiling eyes shining brightly. "That was—"

"A mistake." He finished the sentence for her, before she could say anything too true or too real that would make it impossible to deny the magic between them. "A grave mistake." Although his thickening cock didn't seem to think so.

Surprise, and then what might have been hurt, chased over her face. Before an icy veil shuttered her feelings. "I couldn't agree more. A terrible mistake. Please do try harder to control yourself."

"That shouldn't be difficult. Especially where you are concerned."

She tossed her head. "I'm glad to hear it."

"Didn't you say you were leaving?" He needed her gone so that his cock would calm down. Or so that he could take a hand to himself. Damnation! How could he want to screw someone so thoroughly disagreeable? "And yet here you still are."

"Not for long." She pinched her lips, which were still swollen from his attentions. "The sooner I am out of your company, the better."

"Finally," he called after her, despite his cock still throbbing in protest, "we agree on something."

She responded by slamming his front door hard and loud.

CHAPTER TEN

Raya tromped back to the castle, trampling any wildflowers unfortunate enough to fall in her path.

That cretin! Fury roiled through her, even as the residual effects of his lips confidently taking hers still shimmered through her. She was as angry with herself as she was with Strickland.

She allowed a kiss from a man she abhorred. Not only allowed the intimacy, but sought it out. *Craved* it. What sort of woman yearned to be in the arms of a man she detested?

It had to be the artifacts. That was the only explanation. Any man with an ardent interest in meaningful objects of beauty had to have a certain appeal. Strickland's passion for his field of study stirred Raya, creating a false sense of kinship, of attraction. It was a momentary failing and nothing more.

She climbed over a short stone fence. And then it hit her. She'd lost track of time while touring Orchard Cottage. She was late for a meeting she'd asked Mr. Ward, the steward, to arrange with the late duke's painting instructor. She planned to ask the man to paint over the duke's mural.

Philips greeted her when she reached the castle and informed her that the artist had arrived. She met her visitor in the morning room, but the man who appeared was not a stranger.

"Good day, Miss Darwish," said Alfred Price. "I cannot tell you how delighted I was to receive your summons."

She stiffened. "I am sorry. There must be some mistake."

"I shall be honored to paint your mural."

"You?" She stared at the man who'd unsettled her by intimating Strickland had murdered Deena. "*You* are the late duke's art instructor?"

"I am." His smile was friendly, his manner agreeable. "I'm told you wish to engage my services."

"Oh." The last thing Raya wanted was to have this creepy man hanging about the castle. "I'm afraid there's been a mis—"

"Please do not judge me too harshly." He spoke in a rush before she could dismiss him outright. "I know I behaved badly at our first meeting."

"Mr. Price, I—" She tried to stop him. She didn't want to give this man ready access to the castle.

"I should not have acted as I did," he continued in a conciliatory tone. "I was very emotional. Still, that is no defense for my behavior."

Raya hesitated. Mr. Price's father had been generous when she'd first arrived in England, refusing payment after offering her and Auntie Majida a ride from the inn to the castle.

Mr. Price talked into the silence. "It is just that I was so very fond of Deena . . . erm . . . the duchess."

Raya blinked. "You were?"

"Yes, she was very kind to me."

"Just how close were you?"

"We were friends."

"Oh, I hadn't realized." She took in his lanky form and the soft brown curls that matched his thoughtful eyes. Even though Alfred Price was undeniably handsome, he did not have the same effect on Raya as a certain bad-tempered duke. Yet she could easily see why this man might appeal to Deena.

"She depended upon our friendship once His Grace passed." The words were calm, thoughtful and completely absent of the agitation of their first meeting. "Deena had very few friends in England. She believed people looked down on her because of her foreign origins."

"Including the current duke?" Raya asked. "You accused him of terrible things."

"I should not have said what I did."

"Then why did you? Do you believe Strickland pushed Deena?"

He considered his words before speaking in a careful manner. "I think the duke will do just about anything to get his castle back."

"Including murder? Don't you think that's a little extreme?"

"Perhaps. But I could never live with myself if I held my tongue and then some harm came to you."

"You needn't worry about me. I can take care of myself."

"I thought Deena could too," he said, sadness tinging each word.

Raya's skin tingled. "Did Strickland hate Deena because she inherited the castle?"

"His Grace felt she sold too many of the castle's treasured objects. But Deena said it was necessary to sell some items because the estate was losing money."

"Did she feel Strickland looked down on her because of her foreign origins?"

"She did," he affirmed. "Strickland always made her feel like an interloper. He told her she did not belong here. He was full of rage after Deena inherited the castle. The old duke used to keep Strickland in check, but once he passed, there was no one to protect Deena."

"Did she require protection?"

He shrugged. "Deena had a flair for the dramatic, but she was not a woman given to hysteria. She was uncomfortable having Strickland living in such close proximity. That's why she asked him to leave the castle."

Her eyes widened. "She threw him out?"

Mr. Price nodded. "The duke moved into a cottage he owns on the estate."

Strickland must have been livid when Deena forced him from his ancestral home. "Did the duke make specific threats against Cousin Deena?"

"Not that I know of. But he had much to gain by Deena's death."

"He thought he'd get the castle."

"Precisely, Deena's late husband wanted the castle to remain in the family," Mr. Price said. "Strickland was so confident of his position that he moved back into his rooms in the tower immediately after Deena died."

"But Deena left the castle to me instead. Do you have any idea why?"

"No, but she spoke fondly of you and was looking forward to your visit."

"I see." Disappointment rippled through her. She'd hoped a friend of Deena's could explain why she left the castle to someone she'd never met. "Thank you for your candor, Mr. Price."

"You are very welcome." He paused. "Now, about the mural . . . ?"

"Yes, let's move forward. When can you start?"

They arranged for Mr. Price to begin the following week. He paused before he departed. "The thing about Deena," he said, "is that she loved to surprise people. No one could ever call her predictable. It was part of her charm."

Raya blew out a breath. "She certainly gave me the surprise of my life."

On his way to the forge the following day, Strickland couldn't get Raya Darwish out of his mind. He kept remembering how hot it felt to meld his mouth to hers and how much he wanted to do it again. It was appalling. Working in the forge, fatiguing his muscles, was the perfect way to sweat off the tension riling his body.

Passing the dairy, he stopped by the weaving studio. Strick made a habit of looking in on Betsy whenever he came down. She must be lonely working all alone. Batches of animal hair were laid out on large swathes of cloth drying in the sun. Betsy was busy.

To his surprise, the studio was alive with activity. Several people were hard at work. Strick recognized faces from the village as well as the wives of some of his tenant farmers. Three people were carding the animal hair, preparing it for spinning. Others were busy at spinning wheels, adding fibers to be spun into yarn. Happy memories assailed him. The weaving studio hadn't seen this kind of industry since he was a boy.

"I do hope you are not here to cause trouble," a woman said from behind him.

The sound of Miss Darwish's smoky voice sent a shiver of pleasure down his spine. Strick frowned. He needed to keep his bodily impulses under control. "What is going on?" he asked curtly.

"You told me I could do as I like with your father's goats." She wore one of her favorite working ensembles—crisp white shirt and dark skirt, a leather belt around her waist.

"I did." He paused when realization hit. "They're spinning hair from Father's goats?"

"Yes." She spoke proudly, almost defiantly. "And we are going to sell Tremayne wool to the tourists who visit."

Was there anything this woman would not try to monetize? "What are they making?"

"Wool shawls, scarves and hats with the finer hair and we'll create small rugs with the coarser hair. It's an advantageous situation for everyone," she informed him. "The artisans who make the pieces will be allowed to keep thirty-five percent of what the pieces sell for in our shop."

"What shop?"

"I haven't decided where it will be yet. Perhaps in the undercroft."

"You're going to open a shop in the underground section of the castle?"

"Yes, a gift shop. I think visitors will be pleased to purchase something created with authentic Castle Tremayne wool."

"Is that what you're calling it?"

"Why not? The goats belong to Castle Tremayne. People will feel like they're able to buy a small piece of the castle."

Strick grunted in response. He grudgingly admired her ingenuity. While he'd regarded the goats as a nuisance, she'd (naturally) seen their moneymaking potential. He'd consider keeping Miss Darwish's revamped weaving operation in place once her tourist scheme failed and she departed England.

Suspicion glinted in her dusky eyes. "You don't object to my opening a shop at the castle?"

"Would it make a difference if I did?"

"No." She pulled her shoulders back and tilted her nose at the sky. "Not in the least."

"Then why would I waste my breath?" Once he was rid of her, Strick would close down her gift shop and arrange for the wool goods made on the estate to be sold in the village stores. As was appropriate.

"I have been thinking about Orchard Cottage," she said.

"I'm not renting it out and it's none of your concern."

"If you don't care to lease Orchard Cottage, then why not open the house to visitors?"

"You want me to allow strangers to traipse through my private home and turn it into a curiosity as you are doing with Tremayne?" He might not be able to control the castle—at the moment—but he damn well had a say over his cottage. "No."

"Why not?" she persisted. "Instead of paying someone else to display your collection in London, why not cut out the middleman and exhibit your relics here full-time?"

"Who would come all the way out here to see the collection?"

"Didn't you say people go to London specifically to see your artifacts?"

"Yes, but there are a number of other diversions in Town. The same cannot be said about Tremayne."

"Not yet, anyway," she countered. "But the same people who come to see the castle might be interested in perusing your collection. Two attractions in the same place could entice more tourists to visit."

"Good God, you're serious." He was beginning to understand why people found Americans crass. "Do you never miss an opportunity to come up with yet another moneymaking scheme?"

"It is about time that someone did. If the castle's past residents had put any effort into making Tremayne self-sufficient, we wouldn't be faced with near bankruptcy now."

His mouth twisted. "Our savior. One wonders how Tremayne possibly managed to survive for centuries without you."

"The Roman Empire lasted much longer, for more than a thousand years. But it eventually fell," she retorted. "Nothing lasts forever without proper care and attention."

"The Romans fell due to a string of losses to outsiders. I suppose it is possible that Deena, and now you, could be the outside forces destined to bring Tremayne down."

"Rome also fell apart from within," she countered, "due to overspending by its rulers and a dwindling labor supply. That sounds familiar, does it not?"

Miss Darwish knew her history. And could match Strick point for point. Warmth flooded his balls. There was no denying it. The she-dragon stirred his basest instincts.

"You could open a limited number of rooms to tourists," she pressed. "Your offices and work-rooms would be off-limits to outsiders."

She was like a dog with a bone. "Ah, we're back to speaking about letting strangers into Orchard Cottage for a fee. You never give up."

"Why not try it?" she urged. "You don't live at the cottage. And the spaces and galleries you rent in London charge an entry fee, do they not?"

"They do."

"Why shouldn't you earn the money instead of them? It *is* your collection, after all."

Despite himself, he admired her pluck, her re-sourcefulness. "You really are something, Miss Darwish."

She stiffened. "What exactly does that mean?"

He did not tell her that he found her irritating and frustrating. But also, forthright and intelli-gent. And so damn sexy that he was obsessed with thoughts of screwing her.

He surveyed the workers bustling about the weaver's studio. Miss Darwish might be pushy, but he was beginning to realize that some of her ideas had merit. It would be foolish to dismiss them out of hand. "I shall give it some thought."

"Really?" She gaped at him, her sweet lips parting.

Strick truly was giving Miss Darwish's proposal serious consideration. His treasures were a key part of English history that the public should be able to appreciate. The relics were meant to be seen and enjoyed, not hidden away in a cottage far from London.

Suspicion glinted on her face. "Why are you considering it?"

"Because it is a worthy idea."

She flashed a triumphant smile.

"And," he added, "because I hope to earn enough money to purchase Tremayne and send you on your way."

"Ha." The smile turned cynical, as if a summer blizzard was more likely than Strick finding a way to buy back his family home. "I will not hold my breath."

"WILL IT TAKE long?" Raya watched Alfred Price set up his paints by the mural. "I am eager to open the castle to visitors."

"I have heard," he replied. "It's all anyone in the village can speak of."

"I suppose they are scandalized."

"On the contrary, the villagers are excited." Dipping a brush in paint, he applied broad strokes to the mural. "Visitors to the castle mean new potential customers in the village and more overnight guests at the inn and tavern."

"I hadn't realized." Her mind immediately began turning over potential partnerships with villagers that would make visiting Tremayne even more appealing.

"In answer to your question, the mural could take a couple of months to complete."

"Months?"

"If I work every day. Perhaps you'd care to reroute the tours until I finish painting."

"That's a possibility." It was Alfred's third day working at the castle and she enjoyed watching him paint. Maybe visitors would, too. "Or we could rope off your work area and bring visitors by here. They might find it interesting to watch you create a new mural."

"The late duke's friends certainly did. That's how His Grace got it into his head to paint his friends' faces onto the mural. They enjoyed seeing themselves on the castle walls."

"Did they?" A thought struck her. "Could you add people to the mural, not big floating heads, but perhaps something that would fit into your artist's vision for the piece?"

"Certainly. I was already thinking of adding farmers working in the fields or ladies strolling the castle gardens."

"What if we offered a way for visitors to be immortalized in your mural?"

"At a price?"

"Of course. And you could put their likeness on the people you already intend to incorporate into the mural."

He set his brush down. "It could work."

"And once this mural is full, we could find another castle wall to start new murals with people's likenesses."

"It's a clever idea." He regarded her with open appreciation. "You, Miss Darwish, are very enterprising."

They exchanged smiles, a moment of friendly understanding passing between them. "The responsibility for a castle is a heavy weight for a young woman to bear."

"I am managing. I really have no other choice."

"When you wed, perhaps your husband will help ease your burden."

"Price." The duke appeared. "I see you've already gotten started."

"Your Grace." Coming to his feet, Alfred dipped his chin. "I appreciate the work. Miss Darwish tells me that I am here on your recommendation." Alfred's polite and respectful manner surprised Raya, considering the man's suspicions.

Strickland cut a look between them. "Am I interrupting?"

"Most certainly not," Alfred said.

"We were discussing the mural." Raya explained her latest idea to him. The duke listened without expression.

"As long as their heads are not floating," the duke said after she outlined her proposal, "this scheme is one of your least egregious."

His mild reaction surprised her. "For you, that almost passes for a compliment."

"I would not go so far," he said sternly. "May I have a word?" They left Alfred in the passageway and went far into the Great Room, out of earshot.

"Yes?" she prompted when he paused.

"I do not know how things are done in America, but here in England, it is inadvisable to consort with one's employees."

She frowned. "What do you mean?"

"I could not help but notice you flirting with Alfred Price just now."

"What? I did no such thing."

"Call it what you like but smiling and speaking of marriage to a person who works for you could give people the wrong idea."

"I do not appreciate what you are insinuating," she said coldly. "I may not have been born into nobility, but I am a respectable woman." Back home in Brooklyn, Arab girls were required to be ultra-respectable, to the point of crossing the street to avoid a large group of men on the sidewalk.

"I am merely giving you some friendly advice."

"So now we are friends?"

"You will lose the respect of the servants and others here at Tremayne if you are seen carrying on with Alfred Price."

"*Carrying on?*" Outrage flushed through her. "You are delusional."

His nostrils flared. "I saw what I saw."

"Then I would suggest you get yourself some

spectacles!" Furious, she spun on her heels and marched out of the room, her heart beating furiously. The man had the power to rile her up like no one else.

Despite the strange electricity that arced between them, she could barely tolerate the man and she knew he felt the same. But she caught a flicker of something in Strickland's eyes when he spoke of Alfred that sent shock waves through her.

If she didn't know better, Raya would think the duke was jealous.

CHAPTER ELEVEN

I t's not the worst idea in the world," Hawk said when he and Guy stopped by Orchard Cottage. "You've certainly got enough relics here to open your own little museum."

"I do see the merits," Strick admitted. "These are precious English objects that should be displayed and appreciated by the wider public. Private collections are the height of indulgence."

"And there's money to be made," Guy reminded him.

"But how much? Not many people are going to travel all the way out here."

"One never knows." Hawk picked up a mask to examine more closely. "Touring the castle and viewing your collection could make Tremayne a very attractive destination for some."

They settled in the sitting room to eat the lunch Cook had sent down from the castle.

Hawk bit into his chicken. "Your young American interloper clearly has a head for business."

"You've no idea." He brought his friends up to date on Miss Darwish's wool enterprise, her plans to open a gift shop and her mural idea.

"She clearly has ambitious goals," Hawk remarked. "And what are your plans for the future?"

"How do you mean?"

"Do you intend to go on living in the same house with the girl?" Hawk asked.

"Don't make it sound illicit. Her aunt is a very adequate chaperone."

Guy quirked a brow. "Does Miss Darwish need a chaperone?"

"As far as appearances go, everything is aboveboard," Strick told them. "And, although Miss Darwish is enterprising, I do not believe she will generate enough income to make a real go of things."

"You think she will give up and go back to America?" Hawk asked.

"It's a distinct, and likely, probability."

Guy reached for more food. "Or she could marry for money."

Strick's fork stopped midair. "I hadn't considered that."

Guy regarded him with surprise. "I can't imagine why not."

Because he was a fool. Because he didn't want to envision Miss Darwish in bed with any man other than him.

"It's an obvious course of action," Hawk put in. "There are certainly plenty of wealthy merchants who would love to get their hands on a duke's castle."

The food turned to rock in Strick's belly. Jealousy cut through him. And not just because of his castle. He'd picked up on the friendly energy between Miss Darwish and Alfred Price. He'd suppressed the urge to rip Price's tongue out after overhearing the artist make some reference to marriage. Were they already plotting to wed?

"Or, even worse," Guy said, chewing thoughtfully, "a penniless opportunist could turn Miss Darwish's head, marry her and take control of Tremayne."

Strick shook his head. "The young lady has a good head on her shoulders. She would not be taken in by a fraudster."

"Perhaps you have the right of it," Hawk allowed. "But the fact remains that Miss Darwish is an attractive woman with a castle for a dowry."

"She's a spinster," Strick pointed out.

"A spinster with a castle." Guy smirked. "It won't be long before young bucks in the next five counties beat a path to her doorstep."

Strick couldn't believe he'd been so shortsighted. He'd been so certain Miss Darwish would give up and return home that he hadn't considered the disastrous alternatives. He couldn't let Tremayne fall into another outsider's hands. It was his duty to regain control of the castle and secure the property for future dukes. "I must make a move."

"What sort of move?" Guy asked.

"I need to prevent Miss Darwish from giving up control of the castle to a husband."

"If you want my advice," Guy said, "just turn her head. Flirt, keep her distracted from other men."

"Are you suggesting I take advantage of a respectable young woman?"

"Relax." Guy chortled. "I'm hardly telling you to seduce her. I am merely suggesting a harmless flirtation that will keep potential suitors at bay until you decide how to go about securing your castle."

Strick set his fork down. "I could counsel her to draw up a contract that will prevent any man she marries from controlling the castle."

"That might work in the short term." Hawk swallowed the last of his wine. "But once they have children, she will naturally leave Tremayne to them."

Strick wondered if Miss Darwish's children would have her lively dark eyes. "I must make sure Miss Darwish is long gone from here before she even thinks of bearing children."

"And how will you do that?"

"Perhaps it's time I considered the obvious."

"Which is?" Guy asked.

"Allow the railroad to cut across your land?" Hawk guessed.

"I've already spoken with Foley, the railway representative, to see if they still want to lay rail line over part of Tremayne."

Hawk's eyes shot up. "You've turned him down

repeatedly. Are you really going to allow a railroad on your property?"

"If a railway is the only way to keep Tremayne in the family, I must consider it."

"Did you come to an agreement?" Guy asked.

"Unfortunately, it could take up to a month to make a deal. The railway is still deciding what routes would be most lucrative."

"And the other obvious consideration?" Guy prodded.

"Marrying an heiress." Strick had hoped to turn his estate around on his own once the castle was his. But he was out of time. "My elder sister Claire lives in London. She'll be only too happy to help me find a suitable wife."

"Suitably rich you mean," Guy put in. "Are you certain it's necessary?"

"Unfortunately, I don't have the luxury of even waiting a month for the railroad people." The image of Miss Darwish and Price looking at each other with obvious warmth flashed before him. "Or years to find alternative ways to save Tremayne."

"You intend to wed an heiress who is in the possession of enough of a fortune to buy your castle back," Hawk said.

"I hoped matters would take care of themselves. But now I realize that I cannot leave anything to chance."

"THAT MONEY-HUNGRY AMERICAN is opening our castle to tourists?" Lady Claire paced the sitting room floor in her London townhome. "Next, she'll be hiring the Great Room out for private parties."

Strick wouldn't put it past Miss Darwish, but declined to say so to his sister. "Queen Victoria did open Hampton Court to paying visitors," he pointed out.

Coming to an abrupt halt, she speared him with a furious look. "Are you defending her actions?"

Good God. Was he? "Certainly not. I am merely pointing out that there's a precedent for such a thing."

Claire resumed pacing. "Father is to blame for this. He had no right to leave the castle to Deena. He never earned Tremayne; he did nothing to deserve it. And he just gave it away."

Claire loved Tremayne as much as Strick. The siblings had grown up in the castle's protective embrace, an ancient pile of stones that nurtured them more than either of their parents ever did.

"If it's any consolation, Miss Darwish is nothing like Deena."

Claire faced him. "What is she like?"

"Unlike Deena, she is serious-minded, however misguided her ideas might be."

She blinked. "You like her?"

"Absolutely not. We barely tolerate each other." *But I wouldn't mind bedding her and running my tongue over every curve and indentation on her body.*

She studied him. "Hmm."

"Hmm?" He shoved all indecent thoughts of Miss Darwish out of his mind. "What is that supposed to mean?"

"Are you certain that you dislike her? If you find her the least bit adequate, marry her and get our castle back."

"I just told you she's a harridan." He paused. "You would approve of me wedding an Arab-American merchant?"

She shrugged. "To get the castle back? Absolutely. Is she very dark?"

"What kind of question is that?"

"I suppose it doesn't matter," she said with a dismissive wave. "You will see to it that your children, particularly your heir, are English through and through. Hopefully, they'll refrain from referring to their mother's Levantine roots."

"Miss Darwish seems rather proud of her origins. She might be inclined to mention it to them."

"Nonsense. Any girl with half a brain would rather be an English duchess than an Arab or American nobody factory worker."

"This discussion is pointless because I am not marrying Miss Darwish." He felt a pang of . . . what? *Regret?* What in bloody hell was the matter with him? "She has no money."

"That's a pity."

"But I am here to talk to you about helping me find a wife."

Surprise lit her eyes. "I thought you were against arranged marriages devoid of affection."

"I am. Do you love Floyd?" he asked, referring to her husband of a decade, the second son of a marquess.

"I love the life we have together with our four children. He is a considerate husband and attentive father. I am content."

"You are proof, I suppose, that not all arranged unions are wretched."

"Mother and Father were terribly mismatched. They were bound to make each other miserable from the start."

"Hopefully, I can avoid that fate." Who a man married meant the difference between a lifetime of contentment or interminable years of hell. "Perhaps you can help?"

"Absolutely. I shall put together a list of lovely young ladies who would make a wonderful duchess." Claire was among London society's most celebrated hostesses and tastemakers. "She must have breeding and wealth."

"And a brain would be desirable. And a pleasant countenance if possible."

"What about her looks? What physical attributes are you looking for in a wife?"

Miss Darwish's cool smile crossed his memory. "I'd welcome a nice smile."

She frowned at him. "Is that it? A nice smile?"

He thought of Miss Darwish's full bosom and generous hips. "Curves would be appreciated."

"Now we are making progress. And what else?"

Miss Darwish's uptilted midnight gaze came to mind. "Large eyes. Dark eyes."

She studied his expression. "Do you have a particular woman in mind?"

"Not at all," he half lied. He needed to get Miss Darwish out of his system. Bedding a woman before he returned to Castle Tremayne should do the trick. He hadn't had a woman since before the American arrived, which explained why he got randy every time she looked his way. "I shall leave the rest up to you."

"Very well. I will put together a number of gatherings that will allow you to spend some time becoming acquainted with a potential wife."

"Thank you. I'm most appreciative."

"Not at all. It will be exciting!"

Strick returned his sister's smile and pretended an enthusiasm he did not feel.

CHAPTER TWELVE

In the days that followed, Raya immersed herself in the efforts to prepare Tremayne for tourists.

The duke was in London and she welcomed his absence. She worked much more efficiently when he wasn't around to distract or nettle her. She must be terribly lonely here out in the wilds of northern England to find him the least bit appealing.

Raya made her way to the undercroft. She'd delayed the visit because, next to heights, dark underground spaces—where people were probably tortured a century ago—were among her least favorite places. But it was past time to explore whether the undercroft was a viable space for the Castle Tremayne gift shop.

To her surprise, the cellar wasn't the dark, damp space she'd pictured. The undercroft wasn't even completely underground. Light shone through small high windows along one side of the long, narrow space. She set down the lantern she'd brought with her. This didn't look like any Brooklyn cellar she'd ever seen. And the architecture was charming, with old columns that shot up into arched gothic ceilings.

She could practically hear Baba's voice. *Gothic architecture started with the Arabs.* She remembered Baba discussing it with men at the coffeehouse once when she'd gone to get him. *Just look at the Dome of the Rock*, he said, referring to the ancient mosque in Jerusalem. *It was built in the seventh century.*

Raya would have liked to stay and listen to the discussion. But she and her sisters were not allowed to linger in the neighborhood coffeehouses. It was considered *abe*, shameful, for women, especially unmarried Arabic girls, to spend time in coffeehouses. Raya envied the other women, non-Arabs, who sometimes frequented the establishments.

"Are you scheming where to put your gift shop?" Strickland's voice startled her.

Her heart jumped. He was back. "You've returned," she said, purposely draining all enthusiasm from the words.

"I arrived not too long ago." His intent gaze focused on her face. "Try not to look too overjoyed."

She didn't care for the charge that went through her when he looked at her. "How was London?"

"Uneventful. I visited my sister. And met with my solicitor and banker."

Being alone in the undercroft with Strickland was a mistake. The isolation wrapped them in intimacy. "Still trying to find a way to buy me out?"

"Something like that." He looked around. "What do you think of the place?"

She followed his gaze, relieved to have a distraction from the annoying undercurrent arcing between them. "These arches are actually quite beautiful."

"We have your people to thank for them."

"My people?"

"The Arabs. According to one of England's most renowned architects, Christopher Wren, the gothic style came from the Arabs and the Moors."

"You sound like my father."

"Old? Ancient?"

"That too," she said tartly. "But what I meant is that my father constantly used to rattle off examples of how much the Arabs have contributed to civilization. He would have gotten along very nicely with this Mr. Wren of yours."

She walked along the arched columns, eager to put space between them, to quell the shivery sensation inside her body. "This is not at all what I thought a dungeon would look like."

"There are plenty of pitch-black spaces on the other side where there are no windows. You might be afraid to go there."

"Over here?" She ventured over to the darker part of the undercroft. She wasn't afraid of the dark. Or of him.

He followed. "You really are fearless."

"Hardly." She wandered farther into a shadowy corner. "I just don't happen to fear the dark."

"I'd wager you aren't afraid of anything."

A lump formed in her throat. "You would lose that bet."

He regarded her with interest. "What could a bold young woman who travels halfway across the world to take up the management of a crumbling castle in a foreign land possibly be afraid of?"

"Wouldn't you like to know?" As if she would give him any ammunition to use against her. She tossed the question back at him. "What are you afraid of?"

"Being like either of my parents."

That he would reveal something so personal caught her off guard. "Oh."

"They hated each other and had even less use for their four children. They each pursued their own pleasures and left us to the care of nannies and nursemaids. It's one of the reasons I dislike the undercroft so much. It brings back memories I prefer to forget."

"What kinds of memories?" The hair on her arms rose. "Did you see people being tortured here?"

He laughed softly. "Nothing of the sort. My father was fond of holding his drunken bacchanals down here."

"Here? When he had an entire castle to use for entertaining?"

"It was as far from Mother as he could get, although she was rarely in residence. She mostly stayed in Town. My father enjoyed entertaining down here because the undercroft allowed people to slink off to dark corners where all sorts of depravities occurred."

Images of wickedness flashed in her mind. And all of the men in her imaginings looked like Strickland. The memory of him shirtless in the forge, his muscled and well-defined chest slick with perspiration, assailed her. She swayed.

"Easy now." He caught her, wrapping his fingers around her upper arms. "Are you well?"

His hands branded her skin through her shirt like a hot iron. Their gazes met and his eyes flashed. It was almost as if he could see her thoughts.

She swallowed hard. "Depravities?"

The duke's face was wrapped in shadows but she could feel the intensity of his gaze. "It's . . . We . . . We shouldn't be down here alone."

"Definitely not."

He stepped closer. "All we ever do is quarrel."

"Because you are beyond annoying."

"And you are the most provoking woman I have ever met."

"The feeling is most definitely mutual," she snapped. And yet she wanted nothing more than to feel his kiss again.

His gaze dropped to her mouth. "This attraction between us is a curse."

Raya sucked in a breath. Putting words to the connection, saying it aloud, made the inexplicable pull between them terrifyingly real. "I don't know what you're talking about."

"Liar."

She licked her lips. "The very idea is repulsive."

His pupils dilated as he watched the movement of her tongue. "Nauseating."

"We should keep as far away from each other as possible."

"An ocean would not be far enough away," he growled, "to relieve myself of the affliction of you."

A tropical heat enveloped Raya. "Poor you," she spat out. Everything in her cautioned Raya to get away from him. And yet she remained glued in place.

Waiting.

Hoping.

Yearning.

"You should leave now," he warned. "Go back to your aunt."

"I am not the sort of woman who bolts when confronted by something distasteful."

"You would not find it distasteful." His lips curved, slow and sensuous. "That, I can guarantee."

"Ha!" she said contemptuously. "I doubt that." Oh, but how she wanted him to prove her wrong.

"In fact," he drawled, "you would beg for more."

"You would like that, wouldn't you?" Raya couldn't catch her breath. She was practically panting.

His eyes burned. "I would *love* it."

Later, she would not remember who moved first. All she could recall is that they came together like two waves crashing into each other. He made some primal sound and then his lips were smashing down on hers, hard and urgent as though he would die if he didn't kiss her. Raya felt the same. Instead of shoving him away, she eagerly wrapped her arms around his large muscled form and dragged him closer.

He opened his mouth over hers; she felt the slightest touch of his tongue. She tilted her head so that they fit perfectly and opened for him. His lips moved over hers, giving her long, insistent, drugging kisses that stole the breath from her lungs and the strength from her legs. He showered kisses across her cheeks and down her neck. She arched her body into his, dragging her lips over his jaw, relishing the rugged feel of his skin, and the way it chafed against hers.

He pressed his mouth against her temple, his breath sawing out in quick spurts. "We should not continue."

She pressed her body against his. She ached for him. "We ought to stay a million miles away from each other."

He kissed her neck. "We've lost our minds."

"Clearly." She lifted her chin to give him better access.

"I don't even like you." He nipped her neck.

Pleasure shivered through her. "I detest you."

"You are far too opinionated."

"And, of course, you prefer women to be quiet and submissive."

His hand slid to her breast. "Apparently not."

She pressed herself against his hand. "Perhaps I want to submit just this one time."

Without thinking, she started unbuttoning her shirt. More than anything in the world, she wanted to feel his hands on her flesh. His skin on hers. Before either of them came to their senses.

"Miss Darwish—"

"My name is Raya."

"Raya." He surged forward, kissing her hard. His hands moved to her belt and unbuckled it, dropping the leather to the floor. She tore off her blouse and shrugged out of her corset cover. His hands moved urgently, freeing her breasts from her corset.

"Raya." He put his lips to the tip of her bare breast, mouthing the sensitive flesh, flicking her nipple with his tongue. He started sucking. Pleasure stormed through her. He caught her up to him. "Why the devil can't I resist you?" he murmured, his breath humid against her skin.

God help her. She didn't want him to. He trailed hard sucking kisses up over her décolletage, his hands kneading her breasts, sparking sensation deep down between her thighs. His mouth was over hers again, demanding, exploring.

She wrapped her arms around his neck and kissed him back with equal ferocity. For the first time in her life, Raya let completely go and took exactly what she wanted.

Strickland lifted her against him and she wrapped her legs around his hips, pressing her most private place against his hardened flesh. Gripping her bottom with both hands, he pinned her back to the wall, his hand fumbling under her skirts. He touched her at the apex of her thighs, and stroked her, petting the knot of nerves until the sensitivity became almost unbearable, and she was conscious of nothing but blind sensation driving her to the edge.

Somewhere, a door slammed shut. Strickland froze, his fingers stilling against the wetness between her thighs. He breathed hard against her neck. "We cannot be discovered in this state," he whispered, carefully releasing Raya to the floor.

"Nooo, don't stop." Raya didn't want the enchantment to end. Her body ached for more, the place between her legs throbbed for him. All sublime new sensations she'd never experienced. And might not again. "Not yet."

"We must." Before she could object, he was pulling her corset cover into place and buttoning up her shirt with quick, deft fingers.

"Come back," she pleaded, kissing his neck, her body on the edge of something she was desperate to reach.

He arched his head back, putting his strong throat out of her mouth's reach. "Get ahold of yourself," he demanded in a harsh voice. "No one can see us like this."

Stung, she stopped resisting and watched him find her belt. When he put it around her waist, she shoved his hands away. "I can buckle my own belt."

He studied her face. "You do understand it is for your protection."

"You weren't very interested in protecting me two minutes ago."

His features hardened. "Are you suggesting I forced you?"

He hadn't but she wasn't interested in reassuring him. She was too embarrassed by the way she'd clung to him like a drowning woman. How mortifying. What a *habla.* "What I am suggesting is that I would like you to leave me alone starting right this minute."

"Miss Darwish, I—"

"Let's forget this ever happened. It was awful."

Surprise lit his eyes. "Awful?"

"Terrible," she lied. "I want to erase it from my memory."

He stiffened. "Then we shall pretend this never occurred."

"Excellent."

"Brilliant."

After the way she'd lost control of herself, she couldn't bear to be in his company. "Why are you still here?"

He frowned. "I shan't bother you with my presence any longer."

"Thank goodness."

He turned and strode away without looking back. Listening to his fading footfalls, Raya stood still, hugging her arms to herself, hot embarrassment flooding her. She got so caught up in the moment that the duke practically had to peel her off him. Shame scorched her cheeks.

Unlike Raya, the duke wasn't so caught up in her that he couldn't stop. Still, he did seem to enjoy kissing her. And the other things. The memory of his mouth at her breast tingled through her body. She was so confused. Why was she reacting to Strickland in this way? She couldn't draw on her past experience with men because there wasn't any. Mama and Baba had seen to that.

She peered into the darkness. Silence surrounded her. Whoever slammed a door nearby apparently hadn't come into the undercroft. How far would things have gone if she and the duke hadn't been interrupted? She needed to shake that man out of her head.

She went over to pick up the lantern. She'd come to explore the undercroft and explore it she would. Even though at the moment the last thing on her mind was the undercroft or the Castle Tremayne gift shop.

Holding the lantern ahead of her to light the way, Raya ventured down a dark narrow space and came to a door. She pushed it open and stepped inside. It was a food cellar. Bottles of liquid and jarred foods lined the shelves.

She held the light closer to the jars to see what kinds of vegetables were being preserved for the winter season. A few weeks ago, none of this would have interested her. But, increasingly, everything about the castle piqued her curiosity. Behind her, the door slammed hard. She jumped, the noise surprising her. She went to the door and tugged. It wouldn't budge.

Setting the lantern down, Raya pulled with all of her strength, but it was pointless. The door was obviously locked. She pounded on the door so that whoever locked her in would realize their error.

"Hello! Hello?" she called at the top of her lungs. "Come back! I'm in the cellar! You locked me in!" She heard footsteps. Relief flooded her. Whoever accidentally locked her in was returning to release her. She waited. But the footfalls grew fainter until she could hear nothing at all. Had the person on the other side of the door not heard her?

"Help!" She pounded on the door. "I'm locked in the cellar." She continued for a few minutes until her voice grew raw and her hands hurt from hitting the wood. Giving up, she backed away from the door, plopping down on a sack that probably contained corn, or rice, or wheat. A city girl like her had no clue what kinds of foods were stored in country cellars.

How long before she was missed? Auntie Majida was so used to Raya being out and about that she wouldn't worry until suppertime. And even then, how long would it take them to find her down here? Once they alerted the duke, *if* they alerted him, Strickland would know where to find her. She had nothing to worry about. Unless . . .

What if he locked you in here? a voice in her head asked. *Maybe he wants you to starve to death so he can get his castle back.* She batted the idea away. She'd hardly starve to death in a cellar room filled with food and drink. But what if his intention was to scare her? Maybe he hoped locking Raya in a dark cellar would send her rushing back to Brooklyn. Well, he was wrong.

Someone would come eventually. All she had to do was wait.

CHAPTER THIRTEEN

That evening, Strick smoked a cigarette and sipped brandy.

He tried to focus on a book on Anglo-Saxon antiquities, but all he could think of was Raya Darwish. Kissing her was explosive. He'd never wanted a woman more. He'd also never met a more tiresome woman. He'd been so aroused after leaving her that he'd taken a hand to himself as soon as he reached his apartments. Unfortunately, that did little to satiate his hunger.

The door to his tower apartments slammed open.

Miss Darwish's aunt stormed into his sitting room. She was a short, full-figured, square-shaped woman with dark, angry eyes capable of burning a hole through a stone wall. "What you done with her?"

Strick set his cigarette down and put the book aside before coming to his feet, tightening the belt of his silk smoking jacket. "Good evening, Mrs. Kassab," he said politely even though the woman clearly had no manners. "Have you lost your way?"

She crossed chubby arms high over the prow

of her generous chest. "*Ya* Duke, *fee* big broblem. Raya, her is missing."

"Missing?" Alarm prickled through him. "What do you mean?"

"Her is not coming to dinner. Now I'm worry about her."

"Who saw her last? And when?" He hadn't laid eyes on her since their erotic encounter in the undercroft hours ago.

"Her was coming to lunch."

"You have not seen Miss Darwish since luncheon?"

Suspicion glinted in the older woman's eyes. "Is her here?"

"Where? Here?" What was the woman implying? Surely her niece hadn't mentioned their intimacies to her aunt. "Of course not, why would Miss Darwish be in my apartments?"

"*Ibn il kalb,*" she growled.

He had no idea what she said but the belligerent expression on her weathered face told him it was no compliment.

"Me seein' how you lookin' at her," the aunt accused.

Strick was speechless. First, Guy made unsavory insinuations, then Hawk, and now the aunt? Surely, Strick wasn't that transparent. "Let us find her, shall we?" He strode past the aunt and trotted down the stairs.

"You tellin' the staff to lookin' for her?" the aunt called after him.

"Yes, we must start a search," he said over his shoulder. But before he rallied the servants, he would check the undercroft.

It was pitch-black when he reached the underbelly of the castle. He lifted his lantern and called out. "Miss Darwish? Are you here?"

He waited silently for a response. There was none. His heart pounded. Where was she? He walked slowly through the undercroft, repeatedly calling her name. He checked the storage room last. Surely she hadn't come all the way back here.

"Miss Darwish?" He pushed the door open, holding the light ahead of him to illuminate the darkness. That's when he saw her.

"Miss Darwish!" She was on the floor, curled in a fetal position. He dropped to his knees beside her, propping her upper body onto his lap. "Raya?" He shined the light into her face.

She squinted her eyes open and burped. "Dukey!" she said merrily. The smell of alcohol assaulted him. That was when he noticed the almost-empty bottle of cider next to her.

Amused relief shot through him. "You're foxed."

"You came." She hiccupped, climbing fully into his lap, and settled her plump bottom up against his cock. "I knew you would save me."

Strick instinctively wrapped his arms around her to bring her closer. She was soft, warm and tempting. "Have you ever consumed cider before?"

"Of course! But your apple juice is very strange. It makes me feel funny."

"That's not juice. You're drinking cider."

An adorable frown wrinkled her forehead. "Is it not the same thing?"

"No. This apple cider is boozy, not unlike wine."

"Oh no!" She screwed up her face. "I don't drink spirits."

He tried not to notice the delicious weight of her arse just where he wanted it. "Your aunt is very worried about you."

"Shhh." She held her pointer finger up against her mouth. "Don't tell her where we are."

"What happened?" He feathered a tousled strand of hair away from her face. "How did you get locked in?"

She shrugged her shoulders. "I don't know. I came in here to explore and the door slammed shut behind me. I heard footsteps walking away. I called out and banged on the door but they didn't come back."

He frowned. "Someone locked you in? On purpose?"

"At first I thought it was you," she said in a booze-soaked voice.

"Me?" Surprise rippled through him. "I would never do such a thing."

She cupped his cheeks. "You are rather unpleasant at times."

She said it with no heat. He bit back a smile.

A foxed Raya Darwish was far more congenial than the sober version. "That is because you are so ill-humored."

"And you, sir, are a grouch." Her gaze dropped to his lips. "I want to kiss that frown right off your handsome face."

"You think I am handsome?" He shifted her weight to give his cock less to be happy about.

"Anyhow, you have come to my rescue."

He relished the feel of her holding his face in her hands. He didn't even mind her boozy breath. "Were you frightened?"

"Pshaw." She tossed her head. "I already told you that I am not afraid of the dark. And anyone with half a brain who wanted to starve me wouldn't lock me in a room with food, wine and apple juice." She brought her face closer to his. "Unless your evil plan was for me to eat and drink myself to death. Or to scare me away from your castle."

"Hardly. I know you well enough to comprehend that you do not scare easily." Fury flared in his gut at the thought of anyone trying to harm her. "Why would someone lock you in on purpose?"

"I don't know." She sighed contentedly, snuggling her face into his neck. "Maybe it was the housekeeper. She doesn't like me very much. Or Grasshopper."

"Grasshopper?"

"The butler." The word ended on another hiccup.

"I know it's not very nice of me to say, but you must admit that those bulging eyes make him look like an insect."

Strick suppressed a smile. "I have never noticed that." But now he feared he'd think of a bug every time Philips walked into a room.

"Mmmm." She pressed her lips against his neck. "You smell so good."

"Stop that." He closed his eyes, willing his body not to rise to the occasion. "I've got to get you to your aunt before she alerts the entire village."

"No." She clung to him when he tried to gently dislodge her from his lap. "She will be so angry when she sees me like this. I want to stay with you. Take me to your rooms. I want to see your collection."

"You've already seen it. Surely you recall trespassing into my rooms."

"I hardly had time to see anything because you showed up and barked at me!" She ran her hands through his hair. His scalp tingled at her touch. "You scared the devil out of me. I didn't get a good look at your things. *Please* take me to your rooms."

He paused, trying to think rationally despite the warm, womanly weight in his lap. The aunt could easily suffer an apoplexy if she saw Raya in her current state. And Strick was a little afraid of the old dragon. But being alone with Raya in her boozy, warm and inviting mood was asking for trouble. His mind made up, he set her away from him and stood up.

"You shall just have to deal with your aunt." He could not risk taking this gorgeously plush creature anywhere near his bedchamber. He pulled her to her feet. "Because I am absolutely *not* taking you back to my rooms."

With a firm hold on her elbow, he steered her out of the undercroft. "We'll take the hidden corridors to avoid running into your aunt."

She watched him open a hidden door near the kitchens. "Oh! What is happening?"

"These are entrances and back corridors that allow the servants to discreetly move from place to place while going about their duties."

"That explains how Mrs. Shaw magically appears in our bedchamber even after we bolt the door."

He directed her into a back corridor. "This way."

She stumbled, pressing herself against him. "You feel so good," she purred.

Her tits were plush and tempting against his chest. It took all of Strick's willpower not to devour her with kisses. He gently nudged her away. "Behave yourself."

To his relief, they soon reached the door closest to the family quarters. Otis, who was at his post, straightened when they emerged.

"Please bring some coffee to Miss Darwish's rooms," Strick instructed as he guided Raya toward her quarters. He halted and turned back to the footman. "And some sandwiches. She hasn't eaten since luncheon. Oh, and Otis."

"Yes, Your Grace?"

"Not a word of this to anyone. Understood?"

"Yes, Your Grace."

Once the footman departed, Strick turned back to Raya. Only she wasn't there. "Miss Darwish?" he whisper-hissed. "Raya!" Then he spotted her disappearing around a far corner. He strode toward her. "Come back this instant."

Giggling, she hastened away. "I told you that I want to see your relics."

He closed the distance between them. "Another time."

"Nope." Her ebullient smile made his heart kick. "I want to see them now." She raced up the tower stairs toward his private rooms.

"I'm THIRSTY." RAYA wandered through his rooms, running her hands over his things.

He poured some water. "Drink." He pressed the glass into her hands and wrapped her fingers around it. "And then you are going back to your rooms."

She watched intently. "You have beautiful fingers."

He dropped his hands so they were no longer touching. "*Drink.*"

"Why aren't you married yet?"

"Drink your water."

She ran her hands through her tousled dark waves. She looked like a goddess. "First tell me why a man your age isn't married."

"Drink it while I tell you."

"Okay." She sipped the cool liquid. "Now tell me."

"Naturally, I assumed I'd inherit the castle. I knew Tremayne's finances were in disarray and I wanted to put them to rights before I took a wife."

She stretched, her ample tits straining against her blouse. "Has money always been a problem?"

He swallowed hard. "No. We used to do quite well with farming."

"What happened?"

"It's your fault."

She pressed a hand against her chest. "Mine?"

"The Americans, I mean. You have huge expanses of land. And with your railroads and steamships, you are able to grow, harvest and import certain foods more quickly and efficiently than, at times, we can produce them on our own. Things like wheat, flour and grain. As a result, many farm workers moved to the cities for work."

"Do other grand houses have the same problem?"

"Many of them do. Some just sell their country estates and move to London."

"But not you."

"Even if Tremayne were mine, I have no right

to sell it. My duty is to hold the castle in trust for the next generation. That is what the Dukes of Strickland have done before me. Disposing of this place would betray the trust of the dukes who came before me and those yet to come. Where are you going?"

She sauntered over to the window, the movements loose and easy, lubricated by booze. "I'm restless." She peered out of the window and then recoiled. "Oh, I forgot how high up you are." She about-faced, ambling in the opposite direction. "I love your rooms."

"You do?" The thought pleased him. "I thought the castle was too dark and drafty for your tastes."

"Not your apartments. They're cozy. Being in them feels like being wrapped in your arms."

Damnation. Strick took a deep long breath. He needed to get her out of his rooms.

She glanced around. "You have to get to know Tremayne to really appreciate how special it is."

"And have you?" he asked.

She shot him a naughty look. "I find many things to appreciate here now."

His cock swelled. "Finish your water. I need to return you to your aunt. *Now.*"

"Oh, very well." She petulantly plopped back down on the stuffed chair.

"Why are you sitting? You're not going to be here that long."

Someone banged on the door. "*Ya* DUKE!" The aunt's voice sounded through the door.

Strick cursed to himself. He pointed at Miss Darwish. "Do. Not. Move." He went to the door intent on sending Mrs. Kassab away.

"Excellent news," he said as he pulled the door open. "Your niece has been located and should be back in her rooms by now."

The aunt scowled at him. "Her not there." She tried to look past him. Fortunately, there was no view into the sitting room from the door. "The boy, he bringin' the coffee and he sayin' Raya is back but her not there."

"She is well. She was out walking and insisted on coming back on her own. I assure you Miss Darwish will return momentarily."

"*Hayawan.*" She glared at him. "I'm bromise you if you hurtin' her—"

"I assure you, she is unharmed."

"Yeah?" The aunt didn't look convinced but, to Strick's relief, she turned away. He exhaled. But before Strick realized what was happening, the woman pivoted and stole past him, darting farther into his apartments.

"Mrs. Kassab!" He rushed after her. She was quick on her feet for such a heavy woman. "This is most irregular."

"I'm see for myself," she announced, bursting into the sitting room. Strick's heart drummed. But there was no one there. Miss Darwish's seat was abandoned. "Where she is?"

Strick exhaled. "And as I said—" He broke off as the woman hustled toward his bedchamber. He tried to head her off. But it was too late.

The aunt screamed. A litany of likely Arabic curses followed. Strick raced in behind her to find Miss Darwish sprawled across his bed with her arms flung wide open, completely passed out.

CHAPTER FOURTEEN

"Y ou've got to marry her," Hawk said. "There's no honorable way out of it."

Leaning forward, Strick propped his elbows on his knees and rubbed his eyes. "I have really made a mess of things."

"What did the aunt do when she found Miss Darwish asleep in your bed?" Guy asked. They were gathered in his study.

"She was not asleep *in* my bed. She was sprawled *on top* of my bed, completely passed out. And I was nowhere near her."

Hawk sipped his brandy. "I don't see how that's any better. Your course of action remains the same."

Guy grimaced. "It's possible they don't expect Strick to marry her. Surely the same rules do not apply to American factory workers."

Strick shot him a quelling look. "It does not matter what they expect. It is a matter of my honor. I must do the right thing."

Hawk bottomed out his glass. "Considering this turn of events, you can discard any plan to marry an heiress. The good news is that marrying Miss Darwish means Tremayne will pass to your son."

Guy rubbed his chin. "What if this was all a setup orchestrated by the girl and her aunt?"

"You are not being helpful," Strick said.

"Do not misunderstand me. I find Miss Darwish to be most agreeable, but I think you should consider all possibilities, including that the girl and her aunt schemed to trap you into marriage."

"That's impossible." But was it? The events of the past twenty-four hours clicked through his mind. If inclined, Miss Darwish *could* have plotted with the aunt to lock her in the cellar and then go alert Strick. It was natural to assume he'd return to the undercroft to search for her. And Miss Darwish had stolen away to Strick's chambers instead of returning to her rooms. Strick didn't know the aunt well, but Miss Darwish did not strike him as a conniver. Besides, she held Strick in contempt . . . except when they were clawing off each other's clothes.

"What did Miss Darwish say after the aunt caught her in your bedchamber?" Guy asked. "Did she tell her aunt it was all innocent?"

"She didn't say anything. She was out cold. I still haven't spoken to her. I'll go see her once I leave here."

Hawk set his empty glass down. "And what will you say?"

Strickland exhaled loudly through his nostrils. "There is only one thing I can say." He rose. "And I might as well get it done."

Hawk eyed him. "Is it a terrible hardship," he asked, "the thought of marrying her?"

Given the rapid turn of events—the aunt's screeching and Arabic cursing still rang in his ears—he hadn't paused to consider how it would feel to take Raya to wife.

Yes, a merchant-class American girl of Arab origins might not be a natural fit for the role of duchess, but Miss Darwish was smart and enterprising. And, although she was impossible to deal with, she was very physically appealing. He couldn't get the taste of her soft, seeking lips, or the feel of her gorgeous tits filling his mouth, out of his mind.

Fighting all day and fucking all night wasn't the worst future. Strick was a man, after all, and the prospect of lots of good sex overcame the numerous obstacles that sprang to mind. Yes, Raya said their intimacy was awful and Strick might have believed her if she hadn't been so very reluctant to stop.

"She might be a harridan," he finally said, "but wedding Miss Darwish will have its benefits."

He departed with a grin on his face.

"IBN HARAM!" AUNTIE Majida wailed. "He took advantage of you."

"Auntie, nothing happened." Raya tried to quell the hammering in her head. Majida's carrying on wasn't helping. "I told you ten times that I wandered into his bedchamber because I was confused. I thought it was my bed. I'm not used to drinking apple cider. I thought it was juice."

"Yeeee!" Majida shook all ten fingers out in rapid, jerking motions. A bad sign. Arab mothers and aunties saved that particular gesture for the very worst circumstances. "Your mama is going to kill me," she rattled on in Arabic, "when she finds out you are drinking and sleeping in strange men's beds."

"One man's bed. And I was alone. He was nowhere near me." *At least not last night.*

"And then your uncles are going to come to England and stomp on the duke's stomach for destroying your honor."

Raya rubbed her head. She'd thrown up this morning and slept most of the day away. A hot bath made her feel a little better but Auntie's antics were making her miserable all over again. "Nobody has to know. We don't need to worry Mama."

"I know!" Majida paced away from her. "I am supposed to protect you. It was wrong to live in the same house as an unmarried man. He can't stay here anymore."

Raya's breath caught. "But this is his home."

"He cannot live here. *Abe*, auntie, *abe*! It's shameful!"

Raya considered her options. "If I tell him to leave, do you promise not to say anything to Mama since nothing bad happened?"

Auntie paused. "I won't tell her right away. I

will take time to think about it. But only if you send the duke away. He has his own house. Let him go live there."

The thought of asking Strickland to vacate his tower accommodations made Raya queasy. But she'd rather climb onto the highest rooftop than have her mother learn about last night. Mama would force Raya to leave England and never let her out of her sight again. "Okay then. I will ask him."

"Today," Auntie emphasized. "The minute you see him, you have to tell him to go."

"I'll tell the duke as soon as I see him."

"Wallah?"

"Yes, I swear." A cold shiver went through her at the thought of seeing Strickland again. She had a shadowy recollection of what happened last night. She recalled wandering into the duke's bedchamber and collapsing on his bed. She'd been so tired. But she couldn't remember how she'd gotten from the undercroft to his apartments.

It wasn't hard to envision the drama Majida created when she discovered Raya in the duke's bedchamber. No one executed dramatic wailing quite like Arab aunties.

Raya hoped to put off the meeting as long as possible, but shortly after she promised to evict Strick from the castle, Otis delivered a note from the duke asking to see Raya in the downstairs sitting room as soon as possible.

The duke was standing by the large windows when Raya arrived. Dressed more formally than usual, his form-fitting dark cutaway coat emphasized the breadth of his shoulders. A scarf pin held his snowy ascot in place. He turned at her entrance, the bright light illuminating his aristocratic nose and proud jaw. She sighed inwardly. Why did such an obnoxious man have to be so physically attractive?

Dread filled her at the prospect of telling him he had to leave his home, but Auntie was correct. It was for the best. Raya lost her head whenever the duke came near. She was supposed to be the practical-minded sister. She wasn't given to flighty emotions; that's why she was such a capable businesswoman. She'd never been that girl who swooned when a handsome man walked by. Until Strickland.

The duke lowered his chin in polite acknowledgment. "Miss Darwish." An unexpected air of formality radiated from him.

"Strickland." Her heart slammed against her ribs.

"I trust you are feeling better." The words were sharp and clipped. His accent had never sounded more British.

"Yes. Much." The memory of his mouth on her bare skin rippled through Raya. Followed by a hot flood of embarrassment at the way she latched onto him in the undercroft when he tried to break free. She sharpened her tone. "Is there a reason you summoned me?"

He shot her an imperious look. "Is it not obvious?"

"If it was, I would not be asking, would I?" They were back on comfortable ground. She knew how to argue with the man. It was everything else that threw her.

"Firstly, I must apologize about last night."

"Why?" As hard as she tried, Raya couldn't remember certain parts of the evening. Had she made a fool of herself again? "What did you do?"

A muscle jumped in his jaw. "It was wrong of me to allow you to stay in my room even for a moment—"

"Why was I in your rooms? Why did you not take me directly back to my aunt?"

"I tried. You stole away and took yourself off to my apartments."

"What are you insinuating?" Her cheeks burned. Had she truly been so forward? "Are you saying that I went to your rooms in order to continue . . . what we . . . started in the undercroft?"

He flushed, color arcing high over knife-sharp cheekbones. "You wanted to see my treasure."

"Your what?" Scorching heat rushed to her ears. "If that's how you refer to your manly . . . apparatus—"

"No!" His eyes went wide with horror. "You wanted to see my artifacts. My historical objects. Not my—" He vaguely gestured to below his waist.

"Oh!" Mortification swelled every cell in her body. If it were possible to die of embarrassment, someone would already be digging her grave.

"As I was saying"—he drew himself up, regaining his ducal dignity—"there is only one way to rectify matters."

"There is?" Relief loosened her muscles. He must have come to the same conclusion as Auntie Majida. They couldn't continue living under the same roof. "I hope you don't find it too disagreeable."

"I assure you that I do not. It would be my honor."

She scrunched up her face. "It would?"

"Most certainly. And I think the sooner the better."

"I agree."

"Do you?" he said. "I am relieved."

"As am I." Well, that had gone much better than she expected. "When do you plan to move out?"

At the same time, he said, "I shall speak to the vicar about marrying us posthaste."

"What?" she said.

"I beg your pardon?" he uttered at the same time.

"Marry?" she spluttered.

"Move out?" he asked.

They stared at each other.

"Clearly, we have miscommunicated," he said.

"Clearly."

"It is my intention to set things to rights by making you my duchess."

"Make me what?" The only way she could be his duchess would be—her eyebrows shot up. "Are you *proposing*?"

He went down on one knee. "Miss Darwish, will you do me the great honor of becoming my wife?"

She stared down at him. "Why?"

"What do you mean why?" Exasperation punched through each word. "Is it not obvious?"

"Because you want the castle." Why else?

His lip twitched. He rose. "Because I compromised you and this is the only way to rectify the situation."

"There is no need for such a dramatic gesture. My aunt will keep quiet about what she saw as long as you move out."

"Your aunt wasn't the only witness to you being sprawled out across my bed so intoxicated that you passed out."

Raya winced at that image. She was accustomed to being in complete control of herself. "Who else saw me?"

"The servants. Otis and another footman came running when they heard your aunt's screams. They thought someone was dead."

"Surely they won't tell anyone."

"The entire village has likely heard the rumors. Servants don't keep secrets."

"Well, I don't care what anyone thinks. I won't be forced into marriage because a bunch of strangers might gossip about me." It would be different if she were back home in Brooklyn where she actually knew everyone.

"Respectable people will not keep company with a scandalous woman."

"It is not as though I associate with anyone here. Preparing the castle for visitors fills all of my time."

He massaged his temples. "You misunderstand me."

"Is the idea of marrying me giving you a headache?"

"If it is known that the owner of Castle Tremayne is not respectable, visitors will not come. There will be no tourists."

"That's outrageous." Panic clawed at her throat. Her tourist business could not fail. Revitalizing Castle Tremayne was supposed to be her vindication. Without her new venture, she'd have nothing. "There has to be a better solution than being forced to marry you."

His nostrils flared. "You are the most confounding woman. I am *honoring* you by asking you to be my wife. Any other female within a thousand miles would leap at the opportunity to be my duchess."

"I guess I am not the leaping kind." Frustration trembled in her lungs. "Maybe you should go ask one of those other women."

He stepped closer. "What are you afraid of?"

"Certainly not of you." She squared her shoulders even as her stomach fluttered. "But

I'm not going to agree to marry you to prove that."

"Honor compels me to marry you."

"And you conveniently get control of the castle." It was a trap. It had to be.

His jaw twitched. "I assure you there is nothing convenient about this situation."

"Did you know I was going to ask you to move out?"

"How could I possibly know that?"

"The walls sometimes seem to have ears around here."

"Miss Darwish, put your mind at ease. By law, the castle remains yours even after we marry."

Was he lying? Trying to fool her?

"You can speak with a solicitor if you like," he added after registering the doubt on her face.

"Is this why you took me to your room? So that you could force a marriage?"

He stiffened. "Tread carefully, Miss Darwish. I do not take kindly to having my honor insulted. Nor to having my integrity questioned."

"You wouldn't even think about marrying me if I didn't come with a castle."

"I am offering marriage because I compromised you. I would do the same even if you had not inherited my castle."

"*Your* castle," she echoed. "We both know I am not duchess material."

He released an exasperated breath. "It is true that you are not someone who generally would be regarded as an ideal duchess. You were not bred to be a lady, you have not learned certain manners and etiquette that are normally expected of a duchess. However, circumstances require that we marry to preserve your honor and mine. I am willing to do what is right."

"Even if it means being stuck with me." His words about her wifely unworthiness hit her like a slap in the face. Even though she wanted nothing to do with him. Most of the time. "I suppose you'll just hold your nose at the altar to spare yourself the stench of marrying the New York–born daughter of an Arab factory owner."

"Actually, you smell quite nice."

"Stop flirting with me," she snapped. "The truth is that we cannot stand each other."

"Most husbands and wives of my acquaintance detest each other, so we're already well on our way to being an old married couple."

"That is no way to live. Marriage should be harmonious."

"You underestimate your charms." His voice turned velvety soft. "There is one side of marriage that both of us are bound to enjoy. Very, very much."

The skin on the back of her neck tingled. "Don't be disgusting."

He moved closer to her. "No need to act like a prude." His voice was a low, deep rumble. "I already know that you will not be a puritan behind closed doors."

The scent of him, of masculine vigor and strength, floated over her. "Do not touch me," she warned, her heart thumping so hard that her chest hurt. "I will scream if you do."

"It is my intention to make certain that you scream with pleasure when I touch you."

Her throat tightened. She pictured them naked in bed together, his tongue moving over her skin. "None of this makes any sense."

Did she truly appeal to him? Or was it all an act to get his castle back? She thought of Deena's mysterious death and Alfred's dire warnings. Once they were married, if something happened to Raya, Strick would get his castle back. "How can two people who hate each other also want to . . ." She couldn't say the words out loud.

"Passion apparently has a mind of its own."

"It's much too sudden. I cannot think clearly." She mustn't allow his physical advances to cloud her judgment. Had he planned for this outcome all along, from the moment she arrived? "You must think I'm such a fool. All it took was a few kisses to make me drop my guard."

A storm engulfed his face. He gripped Raya's upper arms like he was going to shake her. "There is nothing foolish about you," he said vehemently. "Stop looking for schemes where none exist. The true reason we are in this predicament is because I find you entirely too attractive."

His fierce gaze made Raya weak in the knees—even now, when she suspected the duke's interest was part of a deliberate scheme.

"Raya." He murmured her name like she mattered, as if she were a thousand times more precious than any of his relics.

"Strickland." She released his name on a long stream of breath.

"My name is Anthony."

"Anthony." Desire glittered between them. Hard and fast. The draw too intense to ignore. Or to resist.

He brought his lips down on hers and she hungrily opened her mouth to accept him. He touched his tongue to her lip and she slid her tongue out to tangle with his. The intimate sparring was pointed yet light, until he intensified the pressure, sliding his tongue along hers, kissing her more purposefully. She wanted to jump out of her skin and into his, to be as close to him as possible. His hands slid down her back, grasping the globes of her bottom, squeezing hard.

He broke the kiss, burying his face in the side of Raya's neck. Her pulse pounded so forcefully that she barely heard his next words. "Don't ever doubt your potent effect on me. I want to fuck you so bad that it hurts. I cannot wait to be inside of you."

Maybe she was supposed to be insulted by the crude words; instead they heated her skin like a fever.

"Say yes." It was both a command and a plea. Urgent need coated his words. "Say you will become my wife."

She inhaled the intoxicating scent of him. Then made a decision she feared she might regret for the rest of her life.

"No," she said. "I will not marry you."

CHAPTER FIFTEEN

Strick abruptly released her. "Why the devil not?"

Raya's refusal surprised him, but what shocked Strick even more was the disappointment that ripped through him.

She licked her lips. The ones that were full and swollen from his kisses. "The list of why we should not marry is much longer than the reasons why we should."

Just when he thought she couldn't be any more maddening. "You are compromised. That's all the reason you need."

"You dislike me."

"Obviously."

"Consequently, it would be natural for me to wonder whether this awkward seduction is a ruse to get your castle back."

"Awkward? I beg your pardon? I have never had any complaints about my amorous techniques."

She all but rolled her eyes. "I shall have to take your word for it."

"Not if you become my wife. We both know you're curious about what you'd experience in my bed."

"Being attracted to you is definitely a major failing on my part. There's no explaining it."

"You will never know greater pleasure than at my hands. And my mouth. And other things."

She blushed. "Stop talking like that."

"I want you to understand that my physical desire for you is very real."

Suspicion glinted in her eyes. "You would say and do anything to get your home back."

"But I would stop short of dishonoring myself or anyone else. To be perfectly candid, one of the reasons I went to London was to find a suitable wife."

"You were looking for a wife? A suitable duchess?" Something akin to jealousy flashed in her eyes. "Unlike me."

"I intended to wed an heiress in order to gain access to enough money to buy the castle back."

"I see."

"Do you? That means I didn't have to seduce you to get my castle back. Which would be a terrible plan because you are not an heiress. You have no money."

"You were going to marry someone you don't love in order to get rid of me," she said flatly. "And now you are stuck with me."

"My only aim was, and always will be, to ensure that Tremayne remains in the hands of the Carey family as it has for centuries. I cannot lose the family legacy on my watch."

"And if you wed me, Castle Tremayne stays in the family. Your son will inherit it."

"*Our* son."

He watched color suffuse her cheeks and ears. Heat flushed through his veins. He couldn't wait to plant his seed deep inside her. "One hopes he won't inherit his mother's argumentative tendencies."

"What if we were to only have girls?"

"Hopefully, they shall be as beautiful as their mother," he answered honestly, "but not as tiresome."

"Stop trying to distract me."

He decided to strike where it really hurt. "It's only a matter of time before the rumors about your questionable virtue reach London and other major cities. No tourists will come within one hundred miles of here if you don't marry me."

"It would make you very happy if no visitors came."

"Not any longer. I have to throw my lot in with yours. The truth is we need that money, at least in the short term, to keep Tremayne from going under."

Surprise stamped her face. "You are in agreement with my opening the castle to tourists?"

"I don't see another way at the moment."

She narrowed her eyes at him. "If this is another ploy . . ."

He sighed. "It is no scheme. I tried to make a deal with the railway people who are interested in laying tracks on my land."

She couldn't hide her interest. "A railway station close to the castle would exponentially increase our foot traffic."

"Perhaps." Her business talk shouldn't be arousing but Strick's blood drummed with need. He wanted to toss up her skirts and put his mouth to her slit, devouring her until she screamed for mercy. "But it will be at least a month before the railway people are ready to discuss a deal."

"We could post advertisements at the Castle Tremayne rail station to entice people who are just passing through."

"Calm down. There isn't going to be a train depot on my land." Making money animated this woman the way a naked strumpet aroused a man. "I am solely considering having tracks laid through an obscure corner of the property. I tell you this so that you will understand that seducing you has never been part of my plan to get the castle back. Marrying an heiress or making a deal with the railway are much smarter ways to secure my home."

She narrowed her eyes at him and he could see her processing her thoughts. "Very well," she finally said.

His pulse sped up. "Very well as in you will marry me?"

"Yes."

He grinned.

"Once we come to terms," she added.

His smile faded. "Must you complicate everything?"

"Actually"—she crossed her arms over her chest—"reaching a business agreement simplifies everything."

"Dare I ask what terms are rolling around in that thorny mind of yours?"

"Be careful. You'll turn my head with such sweet talk."

"What do you want in exchange for agreeing to marry me?" Strick asked irritably. Never in a million years could he have imagined that he, a duke, would have to cajole a virago into marriage.

"I continue to oversee Castle Tremayne Enterprises, the business side of estate operations, without your interference."

"I have already told you that the castle does not become mine if we marry."

"Still, I want all of the conditions set down on paper and signed by both parties in front of a solicitor."

He could see by the firm set of her mouth that Raya would not budge. "Very well."

"Which means I retain oversight of the tourist and weaving operation, as well as any future potential gift shop and coffeehouse."

"What coffee shop?"

"After touring the castle, visitors are likely to be hungry and thirsty. Cook is very gifted. All of her food is delicious."

"I cannot wait until you inform Mrs. Cranch that she'll now be a restaurant cook rather than a ducal chef."

"Let me worry about winning Cook over to the idea. All you must do is pledge not to interfere."

"Very well. Is that all?"

"Certainly not."

He groaned. "I suppose an abbreviated list is too much to hope for."

"You agree to open Orchard Cottage as a museum for paying visitors."

"If you insist." This point was no concession. He had already decided to allow Orchard Cottage visitors so that more people could view his Saxon artifacts.

"And you will allow the railway to come through your land."

"That is hardly fair," he protested. No reason to make the process too easy for her. "Now you are making demands on my land and property? I thought we were only talking about the castle."

"We are discussing both. As you have pointed out, it is all inextricably linked."

He couldn't wait to be inextricably linked to her in bed.

"As I was saying," she continued, "you will direct the railway to establish a depot here on the property to make it more convenient for tourists to reach Castle Tremayne."

"I just told you there will be no station on the property."

"And I am telling you that a depot is one of my terms," she said adamantly. "It can be small and out of the way. You would have final say about its location and design."

"On the very edge of the property. I will not have a railway station within sight of the castle."

"The outskirts of your land? But that will still require an hour's ride to the castle."

"I won't budge on this point. I will not have a railroad cutting through the middle of my lands."

"Very well. We are in agreement."

"We'll wed as soon as the solicitor draws up the document for us to sign." He imagined her beneath him, moaning with pleasure, her hips rising up to meet his thrusts.

"Not exactly."

He resisted the urge to wring her neck. "What now?"

"I need proof that you are able to fulfill your side of the bargain. And that involves us presenting a united front before the servants. They must comprehend that you are now fully supportive of my endeavors."

"Very well. But before I agree, I must demand a concession from you."

She eyed him warily. "And what is that?"

He stepped forward and took her into his arms. "This." Bringing his lips to hers, he nudged her mouth open, gently but insistently, his tongue seeking hers. She opened to him instantly. Loving the smooth cool taste of her, he expertly played with her tongue, a teasing dance designed to excite and titillate. A promise of the pleasure to come. He took his time, making love to her mouth until she was putty in his arms, and he was so aroused he could barely stand.

"There," she said dazedly. "That is enough."

He clawed at her bodice. "Not until I see these magnificent tits again."

"Must you speak so coarsely?"

"I think you like it." He unbuttoned her shirt. She did nothing to stop him. "Some people find dirty talk arousing."

She studied his face. "I don't believe that."

"It's true. It's a form of love play."

"Your grand English ladies enjoy such talk?" she asked doubtfully.

"Not all of them, of course." He spread her shirt wide, baring her corset. "But there was a widowed marchioness that I was once very well acquainted with who demanded dirty talk. And a widowed countess who enjoyed language that was so filthy that even I was a little shocked."

"I don't need a list of all of your past conquests," she said tartly.

"Excellent. Because I would very much rather focus on the present." He freed her from her garments and looked his fill. She was going to be his wife, after all, so he had zero guilt about enjoying the view. And what a view it was. Her large, uptilted tits were a beautiful warm olive color, her soft brown nipples large and distended.

"It is rude to stare," she said blushing.

"When you're my wife, I will do a great deal of staring," he said unapologetically before applying his mouth to one gorgeous nipple that begged to be sucked, while his fingers pinched and teased her other breast.

"Oh," she said. Then, for once, words completely escaped her. And then there were only her shivery moans.

And his own.

THE FOLLOWING DAY, after a restless night, Raya arrived late to the morning meal. Thoughts of Strickland had kept her awake.

She couldn't get the annoying man out of her mind. He certainly had a wicked way with his mouth. She couldn't stop remembering the sensations he aroused in her. Both anger and passion at the same time. And one seemed to heighten the other.

It made no sense at all.

The sounds of Auntie Majida's chuckles coming from the dining room broke into her thoughts. It took her a moment to recognize the sound because Raya's aunt was a stern, serious woman who rarely laughed out loud.

She pushed open the door to find a smiling Strick at the table engaged in conversation with a surprisingly animated Auntie. Both were looking at the embroidery panel that Majida was close to finishing.

"Which one is the moon of Ramallah?" the duke asked.

"That one," she said, their heads bowed together.

"Very interesting." He pointed to another spot. "And this is the one that repels the evil eye?"

"No, no," Auntie admonished the duke. "That one. The triangle moon. And we also showing the nature, like the tree. We sewing things we hoping for."

"Such as?" he asked.

"My cousin's daughter, she have no children. Her want babies, so she sew dolls on her dress and hope her get a baby."

"Did it work?" he asked. "Did she have children?"

Raya had to hand it to Strick. He gave every appearance of truly being interested in Auntie's geometric *tatreez* patterns. Annoyance waved through her. "Good morning."

They looked up in tandem, noticing Raya for the first time. Strick wore an expression of smug delight, his eyes clear and bright, showing no indication that he had any trouble sleeping. And Auntie's smile was radiant enough to make Raya squint. Her stomach dropped. Not only did Majida rarely laugh, she almost never smiled. Something was very wrong.

"Alf mabrouk, habibti!" Auntie beamed. "A thousand congratulations."

"For what?" Strickland had obviously been making trouble in her absence.

"Our betrothal, of course." The duke radiated the cocky delight of a workhouse resident who'd just won the lottery. "Aunt Majida was just showing me the embroidery for your wedding tobe." He glanced at her aunt. "Did I say it correctly?"

"*Thobe*," she corrected before addressing Raya. "See? Your future husband is already learning Arabic."

"He is not my future husband," Raya said. "We are not betrothed. At least not yet."

"Your niece has some conditions that I must meet before she'll agree to wed," the duke informed Auntie, "but I am confident that I shall meet them all."

Majida's expression soured. She frowned at Raya. "Why are you a *habla*?" she asked in Arabic. "Don't be stupid. You must marry him."

"I thought I was supposed to wed an Arab boy from back home," Raya responded in Arabic, feeling on more solid footing now that Majida was back to her usual grumpy self.

"That was before I found you in the duke's bed, *ya hamara*. Don't be a donkey. You are lucky he wants to marry you and save your honor."

"He wants to save his own honor. The duke and I argue all of the time. We can barely stand each other." *Except of course when he was kissing her. Or fondling her breasts.*

"So what?" Auntie scowled. "I didn't like my

husband either. *Allah yerhamo*, God have mercy on his soul. My life was much more peaceful after your *umo* died. May God grant him the highest level of Heaven."

"I don't want to spend my life fighting."

"*Jerrebi ou shoufi*," Auntie suggested.

"Try and see?" Raya repeated, still speaking Arabic. "It's not like the duke is a dress that I can try on and discard if I don't like it. Once I'm married, I'm stuck."

Auntie shook her head. "God help your mother. You've always been a stubborn girl." She rose heavily.

Strick also stood. "Thank you for showing me part of my bride's wedding clothes."

"That is not my wedding *thobe*," Raya retorted.

"Maybe no." Auntie shook her head in the duke's direction. "She very stubborn." Majida shuffled out of the room with her embroidery in hand, pausing just long enough to shoot Raya one last dirty look before leaving them alone.

"You underhanded sneak," she snapped as soon as her aunt was out of earshot. "How dare you involve her?"

"What? I thought it best to become better acquainted with my future family."

She wanted to slap that feigned innocence right out of him. "So much for all of your talk about being a gentleman and a man of honor."

"What is dishonorable about trying to win over my intended's aunt?"

"It's not playing fair and you know it. You told her and got her hopes up to increase the pressure on me."

He didn't bother denying it. "Playing fair was not part of the contract. You are the one who drew up the agreement. There is nothing in there about my staying away from your aunt. When a man courts a woman, he courts her family as well."

"We are not courting!"

"Of course we are," he said smoothly. "However, since it is impossible to conduct a traditional courtship with a woman as pigheaded and opinionated as you, I am forced to improvise."

Raya brightened. Here was her escape. "I will always be opinionated. If you expect a quiet and biddable duchess, you will need to look elsewhere."

And then it hit her. The perfect way to escape. Why hadn't she thought of it before? She would get rid of the duke the way she always sidestepped potential suitors when they came to the house on Henry Street for a cup of coffee to assess whether Raya satisfied their wifely requirements. She'd immediately start discussing business despite the way her mother bit her lower lip in a bid to silently signal her to be quiet. "And I will never lose interest in my business pursuits."

"If that's an attempt to turn me away, you've failed miserably." His eyes gleamed. "If anything, your business acumen is a great turn-on and makes me want you even more. There's nothing more exciting than bending a formidable woman to your will."

"Ha! I will never bend to you."

"I will settle for having you bend over for me." His gaze smoldered. "And you will love it."

Her cheeks burned. "You are expecting things from me that I am not capable of."

His brows drew together. "I don't believe that."

"I am a person who is accustomed to going at it alone in life."

"How can that be? You have a large family."

"Families can be as much of a burden as they are a blessing. It takes a great deal of strength to withstand family pressure to conform."

"I am not asking you to conform."

"I do not do well in partnerships." Her work with her brother was testament to that. "I am used to giving orders."

"And in our marriage bed, I shall be delighted to follow them."

Frustration bubbled up inside of her. "Stop treating this like a joke."

He studied her face and grew more somber. "Why do you feel the need to close yourself off from people?"

"Not people. Just you."

"No, I have seen how you are with others. You keep a polite distance. Why?" His expression changed as a thought occurred to him. "Is it because of your brother's betrayal?"

Life betrayed her. Fate could turn on you in a minute, leaving everything a shambles. A knot formed at the back of her throat.

She'd been at her happiest working at Darwish and Company side by side with her brother, secure in her position and in the full protection of Baba's love and guidance. He was the only person in her life who'd really understood her, accepted her and loved her unreservedly. He alone admired Raya for who she was when almost everyone else deemed her ambition unnatural and unwomanly. Then she lost both Baba and the business within weeks of each other. Two shattering blows back to back.

She looked at Strickland and her stomach tightened at the compassion in his face. She could almost believe he cared. But she'd trusted Salem and look where that got her.

"Our agreement, should you fulfill your end of the bargain, might give you access to my body," she said coolly, "but my innermost thoughts will forever remain my own."

She turned to leave. The only thing worse than arguing with the duke was sharing an emotionally intimate moment with him. She would never give him the power to hurt her as Salem had. Or even Baba. A heart ailment took him unexpectedly far too soon, before he reached his fifty-seventh year.

"Wait," he said from behind her. "You haven't eaten."

Eager to escape, she threw the door open. "I've lost my appetite."

"You ASKED TO see me, Miss Darwish?"

Mrs. Cranch, the castle's sublime chef, appeared in the morning room late that afternoon with her work-roughened hands clasped in front of her.

"Mrs. Cranch." Raya looked up from the ledgers on her desk. "Please do come in."

"Do you have an issue with the menu?" Mrs. Cranch asked.

"No, not at all." Raya forced herself to snap out of her daydreaming. She couldn't allow Strickland to distract her from her goals. She had a business to run and needed to remain focused. "Your food is one of the best things about Castle Tremayne."

Mrs. Cranch gave a small self-satisfied smile. "Then why am I here?" She made little effort to hide her scorn. Yet another servant who acted superior to Raya.

"As you know, beginning next week, we are opening Castle Tremayne to visitors."

"I have heard." Mrs. Cranch's mouth twisted. "Thankfully, that has nothing to do with me."

"That is where you are wrong," Raya corrected. "I plan to open a tea shop in the old malt house in the outer bailey. I should like for you to provide your spectacular pastries and tea sandwiches."

The woman's mouth dropped open. "You want *me* to cook for the general public?"

"I do." Raya held Mrs. Cranch's gaze. "Your food is delicious. More people should have the opportunity to experience it."

"It is precisely because of my superior skills that I am in service to the Duke of Strickland, one of the most important peers of the land."

"Since I am now the owner of Castle Tremayne, you work for me."

Mrs. Cranch gave a derisive sniff.

Raya ignored it. "I will provide you with extra kitchen staff as needed if the tea shop becomes busy enough to warrant it." She threw in a little extra flattery to win the woman over. "Once people sample your lemon tarts and apricot cakes, they're bound to want to purchase some to take home with them."

Mrs. Cranch gasped. "You expect my creations to be sold for takeaway like a common street vendor?"

"Yes. I believe they will sell very well."

"That is hardly the point!" the cook burst out. "My cooking is meant to be exclusive. Reaching the level of serving a duke is the pinnacle for any cook. I have worked hard to get where I am. You are asking me to lower myself to serve the ordinary masses."

"Times are changing, Mrs. Cranch," said a familiar male voice, "and we must change with them if the castle is to survive into the next century." Strickland stood on the threshold wearing a light jacket and carrying a worn leather satchel.

Mrs. Cranch turned to the duke with a desperate look on her face. "Surely Your Grace cannot agree with this."

He lifted a shoulder. "Miss Darwish is mistress here."

"But she wants me to cook for the general public," she pleaded. "I would be no better than a tavern cook."

"Not at all." He set the bag down. "You could become the next Agnes Marshall."

"Who is that?" Raya asked.

"Possibly England's most famous cook," he told her. "She's built an empire selling skillets and food ingredients."

"I had not thought of that," Mrs. Cranch said.

"Perhaps one day you will write a cookbook," Strickland said. "You could call it *Recipes Fit for a Duke* or *Recipes When Your Home Is Your Castle* by Mrs. Cranch."

Her eyes lit up. "I do know very many excellent recipes."

Raya marveled at how skillfully Strickland managed the cook. "And we could sell your book in the tea shop," she added. "And in the castle gift shop."

"Oh," Mrs. Cranch breathed, delight glowing in her face, "that would be something."

"Excellent," Raya said. "We are in agreement. I will consult with you later. In the meantime, please think of twenty or so items you would like to see on the menu at the Castle Tremayne tea shop. Both savory and sweet."

"Yes, miss," Mrs. Cranch said respectfully.

"Thank you, Mrs. Cranch," Raya said. "That will be all."

Once the cook departed, Raya focused on the duke. Was he leaving? "Why are you carrying a satchel?"

"Not even a thank-you for helping you with Mrs. Cranch? You really are a shrew," he said mildly.

"It's nice to see you adhering to the part of our agreement which stipulates that you appear supportive of me in front of the servants."

"As long as you are aware."

"I did notice. Thank you." She gestured toward his bag, surprised by the tug of regret in her chest at the thought of him going away. "Where are you going? Another dig?"

He advanced toward her. "Have you already forgotten that you've ordered me to move out?"

"This is you moving out? That bag only holds enough clothes for a few days away."

"I don't expect to be gone from the castle for overlong."

"You are very optimistic. Or delusional." She turned a page in the ledger, pretending to focus on something other than him. "I haven't decided which."

"Always such flowery compliments from my betrothed."

"Are you quite done?" She was thankful to have the desk as a buffer between them. "I have work to do."

He walked around the desk. "Actually, there is one thing."

"I cannot wait for you enlighten me."

"Where do you plan to open this tea house?"

"In the old malt house. It's vacant."

"All of the buildings in the outer bailey belong to me." He picked up a paperweight and examined it. "The tea shop is not part of our agreement."

She stiffened. "Are you going to fight me on this?"

"Not at all." He set the paperweight down. "Consider my allowing you to open a tea shop on my property a betrothal gift."

"We are not yet betrothed."

He walked behind her. "We will be soon enough."

"We shall see." She didn't turn to look at him. She didn't want to give him the satisfaction, but she sensed him standing right behind her and her heartbeat drummed harder.

"But I will ask for a little boon for my generosity."

Need ratcheted up in her. "Do not touch me," she warned in a reedy voice. "I have work to do."

He put his mouth to her ear. His breath warm and humid. "I want to hear you say my name."

Was that all? "Strickland. There. Now you can leave."

"My name is Anthony." The words were deep, sultry. "Say it," he commanded.

The hair on the back of her neck tingled. "Anthony."

"Beautiful." His breath tickled her ear. She waited to feel his lips on her sensitive lobe. "I cannot wait to be inside you."

She closed her eyes, her nerve endings all firing. Waiting. Needing. Apparently, she didn't hate his coarse language after all. There was no denying that it excited her.

"The tea shop is my special gift to you. But the next time you want something that is mine, I shall demand much more from you." His lips barely brushed her ear. "Be ready."

His lips brushing her neck. Her nipples tightened. Would he slide his strong hands down and cup her breasts, fondling them?

A whoosh of cool air swept over her as he stepped away and reached for his bag. "I shan't bother you anymore for today."

Disappointment streaked through her. He'd incited a riot within her body without doing anything to quell it. She registered his cocky smile. "You did that on purpose . . . you cad!"

"I didn't even touch you," he said with false innocence as he glided out the door. "But the next time I do, it will be because you begged for it."

CHAPTER SIXTEEN

W hat are we doing here?" Strickland asked. "I do not know what *you* are doing here," Raya said as they made their way to the old ruins on the property.

"Me? I am escorting my betrothed, of course."

"How many times must I remind you that we are not engaged yet?"

"A mere technicality. Have you shared our happy news with the rest of your family?"

"Absolutely not." She stepped carefully over a patch of uneven ground. "There is no happy news to share and there probably won't ever be. I doubt you will be able to keep your end of the bargain."

His eyes sparked as he ran a lingering gaze over her body. "Do not forget that I have very strong incentive for keeping my part of our deal."

Warmth slid through her. "Stop looking at me like I am a slab of meat."

"I shall try to contain myself." They set off up a small hill. "You neglected to say why we are going to the ruins."

"Alfred mentioned that the old abbey is very beautiful."

"Alfred?" He frowned. "I did not realize you two are on such familiar terms."

"His is one of the few friendly faces at Castle Tremayne. Almost everyone else looks like they've swallowed a lemon whenever I address them."

"When you are my duchess everyone will treat you with the utmost respect."

Every conversation with Strick circled back to marriage these days. She wasn't naive enough to believe he found her that irresistible. His eagerness was primarily driven by his obsession to repossess his castle.

"If you must know, I am visiting the abbey to see if it would interest tourists."

"Yet another profit scheme. I should have known. You are most definitely a dollar princess."

"Hardly." She trudged upward. The ruins were at the top of the hill. "Isn't that what they call the wealthy American girls who come to England to hunt a lord?"

"You are a variation on the theme." He grabbed her by the waist and pulled her close. "You are all about making a dollar. And, as to landing a lord, you've already snagged a duke. I am the most eligible noble under the age of seventy in all the land."

"There must be a sixty-nine-year-old minor noble out there who is far less irritating than you." Raya pulled away as she spoke, ignoring the thrill that went through her whenever Strickland touched her.

Undeterred, he came up behind her and nibbled on her neck. "But would you want him to do this?" He slid a hand around to cup her breast. "Or this?"

She suppressed a shiver of pleasure. "Stop pawing me. I am not here for your—" The words died on her lips when she realized they'd reached the top of the hill and the abbey came into view.

The imposing solid stone structure was a majestic combination of columns and arches. A lantern tower soared above the rest of the abbey, adding flair and drama. "*Those* are the ruins?"

He wrapped an arm above her upper chest, his hand gently clasping her shoulder. "The abbey is quite a sight, is it not?"

"It's in far better shape than I envisioned." She allowed her body to relax back against the warm strength of his as she took in the view, momentarily forgetting that Deena had died here and some villagers blamed the duke. "It is stunning."

"You should see the view from the lantern tower. It is truly spectacular."

Raya tried not to flinch at the thought of being up so high. She reassured herself that even if Strickland were capable of murder, he'd at least wait until they were wed, to assure his inheritance, before harming her.

She pulled away to have a closer look. Only the outer walls had withstood centuries of nature's battering, leaving a shell overgrown with grass and handfuls of bright wildflowers.

"As you can see, the inside isn't as impressive as the exterior," he noted, following her inside.

"I think it's splendid." She sat on an old stone bench, surrounded by immense arch-shaped old windows. She could well imagine the colorful stained-glass panes that used to adorn them. When had she started developing an appreciation for archaic structures? "The grass and the wildflowers are lovely. It has the feeling of a park with spectacular views."

"My sisters and I used to play here all the time."

"This would definitely appeal to visitors. We must add it to the tour."

His eyes twinkled. "Haven't you forgotten something?"

"Have I?"

"The ruins are technically mine. They are on my land."

She blew out an exasperated breath. "Not this again."

"What can I say? The abbey is not part of our agreement."

"How could they be? I hadn't yet seen them when we made our deal."

"Still. You set your terms. I agreed to them. The abbey is not included."

She narrowed her eyes at him. "What do you want in return for allowing me to add the abbey to the tour?"

He shot her a wolfish grin. "I thought you'd never ask."

She braced herself. Would he lay her down in the grass and do delightfully wicked things? "Well?"

"In exchange for allowing you to add the ruins to the tour, you must agree to return here tomorrow with me."

"Whatever for?"

"We shall come an hour before sunset and you agree to spend at least two hours with me."

"One hour is more than enough."

He waggled his eyebrows. "Not for what I have in mind."

"One hour and fifteen minutes."

"You truly are difficult. One hour and thirty minutes. That's my final offer."

"Very well," she said sullenly. "And not a minute longer."

"Excellent. Now that the haggling is out of the way, shall we go and see the view from the lantern tower?"

"No." She came to her feet. "I have had enough of you for one day."

"It is ridiculous to come out here just before sunset," Raya grumbled the following day as they hiked back to the abbey. "We will be returning to the castle in the dark of night, which is pure folly."

"Stop being such a harpy." Strick had spent all day arranging his surprise. He couldn't wait to see her reaction.

"One of us could twist an ankle in the dark." She shot him a suspicious look. "Or fall and get seriously hurt."

"Relax, Miss Darwish." Strick wasn't sure whether he wanted to gag the harpy or lay her down beneath him and have his way with her. "We will both be perfectly safe."

"Didn't Deena die at the abbey at night?"

"She fell from the lantern tower. Even if I wanted to push you off the tower to silence your incessant nagging, I couldn't possibly drag you up all of those steps."

"I am not going up to the tower," she informed him. "If that's what you have in mind for this outing, you may as well forget about it."

"Noted." It confounded him that he was actually eager to make this harridan his wife. That's what happened when a man thought with his cock.

"Do *you* think Deena's death was an accident?" she asked.

"I have no reason to believe otherwise." He'd wondered when, and how, she'd bring up the rumors. People gossiped about dukes. The allegations were ridiculous and, to his knowledge, no one took them seriously. "The only person I know who hated Deena was me," he said candidly, "and I did not lure her up to the lantern tower to push her to her death. We are not living in a gothic novel."

Her dark brows shot up. "You certainly are direct."

"Why be otherwise? You basically just asked me whether I killed your cousin."

She flushed. "I did no such thing. Stop putting words in my mouth."

He could think of other things he'd rather put in her mouth. Although she might slice his cock right off with that sharp tongue. "I am obviously aware of the absurd lies floating around."

"The rumors don't bother you?"

"I wouldn't mind finding the source of the gossip and having a word with them. But I am a duke and we live in a quiet village in the wilds of England. It's to be expected that people will invent things to talk about to pass the time."

They reached the ruins and he led her inside. Her eyes lit up when she caught sight of his surprise. "What is this?"

At Strick's direction, the servants had laid out an elaborate picnic atop a low-to-the ground table. Vases full of wildflowers adorned the table. He and Raya would sit on the blanket on the ground to enjoy their supper.

"Surely you've seen a picnic before," he said. "Or do you have no picnics in New York?"

"I know what a picnic is." She eyed the porcelain plates and silver serving dishes. "This is obviously a duke's version of roughing it." Her eyes widened as she surveyed the scene. "Oh my."

"I see you've noted the rest of my surprise." He'd directed the gardener to plant more wildflowers throughout the ruins. Shoots of pink, purple, blue, white and yellow abounded. "I don't know your favorite color, so I had every shade planted."

"Purple flowers are my favorite but this array of color is gorgeous." She rested her hand against her chest as she surveyed the scene. "This is so . . . thoughtful."

He beamed, feeling ridiculously pleased with himself. "Careful, Miss Darwish, that sounds suspiciously like a compliment."

She strolled among the flowers. "It might be," she said back over her shoulder. "The view is wonderful."

His eyes dropped to her curvaceous backside. "Spectacular."

She faced him. "I am hungry."

The glow of the late afternoon sun bathed her face in golden light. The dark catlike eyes, the austere cut of her cheeks, the determined set of her lips. He realized with a jolt that Miss Darwish was a beauty. Only hers was the type of beauty that took time to fully come to appreciate. "I am starved."

"Stop looking at me as though I am the meal." She pointed to the spread on the table. "That's what we are eating."

"I cannot wait to eat a great deal more than that," he murmured. He imagined feasting between her legs until she came at least twice.

"I do not know what that means and I am certain that I am better off that way," she said, lowering herself to the ground at the table.

He sat beside her.

"Must you be so close?" She frowned. "Why not take a seat across from me?"

"Absolutely not." The table was set before an enormous archway where a set of double doors used to be. "As we eat, we shall watch the sun set through that opening. It's a spectacular sight from up here on the hill."

He served her a little bit of everything because he did not know what she liked. Raya was not a dainty eater. She enjoyed her food.

"Food is very central to an Arab household," Raya told him. "It means love, welcome and hospitality."

"And here I thought food was just food," he said, adding more lamb to her plate. "What are your favorite dishes?"

"My very favorite meal is an Arabic dish called *musakhan*. It is basically chicken and bread with lots of onions."

"Chicken and bread? That doesn't sound particularly exciting."

"The onions are caramelized, sautéed in olive oil. That's a very important part of the meal. And they are flavored with sumac."

"I have never heard of it."

"It's a spice. It's deliciously lemony, tangy and a little fruity. There's nothing tastier in my opinion. I really do miss it."

The meal was surprisingly harmonious, with Raya answering Strick's questions about her siblings and parents. She asked him about his sisters and his childhood at the castle. The duke proved to be an unexpectedly entertaining dinner companion. They quieted as the sun began to fall below the horizon in a glorious swirl of red and gold.

"It's breathtaking," she said. "Thank you for arranging this."

"Maybe one day you will consent to go up the lantern tower. This view is lovely but the one from the tower is unparalleled."

She flinched. "No," she said sharply. "I will never go up there with you."

He stiffened, shocked by her reaction. She *physically* recoiled from the idea of going to the lantern tower with him. There could only be one reason why. She actually believed him capable of murder.

"As you like." He set down his drink and came to his feet, the amiable mood shattered. "We should return now."

"Already?" Disappointment flickered across her face. "But the sun hasn't completely set yet and we haven't had dessert."

"When a duke calls for the end to an event he is hosting, Miss Darwish," he said stiffly, "the event is concluded."

"You said you wanted ninety minutes. We've barely been here an hour." Tilting her head to the side, she gazed up at him. "Why are you being like this?"

"Suit yourself," he said when she didn't rise. "I shall send Otis back to escort you home."

She popped up, her eyes glittering. "You, sir, are no gentleman. To even think about leaving me out here alone in the dark is reprehensible."

She thought him capable of murder yet expected him to be a gentleman? "You are the most mystifying woman of my acquaintance." He offered his arm. "Ready?"

She marched by him, ignoring his proffered arm. "I am more than ready to be out of your company."

"I assure you, my dear virago, the feeling is completely mutual."

CHAPTER SEVENTEEN

S hould you wed, the law is on your side," Mr. Combs informed Raya. "You retain control of the castle as well as any income that the property generates."

"Even if I marry a duke?" she asked.

"Who you wed has no bearing on your rights. Parliament passed the Married Women's Property Act a few years ago. It allows you to keep all inherited property. You also have the power to sell the castle, should you wish."

The solicitor appeared in the morning room three days after Strickland abruptly ended the picnic supper. Raya had not seen him since, but the duke would have to make an appearance today. The document outlining the terms of their marriage agreement was ready to be signed. If he was still interested.

Raya told herself that Strick's absence was a positive occurrence that allowed her to focus on the impending opening of the castle to visitors. Yet part of her was disappointed he hadn't manufactured some excuse to see her. She missed the irksome man's presence. There was no explaining it.

"You and His Grace considering marriage is certainly a surprising turn of events," the solicitor said as they waited for Strick to make an appearance.

"Do you know why we are marrying?"

The solicitor squirmed in his seat. "Well, I . . . erm . . ." His uncomfortable reaction appeared to confirm what Strickland predicted. Talk of Raya being compromised had spread.

"You will have heard about my being found in an indelicate situation."

Mr. Combs looked everywhere but at Raya. "There has been . . . I haven't given any credence to—" He stumbled over his words.

"I can assure you that nothing untoward occurred. But I understand that even the appearance of impropriety can damage my reputation."

"But His Grace is doing right by you so all will be forgotten," Mr. Combs assured her. "You are a very fortunate young lady."

She wasn't sure about that. Strickland's abrupt dismissal of her at the ruins left her with more questions about his intentions than ever before. "If we do not marry, in your estimation, would people still visit Castle Tremayne?"

"If I may speak frankly," he said hesitantly.

"Please do. I expect nothing less."

"If you do not wed, many people will stay away. There is a big difference between attending an enterprise run by a duchess and one run by a woman of questionable reputation."

Raya exhaled. She truly was stuck. Castle Tremayne could not fail. She couldn't bear to lose another business enterprise.

"Combs." The duke stood on the threshold wearing a thick wool sweater and jodhpurs with riding boots. Raya's heart sped up. But he did not acknowledge her. "I trust you have the agreement."

The solicitor came to his feet. "Indeed, Your Grace."

Strickland briefly looked Raya's way and it was as though all sunshine vanished. His cool gaze whipped through her like a Nordic breeze. He barely dipped his chin before focusing on the agreement Combs laid out on the table for him.

"This is not the agreement I sent you," he remarked as he read through the document.

"Miss Darwish requested some changes." Mr. Combs's curious gaze darted between Raya and the duke. There was no missing the tension hovering in the air.

Raya spoke up. "I sent word to Mr. Combs two days ago asking him to make the changes we agreed on. The tea shop in the courtyard and your consent for paying visitors to be allowed to tour the ruins."

"Naturally you felt compelled to add them to the agreement"—the duke's attention remained on the document—"because my word alone is not satisfactory."

"It is nothing personal." Raya knew better than to trust any man's word. And yet she felt a sprinkling of guilt. "This is a business agreement and business agreements should be as thorough as possible."

He did not respond nor show any sign that he'd heard her. Reaching for a pen, he signed the document. "Is there anything else, Combs?"

"No, Your Grace. Miss Darwish has already signed. The agreement is now in force."

"It is done then. Good day." The duke departed without another glance in Raya's direction.

Mr. Combs watched after the duke for a moment. He turned to Raya with sympathy in his eyes.

"Well," she said lightly, despite the disappointment roiling her chest, "as you can see, it is not a love match."

AFTER MR. COMBS's departure, Raya tried to get her mind off Strickland by sorting through the mail Otis brought in earlier. She was surprised to find a letter from New York. Her brother Salem had written to her.

Her stomach clenched. No one had deliberately hurt Raya as badly as Salem. After his betrayal, what could he possibly have to say?

The contents of the letter were so unexpected that Raya had to read the missive twice before its contents started to sink in. It was an apology and an offer. Salem regretted tossing her from the business. It was childish and a bad business decision, he wrote. He now realized that she was a critical part of the enterprise. He'd allowed the shock of Baba's death and Mama's influence to color his judgment.

Would Raya consider coming back and working alongside him as Baba had wanted? He would sign a contract, Salem said, assuring her a place in the company for as long as she wanted.

Raya's heart raced. Not so long ago, Salem's offer would have been the answer to her prayers. Her path to redemption. A way to return home triumphant.

Auntie Majida wandered in just as Raya finished reading the letter for a third time. "Have you come to your senses and agreed to marry the duke yet?"

Raya stared at her brother's words. "Not yet."

"What are you reading?"

"A letter from Salem." She looked up from the letter. "He wants me to come back and work at the business."

Majida frowned. "Why?"

"Maybe because he realizes the business is not as successful without me."

"Don't be thick blooded." Auntie made a moue of distaste. "Nobody likes a girl with a big head."

"What you mean is that nobody likes a girl who knows her worth." Raya pondered the unexpected offer. A signed employment agreement meant security. Her position at Darwish and

Company would no longer be subject to Salem's whims. She and her brother had worked well together before. Could they again?

"You are going to marry the duke. You can't go back home."

"Why not? No one in America will know of the scandal."

"*I* know!"

"And if you keep it to yourself, everything will be fine. *If* we go back."

"Are you considering Salem's offer?"

"I am not sure. Not so long ago, I would have jumped at the chance to return to Darwish and Company." Raya would have done just about anything to escape the crumbling castle. But her thinking had changed now that she was on the verge of steering the old fortress back to profitability.

"And now?" Majida asked.

"I am my own boss here." And she thrived on it. "I own a castle and all of its associated business enterprises—the tours, the weaving shop, gift shop and tea shop. I am not sure I could work for somebody else now."

Majida looked heavenward. "Deena ruined you by leaving this castle to you. And you do not know if any of it, the tours, the tea shop, will make any money."

"I believe in myself and in Castle Tremayne." Raya realized she'd become invested in the castle. She felt the pride of ownership and couldn't envision a greater, more satisfying challenge than building her related business ventures from the ground up, eventually earning enough income to fully restore Tremayne. What a sight that would be. "Working with Salem means he would always have the last word."

Auntie tapped her pointer finger against her right temple. "If a woman is smart, she lets the man think he has the last word, but in truth the woman will be running things."

Raya's eyes widened. "Auntie! You always say the man should be the boss."

"Of course. From the outside, the man must rule the family. That is how he saves face. But women are the true authority in a family."

"Why should women have to hide their strength?"

Auntie shook her head. "It is the way of things. I am going back to work on your wedding *thobe*."

"Are you really making that for me? You've been stitching it since we left Brooklyn."

Auntie nodded. "That's why I added some blue to the red flowers. And there will be children on the back panel. It's a wish for you to get married and have children. And look. It worked. The duke wants to marry you even though you are old."

"He wants his castle back."

"So what?" Majida said as she disappeared out the door. "You become a duchess and he gets the castle. It's a good exchange."

After Auntie left her, Raya pondered her options. Did she want to expend energy making Salem more comfortable with her competence when she could stay at the castle and run her own business? But then she considered Strickland and how, in a flash, his demeanor could change from flirtatious and attentive to cold and disdainful.

There was no question the duke excited her physically. And she'd even begun to enjoy their verbal sparring. But, beyond that, how well did she really know the man? How far would he go to get what he wanted? What if the cold, aloof man of late was the real duke? Would he treat her with contempt once he secured the castle for his future heirs?

The alternative was to return home where no one would know of the scandal. She wouldn't be forced into marrying a man who ran hot and cold on her. A man whose motives remained dubious. The more she thought about it, the more sense it made to accept Salem's offer.

Her chest ached at the thought. She realized with a jolt that she'd miss both Strickland and Castle Tremayne. Somewhere along the way the old stronghold had begun to feel like home.

But it wasn't.

Castle Tremayne had belonged to the Carey family for centuries. This was Strick's home. Once the railway came through, he'd be able to start making payments to buy the castle back. Maybe her true place was back home in New York working in the business she'd poured so much effort into making a success.

But, before she could even begin to envision returning to her old life, certain conditions had to be met. Reaching for her fountain pen, she started to write.

Dear Salem, she wrote, *the only way I could consider returning is if I have a true stake in our family company . . .*

PHILIPS PURSED HIS lips. "This just won't do, Miss Darwish." The butler stood at the entrance to the tea shop.

Raya surveyed the scene with satisfaction. The old malt house had been transformed. The vacant outbuilding had been cleaned out and tables and chairs from various castle rooms were arranged in a pleasing fashion. The cozy stone structure would be ready to receive tea shop visitors when the tours began in four days' time.

"Why not?" she said. "I think the arrangement looks very pleasing."

"The furniture belongs in the castle. Not in an outbuilding."

Raya kept her temper despite the urge to lash out. She was weary of being challenged by the servants at every turn. "We need someplace for tea shop visitors to sit and tables for them to set down their tea."

"These pieces have been in the castle for decades, some of them for centuries." The other lower servants who'd been helping set up the tea shop slowed at their work, listening to the lead servant, their superior, spar with the interloper mistress of the house.

Raya straightened her spine, making sure her voice was loud, clear and authoritative. "None of these items came from public castle rooms."

The tables and chairs were from service areas of the castle, where the pieces were regularly subjected to wear and tear. The tables she found in the pantry, larder and buttery. The chairs were discovered in vacant old guardrooms and the gatehouse.

"That is just it," Philips said. "For this old furniture to be what the public sees of Castle Tremayne is an assault on this fortress's magnificent past. These pieces were in back rooms, unseen by castle visitors, for a reason."

Raya saw no other way to furnish the tearoom. She couldn't risk damaging heirlooms by using furnishings from the main rooms. Besides, in her view, the time-worn nature of the pieces she'd borrowed for the tearoom were part of their charm. "I have asked the carpenter to come by and do what is needed to make these chairs and tables look their best."

"I am certain His Grace would not approve." The room had gone completely silent. The servants, no longer bothering to pretend to attend to their tasks, watched openly. "Someone of your background might not understand the nuances of such things."

"Someone of my background?" The back of Raya's neck burned. "What exactly do you mean by that?"

"Americans barely have any history to appreciate," he said, "and the Arabs . . ." His voice trailed off but his skepticism came through loud and clear.

Anger swirled in Raya's chest and, even though she'd rolled her eyes whenever her father rattled off Arab contributions to the modern world, she found herself reciting facts her father used to be so proud of. "The origins of the alphabet you use to write your precious English was created by the Arabs. An Arab woman created the very first university in the entire world. So, if you please, do not presume to lecture me about who is and isn't civilized."

"You are wrong." Strick walked into the tea shop.

Raya's ears burned. How dare Strickland contradict her in front of the servants? She drew herself up, ready to spar with the duke. But he stared at the butler.

"I absolutely approve of Miss Darwish's use of these tables and chairs for her tea shop," he said, a sharp edge to his words. "And in the future, do not presume to speak for me."

Philips's gaunt face lost all color. "I did not

mean to speak for you, Your Grace. I would never be so impertinent."

"If any of you is confused about my thoughts regarding Miss Darwish's tea shop or any of her other enterprises here at Castle Tremayne, allow me to clarify my position." Strick directed his words at all of the servants in the shop. "I am in full support of Miss Darwish's efforts. That is why I allowed her to set up her tea shop here in the outer bailey, which remains under my complete ownership and control. In the future, any disrespect shown to Miss Darwish will be viewed as an affront to me. Do I make myself clear?"

Murmurs of "Yes, Your Grace" and other words of assent came from the assembled workers.

"Very well." He departed as quickly as he'd appeared.

Raya went after him. "Strickland."

"Yes." He kept walking.

She hurried to keep up with him. "Thank you for that."

He did not look at her. "It is nothing personal. I am merely fulfilling my part of our agreement."

"Are you saying you weren't being honest back there?"

"Miss Darwish, we are now on a course that will inevitably result in your becoming my duchess. What I said back there was perfectly true. It would be an affront to me if my duchess were to be disrespected."

"Your duchess?" Any warm gratitude melted. "So your words of support had everything to do with enhancing your own consequence and nothing whatsoever to do with me."

"Interpret my actions as you like. You always do anyway," he said before quickening his pace to leave her behind.

"You really are a *jehish*!"

He pivoted. "And what exactly is that?"

"A mule," she shot back.

He looked so shocked that Raya almost laughed. "Nobody calls a duke a mule."

"Well, I am somebody. And I am calling you, Anthony Carey, a mule. An animal not exactly known for its brains." She jabbed her pointer finger in his chest. "What are you going to do about it? Throw me into your dungeon?"

"Stop poking me." He grabbed her hand. A jolt went through her at the skin-to-skin contact. "Since you insist on behaving like a brat, I should take you over my knee and spank you."

She snatched her hand away. "I'd like to see you try."

Something sparked in his eyes. And it wasn't anger or annoyance. It was hunger, interest, *desire*. The burning intensity of his gaze prompted Raya to fall back a step. "Don't."

"Don't what?" he murmured. "Bare that luscious ass of yours and have my way with it? And with you?"

Need surged inside of her. "You are disgusting."

"And you can't get enough, can you?" With a mirthless smile, he strode away leaving Raya staring after him with quivering legs and a pulsing sensation between her thighs.

CHAPTER EIGHTEEN

"This is a pleasant surprise," Strick said when Guy and Frances paid an unexpected call at Orchard Cottage.

Guy escorted his sister inside. "For some unfathomable reason, Frances is eager to see your dusty old scraps."

As they entered the main salon, Frances surveyed the room with interest. Strick had most of the furniture removed to make way for additional tables and shelving to display his objects. Organizing the exhibits for public display was more gratifying than Strick could have imagined. He enjoyed making the groupings, deciding which pieces to put together, and awaited his first visitors with anticipation.

Frances examined the masks on the wall. "When Guy mentioned you were putting your collection on display, I thought we should be among your first visitors."

"You are most welcome to view my Saxon artifacts at any time," Strick told her warmly before cutting a sharp look at his friend. "However, I might require that your brother pay the entrance fee."

Guy guffawed. "As if I'd spend perfectly good money to see your odds and ends. It is beyond belief that people actually spend money to see half-broken old things. I prefer objects that are shiny and new."

"Don't mind my brother," Frances said.

"I never do," Strick assured her.

She walked over to the nearest table display, surveying the patterned bowls, decorated vases and assorted figurines. "This is wonderful, Strickland. Were these pieces discovered on your digs?"

"Some of them, yes. Others I acquired here and there."

"Wonderful?" Guy asked before glancing over at Strick. "You do know she is just trying to be polite."

"I am not," Frances protested. "These relics are pieces of art influenced by Germanic tribes and the Celtics."

Strick regarded Frances with surprise. "I didn't realize you had any interest in or knowledge of the Saxons."

She smiled brightly. "How could I not? The metalwork is so sophisticated and beautiful."

Guy stared at his sister as though she'd grown two heads. "Who are you?"

She reached for a gold brooch with interlaced geometric designs and examined it. "I know it must come as a shock, Guy, but ladies do grow and learn and develop interests beyond needlework and watercolors."

"If you say so." He turned his full attention to Strick. "Are you a betrothed man yet?"

Frances dropped the brooch with a clatter.

Guy looked over at her. "Did you come here to scatter Strickland's so-called precious objects all over the floor?"

"Oh! No! Of course not." Flushed, she knelt to retrieve the brooch. "Did you say someone is betrothed?"

"Strickland," her brother told her.

Frances's head swung in Strick's direction. "Is that so?"

Strick dipped his chin. "I intended to keep the matter private until it was official. Unfortunately, your brother has a loose tongue."

"I see." Her fingers went white as she clutched the brooch. "Who is the lucky lady?"

"Miss Darwish."

Her brows went up. "The American?"

"Yes," he said.

"I had not realized that the two of you had developed an affection for each other."

"We have." He refrained from expanding on the circumstances surrounding his proposal. In public he intended to act besotted, at least for the first few months of their marriage, in order to dispel any rumor he'd been forced into marriage to a woman of questionable virtue. "I am a very fortunate man."

Frances swallowed hard. "This is very unexpected."

"There is no controlling the heart," he responded, trying to sound like a man in love. "It demands what it wants." At the moment, his heart demanded he stay as far away from Raya as possible. It grated that he was about to wed a woman who thought him capable of an abhorrent act of violence.

"Does it?" Frances said politely. "May I offer my very best wishes?"

"You may. I do hope you will help Raya feel welcome. You are the nearest lady for many miles."

"Miss Darwish is charming, of course. But it will be difficult for her to fill the role of duchess as she was not raised in society."

"Perhaps you will be kind enough to show her the ways of a lady." Frances's manners were exquisite. "I can think of no one more suited to the task."

"Of course, Strickland." Frances smiled serenely. "There isn't anything I would not do for you."

RAYA WANDERED OVER to the corridor outside the Great Room to check on the mural's progress and to distract herself from thoughts of Strick. She found Alfred hard at work as usual.

"It is coming along nicely," she said, watching him apply paint to the scene.

"The castle has never looked better," he said. "You are to be commended for all you have done." She was proud of her work. The castle was practically sparkling. The gardens were trimmed and neat, with lush green grass and bright pockets of flowers. Everything was set for the arrival of the first visitors in a few days' time.

"I have decided to add the abbey as a stop on the castle tour," she informed him. "You had the right of it. The abbey is stunning."

"You went to see it? Who showed you the way?"

"Your directions were excellent. It wasn't hard to find at the top of the hill. But the duke accompanied me as well."

Alarm flickered across his face before he masked it. "I see."

"He had wildflowers planted inside the abbey. It's truly beautiful. Especially when the sun was setting."

"You were at the abbey with His Grace in the dark?"

"We left just as night fell."

He kept his attention on his brushstrokes, streaks of soft blue sky. "I hope you had a care." His voice was purposefully bland. "It isn't safe to visit the ruins at night."

"What happened to Deena isn't going to happen to me," she assured him.

A haunted expression fell over his face. "I will never understand why she was there at night. It was unlike her. She never went to the ruins."

"You think she was lured there." He did not say it aloud this time but she knew Alfred thought

Strick was the reason Deena visited the abbey the night she died.

"I do."

"The duke has heard the rumors."

"Has he?" Alfred kept his attention on his task. "He thinks it is to be expected that people would gossip about him."

"Few dukes are thought to be guilty of murder."

Realization hit Raya. And suddenly she understood the reason for Strick's coldness and his abrupt withdrawal from her. "I have to go."

"Leaving so soon?" Alfred was accustomed to Raya staying for a while to chat while she watched him work.

She needed to set things right with Strickland. But there was only one way to truly fix relations between them. And that meant trusting the duke with one of her most closely held secrets.

"Yes, there is someone I have to see."

ONCE HIS GUESTS departed, Strick went upstairs to retrieve another crate of relics. He carried them down to the salon to unbox the pieces when he heard the front door open and close.

"Did you forget something?" he called out, assuming that Guy and Frances had returned. Instead, Raya appeared wearing an apprehensive expression, her dark liquid eyes watching him intently.

"I knocked," she told him. Instead of her usual work uniform of white shirt, leather belt and dark skirt, she'd put on a pink gown that flattered her dark hair and warm skin tone. And her beautiful curves.

"And when I didn't answer, you decided to let yourself in." He continued his task. "That's becoming quite a habit for you."

She surveyed the room. "You have turned this place into a true museum."

"As you wanted."

A pause. "Will you stop what you are doing for a moment?"

The soft vulnerability in her voice caught Strick off guard. He ceased his efforts and gave her his full attention. "Very well. What is it?"

The cords of her throat moved. "I would like to clear up something between us."

She was nervous. Against his better judgment, he felt a pang of empathy for her, a woman who thought him capable of taking a life. "Would you like to sit down?"

She shook her head. "No, thank you."

"Very well. Go on then," he urged in a gentle tone. "I am listening."

"At the ruins—" She faltered. "You thought I was afraid to go to the top of the lantern tower with you."

He stiffened. "You made your feelings quite obvious. You literally cringed when I mentioned going up."

She looked down. "It is not you that I am afraid of."

She had never seemed fragile to him before. Normally, the fierce lioness bared her claws when anyone dared overstep.

"What was it then?" he asked, surprised by just how badly he wanted to know. She was not a woman to reveal intimacies of the heart and mind. That she deigned to share something personal with him was a gift he felt privileged to unwrap. "What are you afraid of?"

"Being up high." She swallowed against the tightness in her throat. "And falling."

"Ah."

"No one outside of my family knows."

"I certainly won't tell anyone."

"I used to be fearless."

"You are saying that it was fear of going up high that made you flinch." Understanding dawned. "Not the idea of going up with me."

She nodded. "As children, we played on the roof of our three-story row house in Brooklyn. One time, we were playing tag and my cousin Adnan tagged me." She closed her eyes. "When I remember that day, I can still hear the sounds of me and my cousins screaming and laughing. We would dart between the flapping laundry drying on the rooftop clotheslines. I can feel the cool sting of the damp garments slapping me in the face."

"And then what happened?" he prompted, soft-voiced.

"He was running so fast. I was too close to the

edge. The force of him tagging me, the momentum behind him, almost pushed me off the roof." She rubbed her chest. Her heart felt like it was collapsing in on her. "I lost my footing and almost stumbled off the roof. Adnan caught me, he grabbed my dress, and after some tugging, finally managed to drag me back to safety. But, for a few seconds there, I really thought I was going over. I'll never forget that feeling of teetering on the edge. It seemed to last a lifetime."

She stared past him, terror stamping her face. As if she was back there again, the New York street spinning beneath her, her arms flailing as she tried to keep from plummeting to the ground.

"It's over now." He rested a strong comforting hand on her shoulder. "You're safe. You didn't fall."

His warm, gentle voice seemed to cut through her haze. She drew a deep breath. "Since then, I can't be anywhere high up. If there was any reason for one of us to go to the roof, one of my sisters or my brother would have to do it. You must think me a silly girl."

"No, I do not. You are an astounding woman." Facing her, he planted both his hands on her shoulders to press his point. "Few women, or men for that matter, could have resurrected Tremayne's weaving enterprise the way you have. And your idea to display my relics for the public has true merit. As does opening the house to visitors."

"Careful, Strickland," she warned. "Someone might mistake you for being nice."

All he ever wanted was to be nice to her, to surround her with the nicest things. "I can be very nice. If you would allow it. Instead, you push me away."

She kept her gaze steady on his. "I am not pushing you away now."

His blood heated. He hoped it was an invitation. And he intended to take her up on it before she changed her mind. They came together, meeting in the middle, dancers moving in sync.

Their lips touched sweetly, tentatively, as if they were exploring one another for the first time. And in a way they were. The honesty of the moment raked Strick's chest. Even though it was Raya who'd revealed one of her most closely held secrets, Strick felt exposed.

Cupping the back of her neck, he brushed his mouth against her lips, slowly increasing the pressure until his lips caressed hers. She allowed it, returning the kiss tenuously. Her hands moved up his back and he trembled at the feel of it.

Strick kissed her as he'd never kissed a woman before. With exquisite tenderness, pouring his unspoken feelings into the intimacy. It was the first kiss of his experience that wasn't purely for physical gratification. It wasn't the initial step in pursuit of the ultimate goal of screwing a woman. With Raya, he wanted to savor the moment, to wrap her in safety and security after she'd opened herself up to him.

He kept the kiss soft and slow, sensual, gently biting her lip and then soothing the plush curve with easy kisses. His hand slid down from her neck, over her back until he reached her waist to pull her closer. She moaned and parted her lips.

Taking his time, Strick delicately touched his tongue to hers, allowing his deepest feelings to take over. An intimate energy flowed between them. It was as if she sensed his emotions and experienced them herself. After the weeks of tension building between them, a sublime sensation of full surrender on both their parts overtook him.

A coolly argumentative Raya made desire burn up his blood, but the soft, vulnerable woman in his arms clutched his heart. He kissed her as if it was his first kiss. And the last. It went on and on until he was breathless and dizzy, and Raya was swaying on her feet.

"Well," he said when they finally came up for air. Because there were no words to adequately describe what he'd just experienced. "That was . . ."

She gazed up at him with sparkling eyes and radiant cheeks, her lips pink and swollen. "Yes," she agreed. "It was."

CHAPTER NINETEEN

"W hat do you think?" Mrs. Cranch asked the following day when Raya sat down to taste the final menu selections in the tea shop.

"The rose almond cake is delicious." Raya tried to focus but it wasn't easy. To her consternation, she was still floating from Strick's embrace. "And the gingerbread nuts are divine. It is hard to select a favorite."

"You approve of them all for the menu?" the cook asked.

"I do. I think we shall be ready when we open tomorrow."

Mrs. Cranch beamed. "If you will excuse me, I have much work to do to prepare for opening day."

After she departed, Raya sipped her tea and nibbled on the gingerbread. The tea shop was ready. The old malt house had been scrubbed down so well that it practically sparkled. The tables and chairs were arranged in an orderly manner.

But, for the first time in her life, Raya was having a hard time staying focused on business. She kept replaying *that* kiss. It was nothing like her previous embraces with Strick, which were driven by mindless animalistic desire. Yesterday's caress teemed with feeling. It was like they touched each other's soul. She might not dislike Strick after all. Surely it wasn't possible to feel such a close connection to someone she hated.

"There you are." A friendly female voice cut into her thoughts. "Philips told me you would be here."

Raya greeted the striking redhead. "Miss Vaughan."

"Please, you must call me Frances." She was resplendent in an emerald gown that set off her fiery hair. "I do hope we shall become friends."

"As do I." Raya realized she would very much like to have a friend in England. "Will you join me?"

The ceiling creaked. Frances looked upward, a dubious expression on her face. "Is it safe?"

"Yes, quite. Or so I have been assured. One of the ceiling beams appears to be loose but I've asked that it be fixed before any castle visitors arrive tomorrow."

Frances surveyed the plates piled with sweets. "Are you having tea out here?"

"I am sampling the final menu selections for the tea shop." She gestured toward the plates of cakes, tarts and wafers. "As you can see, Mrs. Cranch prepared far more than was necessary."

"If you are certain that it is safe, then I should

love to join you." Frances settled in the seat opposite her and reached for a wafer.

"Wonderful." Raya poured tea for her guest. "It is lovely to have someone to enjoy Mrs. Cranch's divine creations with."

"Dare I ask how Mrs. Cranch reacted when you informed her she'd be cooking for the general public?"

"She objected very loudly. Until the duke encouraged her to see reason."

Frances's green eyes widened. "Strickland convinced Mrs. Cranch to cook for your tea shop?"

Raya nodded. "He was very helpful. You and Strickland think alike. The duke knew immediately that Cook would object, which hadn't even occurred to me."

"English customs and societal rules can be complicated for an outsider." Frances caught herself. "For a newcomer, rather. You are hardly an outsider, especially now that you and Strickland plan to wed."

Surprise shot through Raya. "He told you?"

"He did," Frances said with a smile. "We have been friends for a very long time."

"It is not official. I am still considering his proposal."

"Truly?" Frances blinked. "There are few women in England who would turn down the chance to marry a handsome duke and become a duchess who could rule over most of society."

"Do you include yourself in that number?"

Mischief flickered in her radiant gaze as she leaned closer, lowering her voice conspiratorially. "I must confess I would welcome the opportunity to rule over all of society. It is the only power a lady can hope to wield."

"Oh," Raya said. "That is quite sad."

Frances leaned back. "Isn't it? Society expects perfect manners and boring behavior from ladies of our status. As you will soon learn."

"Oh, I don't anticipate moving in society overmuch." The thought had never really occurred to her. Even though, of course, it should have.

Surprise flashed in Frances's face. "Hmm. I see."

"Why?" The other woman's reaction alarmed her. "Does Strickland move about much in society?" The idea of attending balls and parties with a sea of noblemen sounded daunting. And boring.

"Strickland is a duke," Frances explained patiently. "A duke is a leader in society, someone who is highly respected and who will be expected to take his place during the Season."

Raya reached for a cake. "But he barely goes to London now."

"He attends to his duties in the House of Lords as needed. But many noblemen truly take their place in society after they wed."

"I shall be busy managing castle operations." Panic blossomed in her chest. "I won't be able to be away from Castle Tremayne for long."

Frances nibbled daintily on the wafer. "That might be a surprise to Strickland."

Raya couldn't imagine why. It was practically written into their agreement that she would run Tremayne's business operations. "I think the duke understands that I will be busy overseeing all of the castle enterprises." She spoke with more certainty than she felt. "Why? Did Strickland say something to you?"

"Nothing explicit. He simply asked me to help you learn how to become a duchess. I assumed it was to prepare you to take your place in society, but perhaps I misunderstood."

The cake in Raya's mouth lost all flavor. "Strick asked you to do *what*?"

"Oh, nothing too taxing. Do not worry." She patted Raya's hand. "I do not feel at all put out. It will be amusing to teach you how to be a proper English lady."

"The duke asked you to make a proper lady out of me?"

"Of course, he did not speak quite so bluntly. He simply wants me to offer you some guidance, on manners and etiquette. Surely you understand."

"I am beginning to." Stung, Raya swallowed hard, the cake dry in her throat. "When did he ask?"

"Just yesterday when my brother and I paid a call at Orchard Cottage."

Yesterday. After the kiss that felt like they'd reached a new, intimate understanding? Raya silently castigated herself for feeling betrayed. What did she expect? Like Salem, Strick was a man. Only a *habla* would place complete faith in the opposite sex after what Raya had been through.

"Enough about that," Frances said with a wave of her hand. "Tell me all about your plans for opening day."

The last thing Raya wanted to do was continue chatting. But she hid her disappointment and rallied. "To begin with, we are offering half-price entry to everyone who comes on our first day." And she launched into the full list of activities that she had planned.

WHEN STRICK ARRIVED at the castle late in the morning on opening day, he found several visitors streaming through the bailey.

Servants bearing trays of wafers and gingerbread wandered through the grassy courtyard enclosed by the protective curtain wall. The sounds of laughing children drew his attention upward to the parapet walk. A couple of boys poked their heads through the squared openings of the low barrier at the top of the castle's outermost walls. Strick smiled at the sight. It reminded him of the times he and his sisters played along the top of the curtain wall.

He'd worried that opening the castle to strangers would tarnish the noble history of the centuries-old fortress. Instead, the castle felt alive again. Raya had managed to imbue the ancient stronghold with new energy and vitality. Perhaps, like his Saxon relics, the castle was a piece of history meant to be shared with the public.

Inside the castle, he came across Mrs. Shaw leading a half-dozen visitors through the Great Room. A couple of guests lingered to watch Alfred Price paint the mural in the passage. Eager to see Raya, Strick strode from chamber to chamber, stopping in the morning room, in case she'd retreated there, but there was no sign of her.

He finally ran Raya to ground in the undercroft, where he found her tidying items displayed on various tables and shelving. She didn't immediately notice him. She was engaged in an animated conversation with the clerk running the shop. Not wanting to interrupt, Strick stayed in the background and took the opportunity to look around.

There were far more items than the wool shawls, scarves, hats and small rugs made with his father's goats. Other objects available for purchase included hand towels and linens embroidered with the castle's likeness.

Raya had obviously dressed for the occasion of opening day. She was resplendent in a violet gown that hugged her in all of the right places. An old notebook with tattered edges was tucked under one arm. He marveled at her accomplishments, pride and admiration surging through him.

She glanced over in his direction and his heart jumped a little. He smiled, eager to speak with her, to be fully in her company again. What a mystery the heart was. His had little involvement in his previous interactions with women. But now it beat solely for the smallest hint of affection from the fiery American daughter of an Arab merchant.

Raya's eyes did not light up when she realized he'd entered the shop. Nor did she exchange a secret, meaningful glance with him. Instead, Raya barely acknowledged his presence before refocusing her attention on the clerk. Strick was disappointed but understood. An overly friendly reception would be fodder for gossip.

He couldn't wait until he and Raya were betrothed and he could publicly claim her. Strick never anticipated wedding a woman who completely besotted him, who appealed to both his mind and body. He felt like he was on the verge of capturing the most magnificent prize.

When Raya finished her business with the clerk, the man started when he finally realized the Duke of Strickland stood in the shop. With wide eyes, he greeted Strick respectfully.

"Cuffe." Strick recognized the owner of the sundry store in the village. "What are you doing here?"

"Miss Darwish offered me a partnership of sorts," Dennis Cuffe explained. "We will be stocking items made with authentic Castle

Tremayne wool and as well the linens embroidered with the castle's likeness."

"Are you also running the Castle Tremayne gift shop?" Strick asked.

Raya interjected, speaking briskly. "Mr. Cuffe kindly agreed to train a couple of our staff on how to run a store."

Strick enjoyed the way she said *our* staff. And not *her* staff. Raya was already behaving as if they were betrothed. "That's very good of you, Cuffe."

"Certainly, Your Grace. It is my pleasure."

They departed the shop, Strick following Raya as she walked purposefully beneath the undercroft's numerous gothic arches. "I have been looking for you," he told her.

She paused to consult her notebook. "You found me."

"Are you pleased with how opening day is proceeding?" He found himself eager to speak with her, to hear her thoughts, to share this victory with her. "You must be very proud to see your efforts come to fruition."

"Yes, I think we're off to a promising start." She scribbled something in her notebook. "It's not a huge crowd but it's fair enough for our first day."

"You are to be congratulated." He looked around; being in the undercroft brought back pleasant memories. "We are in the undercroft."

"So we are." She resumed walking.

"Do you recall the last time we were here together?" When he'd half undressed her. And kissed her all over.

"Barely. I was drunk."

"Before that."

"Before that someone locked me in the storeroom."

"I have fond memories of finding you in the storeroom."

"I have no recall of it at all." She started up the stairs.

"Is something the matter?"

She finally looked him in the eye. "Whatever could be the matter?"

His neck muscles tightened. He understood the female mind well enough to comprehend that he was supposed to know the answer. "If I knew, I wouldn't be asking."

She released an irritated breath. "I don't have time for this, especially not today of all days. I have a million tasks to see to."

He laid a hand on her arm. "Have I done something to offend you?"

She directed a cool glance to where his hand rested on her sleeve. Then blinked her gaze up to meet his. "If you do not know the answer to that, then I cannot help you."

There was no trace of the intimacy, the closeness, they'd shared yesterday. Raya reverted back to the same cool, detached—and contrary—woman from their first meeting at the reading of Deena's will. How had he lost this splendid prickly creature before he'd had a chance to properly win her?

"Dammit, woman!" He tried to keep the desperation from his voice. Yesterday he felt gloriously connected to her. Yet today she treated him like a turd on the bottom of her shoe. "Must you speak in riddles?"

"We will always be who we are," she answered. "Neither of us should forget it."

He gritted his teeth. "Another riddle." His voice softened. "Yesterday, I thought we reached a new understanding."

"As did I," she said. "Unfortunately, I was wrong."

"What the devil happened in the last twenty-four hours to change your opinion?"

"Miss Darwish?" Otis appeared in the undercroft.

"Yes?" She gave the footman her full attention. Strick saw it for what it was. An excuse to look at anyone but him. "What is it?"

"There is a situation in the tea shop with Mrs. Cranch. She asked that you come."

"Certainly," she said. "Lead the way."

She followed Otis out without another word to Strick.

CHAPTER TWENTY

Raya girded herself before walking into the duke's castle apartments.

After successfully evading Strick for most of opening week, she had no choice but to seek him out. There was business to attend to.

His essence engulfed her the moment she entered his inner sanctum. The scents of smoke and books, a hint of his spicy cologne washed over her, making the duke's presence known before she laid eyes on him.

She strode into his sitting room to find Strick settled in a deep chair with an open book on his lap, one ankle crossed over his knee. "Excellent," she said. "You're here."

"You did ask to see me." He sprang to his feet, tossing his reading material aside. He was casually dressed, his golden hair neatly combed except for the wayward cowlick at the back of his head. "As always, your wish is my command."

She ignored the way her heart fluttered. "If only that were true."

"You could always test me." His golden-brown eyes twinkled. "What is your command? Would you like me on my knees?"

Raya forced herself to look away, resisting the urge to fully take in the sight of him. The man could easily entice her back into his orbit. The athletic vigor, the easy grace he displayed when bounding to his feet, was enough to make her body tingle in the most intimate of places.

She spoke briskly. "My command is that you put some of your relics on display here in the castle."

His forehead puckered. "Why would people bother to go to Orchard Cottage if they can view my artifacts here?"

"Because not enough castle visitors are opting to pay the extra fee to go to Orchard Cottage."

"That's to be expected. Not everyone who wants to tour a castle is interested in Saxon relics."

"That's just it. They don't know what they're missing." She made for the nearby room where he kept the case containing his Saxon jewelry. Her breath caught all over again when she spotted the patterned gold-and-garnet bracelet that had mesmerized her the first time she saw it. "If some of these pieces are put on display in the front hall, or somewhere along the tour, it would certainly entice me into wanting to see more."

He paused, watching her, the powerful connection between them charging the air.

"Well?" she said, trying to break the spell. "What do you think?"

"Try it on."

"What?"

"I think you should try the bracelet on."

How did he know that was the piece that drew her the most? "There is no need for that."

"Try it on and I'll seriously consider your suggestion."

She looked heavenward. "Very well. Be quick about it."

He was anything but quick. Moving slowly, almost languidly, he unlocked the case and withdrew the piece. The gold sparkled and winked as it played with the light. He reached for Raya's hand. The hair on her arms rose the instant Strick touched her.

He slipped the bracelet on her wrist, the gold cold and hard against her sensitized skin. He held her fingers as they admired it together, his thumb feathering ever so slightly across the back of her hand. She shivered at his touch. "It's beautiful."

"It becomes you." He reached into the case for a necklace with detailed swirling designs resembling snakes. Stepping behind her, he strung the extravagant piece around Raya's neck, his fingertips lightly brushing the skin of her nape. He angled her toward the full-length mirror so she could see. "You should always be adorned in gold. Take a look."

Mostly what she saw was him. Behind her, engulfing her.

"You make the jewels shine," he said.

She laid a hand against the cool metal. "It is

our tradition for an Arab bride to be dressed in gold. The groom puts the pieces on her, sometimes with the help of his mother or sisters."

"I don't require any assistance while dressing my future bride in jewels." His breath was humid against her neck. He touched his lips to the curve of her neck. "What did I do," he whispered against her skin, "to lose your favor? Please tell me."

She hardly remembered anymore. She couldn't resist leaning back into the hard strength of his body, setting her head back against his chest. He wrapped his arms around her, pulling her closer. He nipped her neck and her knees almost buckled. "Don't abandon me, Raya. I need you."

Me? Or my castle? Then his hands closed over her breasts and she didn't care what the answer was. He kneaded the plump flesh and tweaked her nipples. She moaned, watching in the mirror as he played with her. He slid one hand slowly and purposefully down her body, over her ribs and stomach, stopping at the place between her legs. Giving her time to protest, to resist, if she wanted.

She put her hand over his, where he fondled her breast. "Yes," she said on a sigh.

He growled with delight, his touch firm and insistent against her most private place. He rubbed and teased her through her clothes. She squirmed from the frustrating pleasure of it, desperate to rip her dress off so she could feel his touch. She parted her legs to give him better access.

"Not yet." His voice was a low rumble in her ear. "First, I must dress my bride in her jewels."

Raya groaned. "Later."

"Patience, my love. It will be well worth it." He nipped her ear. "I promise."

She watched in the mirror as he slowly undressed her. "I thought you were putting more gold on me."

"I am." He brushed his lips against her cheek. "But I must bare the canvas so the jewels can shine as they were meant to."

Her gown fell around her shoulders. He took his time unhooking her corset, moving at a leisurely pace while removing her chemise and petticoats, discarding her clothing until she wore nothing except her loose white drawers that stopped a few inches above her knees.

"Look at what you've been hiding." He ran a hand over her bottom and squeezed. "I knew you had spectacular tits but your legs are superb. What a shame to keep them hidden."

His hands trailed upward to toy with her bare nipples, twisting them gently, pulling on them, all while they watched in the mirror. Raya squeezed her eyes shut. She was not used to lingering when she looked at herself.

"Open your eyes," he commanded. "The pleasure is heightened if you watch."

She did as he asked, fully under his spell. He loosened her drawers and they dropped to the floor. She was completely bare, her breasts heavy and full, the soft slope of her belly giving way to the dark curls between her legs. "You are a goddess," he whispered in her ear. "I cannot wait to fuck you."

Desire pooled between her legs. She felt him hard and heavy in her lower back. She ground back into him.

He smacked her lightly on her bottom. "Don't be naughty. We are not rushing things. My evil plan is to give you so much pleasure that it ruins you for any other man."

The sting on her bottom heightened the experience. He withdrew another bracelet from the case and slipped it onto her wrist. Then another and another. Until both forearms were heavy with gold. He put a second and then a third necklace around her neck, brushing his lips against her shoulder each time. He slid ornate rings onto each of her fingers, and dressed her in dangled earrings. He took her hair down, where it fell in thick, wavy dark curls, and pinned a brooch into it.

"There," he finally said, admiring her in the mirror. "My beautiful Arab queen."

Raya studied herself in the mirror, fully naked except for the heavy jewelry. Adornment as armor. Strick was right. The woman reflected back at her was beautiful and powerful. Strick's large, strong hands settled on her shoulders and slowly slid down her arms over her bracelets. "The Saxons thought gold had magical qualities."

Raya believed it. Everything about this moment felt otherworldly.

His hands traveled over the sides of her hips, over her waist. "Gold was an important status symbol. It was worn to show wealth and rank."

He feathered the back of his hand down over the gleaming necklaces, deliberately, teasingly brushing her peaked nipples. "My relics have never shown to greater advantage. If we could display these pieces in the front hall just like this, Orchard Cottage would be overflowing with visitors."

Raya stared at her reflection. At the woman in the mirror who looked like someone in control of her destiny.

Destiny. Fate. The words reverberated in her mind.

That's when she knew.

Turning to face Strick, she wrapped her arms around his neck. Their mouths met in urgent need, kissing slowly and fully, taking their time tasting and devouring each other.

"Turn back around."

She protested but he insisted. He dragged a stool over with his foot. "Put your leg up on it."

She did as he asked.

"Watch me pleasure you."

She leaned back against him, watching in the glass as his hands traveled down her stomach. Until he reached the place between her legs. He spread her with his finger so they could both see her folds. He put his hand on her thigh, widening her stance, baring more of her privates. "Do you like watching me touch you?"

"Yes." Her skin was an inferno. She was so needy for him.

"Play with your tits." He watched her intently. "I want to see it."

She dragged both hands up over her stomach, cupping each of her full breasts, rubbing the pad of her thumbs over her engorged nipples. She pinched her nipples and moaned. Her body had never been so sensitive, so eager, so desperate.

He inhaled sharply. "You're so fucking gorgeous."

His long strong fingers worked between her legs, stroking, petting, slowly making his way to the knot of sensitive nerves high atop her sex. Watching in the mirror through lowered lids, Raya felt frenzied for more. "Hurry," she panted. "Stop teasing me."

"Be patient. It'll be worth it." He nibbled on the outer curve of her ear. "You're nice and wet. So slippery."

Her entire body strained for more. "Anthony," she pleaded. "I need—" She didn't know exactly what she was striving for.

"I know what you need." Strick's heart beat hard against her back. He pressed his erection into the small of her back. "Can you feel my cock?" he murmured, his tongue flicking inside her ear. "You make me so hard."

His fingers finally caressed the most intimate part of her, offering persistent, rhythmic stimulation just where she needed it. Her body was deliciously on edge. He tweaked and rubbed the sensitive knot, tracing circles around it. His finger dipped inside her in a swirling motion, sending pleasure streaking through her body. Her legs gave out. Strick caught her and swept Raya up into his arms as though she weighed nothing.

He carried her to his bedchamber and tossed her onto his mattress. "This time, you will not be falling asleep in my bed." The cool bed linens felt silky and luxurious beneath her. "At least, not until after I'm through pleasuring you."

He stood back to admire her. "Spread your legs."

She pouted. "This is hardly fair. You are still dressed."

"Open your legs wide. You will not be disappointed."

She had no resistance in her. She wanted it all.
Fate.

She obeyed his command.

Hunger flashed in his eyes. "I am going to worship my queen with my tongue." He crawled up over her on the bed and kissed her long and hard. She whimpered when he broke the kiss.

"Shhh," he soothed, kissing his way down her body, stopping to suck her breasts, his tongue flicking the hard tips. She bucked when sensation shot from her breasts straight to the place between her legs as if a taut cord connected them. He kept moving lower until he settled between her legs.

She felt him use his fingers to part her. And then his tongue was doing things that made her body come up off the mattress again. And again. She had no words. This was all pleasure far beyond any of her imaginings. Or her most secret fantasies. She could never have conceived of such delights.

"I love the way you taste," he murmured against her folds. "I could stay here forever."

He sucked and licked and nipped and teased until she screamed from the painful pleasure of it, a tension too intense to bear. And then her insides were bursting. The tightness in her muscles released, a sense of warm well-being flooded her. Gratifying contractions pulsed between her legs.

Wearing a satisfied expression, Strick rose, tearing his shirt off and making quick work of his trousers. Raya stretched, feeling languorous while feasting her eyes on his muscled arms and taut stomach. Her perusal stopped at his hard and thick penis.

He climbed on top of her. "I need to be inside of you *now*. Unless you tell me to stop."

It seemed the most natural thing in the world to part her thighs as he settled himself between her legs. He slid into her, the feeling tight and uncomfortable.

"Okay?" he asked.

"I think so." It was a curious sensation. Only slightly painful. He filled her, the feel so snug that it seemed that he wasn't meant to fit. But she knew she was made for him. And he for her.

Her mother and aunts had always said when her *naseeb*, the man destiny meant for her, came to her she would instinctively know him. Raya hadn't believed it. How could she? She reached the age of twenty-six before he appeared when almost everyone around her, except for her sister Naila, married by eighteen.

But now she knew the timing was perfect. She'd been waiting for this man. As he had waited for her.

Strick moved inside her, slowly at first, measured and rhythmic. "Move with me, Raya. It is best when we move together. Bring your hips to meet me."

She experimented, adjusting until they moved in rhythm, her hips curving up to meet each thrust. When she tilted the right way, he was deeper inside of her. And it was everything—more than everything—she'd ever imagined joining with him could be. Her gold bracelets clinked as they moved, the music of their lovemaking. Her heart felt so full she wanted to cry. His hand moved between them and he was playing with her, causing the physical tension to rise in her again. She marveled at the way her body responded to his.

She arched up under him and cried out.

AFTER, THEY FELL asleep in each other's arms.

It was a first for Strick, who normally bedded a woman and lingered a little afterward to be polite, before slipping away back to the cozy comfort of his own bed. He was a light sleeper and preferred to sleep alone once the screwing was done.

But now, watching Raya doze, he couldn't envision ever sleeping without her again. She'd discarded the jewels but a woman like Raya needed no adornment. Dark luxuriant lashes fanned across her cheeks. Her hair was strewn about the pillows in thick silky strands. His heart had never felt so full.

Her eyes blinked open. It took a moment for her to orient herself. Understanding flashed in those dark depths. She smiled and stretched, her breasts arching into the air. "It wasn't a dream."

He shook his head. "Most certainly not. But we can do it again just to make sure."

She giggled, propping herself up on one elbow. It was his first time hearing her giggle. She'd never been carefree enough to in his presence. "Let us hope Auntie doesn't come looking for me again."

He leaned forward to give her a lingering kiss. "In my heart, you are already my wife."

She tilted her head, giving him a considering look.

"What is it?" he asked.

"Duchess lessons. Truly?"

"What are you talking about?"

"Frances said you asked her to give me duchess lessons. On account of my being a rough merchant-class American daughter of foreign immigrants."

He sat up, staring down at her. "Frances said that?"

"Not exactly. But that was the gist of it."

"Wait one moment." Realization hit. "Is that why you've been cold to me?"

"Being told that I'm not good enough isn't exactly endearing."

"That is not it at all. As stubborn and tiresome as you are, you are everything I have ever wanted."

She sniffed. "You should marry a true lady like Frances."

"If I wanted Frances, I'd be wed to her."

"She doesn't require duchess lessons."

"All I asked of Frances is that she act as a guide should you have need of it, should you ask for it." He played with her hair. "I want you just as you are. You could walk through the Great Room wearing nothing but gold adorning this ravishing body of yours and I would still think you the best duchess Tremayne could ever have."

She turned on her back, smiling up at him. "Have a care, Your Grace. It almost sounds as though you are saying I am perfect."

"You are perfectly imperfect."

"I'm not sure whether that's a compliment or an insult."

He lay back down and she turned on her side to tuck herself against him, her back to his front, his cock nestled into the warmth of her arse crack. He wrapped an arm around her and pulled her closer, cupping one of her breasts. What an extraordinary privilege it was to touch her as he pleased.

"You don't really expect me to go into society, do you?" she asked.

He was tempted to lie to her, to smooth things over, to ensure she would stay by his side. Instead, he told the truth. "I am a duke. I will have to appear in society from time to time. And I hope to have you by my side at least some of the time."

"I shall be very busy here managing castle operations. It truly requires my full attention."

"Imagine how much business you'd drum up if you go to London. You will be meeting dozens and dozens of people. You could charm them into coming to Castle Tremayne."

She glanced back over her shoulder at him. "It is frightening how well you know me."

He kissed her. "I am learning the language of money and commerce."

He felt himself thickening and lengthening again. A better man would not take a woman again so soon after her first time. He should go easy on her. But then she snuggled up back against him.

"Mmm," she said dreamily. "Please don't ever stop."

"That is a tall order," he said happily as he mounted her, "but I shall give it my all."

CHAPTER TWENTY-ONE

Combs, this is a surprise." Strick ushered the solicitor in, still cheerful after a splendid afternoon spent in bed with Raya.

He was feeling magnanimous, despite the fact that Combs interrupted his search for his mother's emerald ring, which had passed from one Duchess of Strickland to the next for generations. This time, his proposal must be well thought out. He intended to banish his uninspired perfunctory first proposal from Raya's mind.

"Good afternoon, Your Grace." Combs appeared in the company of a man who looked like a younger, thinner version of the solicitor. The younger Combs worked with his father but had a reputation as a rather dim bulb.

"You told my butler that you have urgent business with me?"

"Yes, Your Grace." Combs fidgeted, shifting his weight from one foot to the other. "I do beg your pardon for calling without an appointment."

"What is so dire that you felt compelled to appear without notice?"

Combs was perspiring. "We bring excellent news, Your Grace. I felt certain you would want to hear of it right away. You will remember my son, Keith."

"Yes, of course."

The younger man flushed. He'd never been to the castle before. "Y-Your Grace," he said, licking his lips, darting an uncertain look at his father.

"If you bring good news," Strick said, "why do both of you look like you're about to spill the contents of your stomach?"

Combs took a deep breath. "It seems there's been a mistake with the late duke's will."

Strick frowned. "Are you referring to my father's will?"

"Precisely."

"What kind of mistake? Did you read the wrong will?" he asked sardonically. But the other men did not laugh. Instead, they exchanged an uneasy look.

"Not exactly," Combs hedged. "The will that gave Castle Tremayne to your late stepmother was the correct document."

"Then why are you here? If my father truly left Tremayne to Deena, then there isn't much else in his will that I care about." He reached for the bellpull so that the butler could see them out, and Strick could go back to thinking about how to properly propose to Raya.

"What we didn't read was the codicil," Combs said.

Strick released the rope. "What codicil?"

"As you know, a codicil is a supplement to a will."

"Are you saying my father made an addition to his original will?"

The elder Combs licked his lips. "He did."

"Why am I only hearing about this now? My father has been dead for two years."

"He made the codicil about a month after I drew up the original will for him," Combs explained. "However, I was away on holiday when he wanted to add the changes so Keith wrote up the codicil for the late duke."

"And he swore me to secrecy," Keith Combs put in. "I did not tell anyone."

Combs shot his son an exasperated look. "I have told Keith that his pledge of secrecy should not have included me, his father, as I was the duke's primary solicitor."

"And you've just learned about this supplement to my father's will?"

"Yes, Your Grace," the elder Combs said. "I was going through our files searching for another document and found the codicil quite by accident."

"What is in this supposed codicil?"

"The late Duke of Strickland stipulated that after Deena Darwish's death, Castle Tremayne was to pass to his son and heir."

Everything went silent, except for the ticking of the mantel clock, while Strick processed the solicitor's words.

"What are you saying?" he finally burst out, disbelief streaking through him. "Does this mean the castle belongs to me?"

"That is precisely what it means," Combs said.

"And the codicil is a sound legal document?" Strick doubted Keith Combs could properly execute a legal document.

The elder Combs understood. "Yes, your father signed it, as did two witnesses. I have spoken with the witnesses myself."

Strick was dubious. "Who are they, these witnesses?"

"One is a very trustworthy and reliable clerk in my office and Dr. Michaels."

"I see." Could it really be true? He'd never wanted anything as much as the castle. But that was before Raya.

Combs beamed at him. "This means Raya Darwish has no claim at all on your home because Deena Darwish had no authority to leave the castle to her."

Strick slid into the nearest chair. "Castle Tremayne is legally mine," he said, dazed. "And has been since Deena died."

"That is correct. You have the authority to eject Miss Darwish today."

"I can shutter all of her business enterprises here at the castle if I so choose." Strick spoke more to himself than to his visitors. There was a time, not too long ago, that he wanted nothing more than to quash Raya's moneymaking ventures.

"Yes. Absolutely," Combs confirmed. "It is well known in the village that you were not in favor of Miss Darwish turning this venerable old fortress into a commercial enterprise. Now you have the power to stop her."

Strick felt light-headed. "This changes everything."

"Now that I have told you, I will go and inform Miss Darwish."

"No." Strick snapped out of his daze. The truth would upset the delicate balance of his relationship with Raya. If she didn't own the castle, she might decide she had no reason to stay in England.

Surprise flickered in Combs's face. "Your Grace?"

"You heard me," he said forcefully. "Not a word of this to Miss Darwish or anyone else."

"But Your Grace, it is my duty to inform—"

Strick cut him off. "It was also your duty to tell me about Father's codicil in a timely fashion. What has happened here, this two-year delay, is gross malpractice."

The younger Combs uttered a sound of distress while his father paled. "It was not intentional, Your Grace. Surely you understand—"

"What I know is that you caused me great distress by allowing me to believe that my father disinherited me."

"It was an honest mistake," Keith croaked.

"You also misled Miss Darwish, an innocent woman who would never hurt anyone, to believe she inherited a windfall. You upended her life."

"Very well." Combs swallowed. "If you prefer to inform Miss Darwish yourself then I will stand down, as you request."

"And you will make sure that your son and the clerk who served as witness to the codicil tell no one."

"You have my word. And I am certain that you can rely on Dr. Michaels to be discreet. In all likelihood, he isn't aware of the exact contents of the codicil."

After father and son departed, Strick's mind whirled. Now that he had the power to stop Raya, he no longer wanted to. When he told her that Tremayne could have no better duchess, he'd spoken the truth. Raya was critical to Castle Tremayne's future. She *was* the future. Her business acumen would ensure Castle Tremayne's continued solvency for decades to come.

Strick firmed his mouth. It was decided. There was no reason to tell Raya or anyone else the truth. He would proceed with plans to make Raya his wife, giving Tremayne the duchess it deserved. Their son would one day take possession of the fortress. All would be as it should. The succession assured.

And Strick would take what he learned today to his grave.

THE FOLLOWING DAY, Raya walked to the village to meet with Mr. Cuffe. They planned to inspect his inventory to see what items in his sundries shop she might want to stock in the Tremayne gift shop.

As she followed the path away from the castle, Raya took inventory of Tremayne matters. The business was running smoothly. Castle Tremayne wasn't overrun with visitors but they were off to a respectable start. She was heartened that the people who came for the tour enjoyed taking advantage of almost everything the castle had to offer, including the tea shop where they could eat delicacies prepared by a ducal chef. The gift shop was also doing well. Visitors wanted to take a piece of the castle with them in the form of the linens embroidered with the castle's likeness or with an accessory made from genuine Castle Tremayne wool. Hopefully, traffic would also pick up soon at Orchard House.

And then there was Strickland. She exhaled, wary of believing too deeply in him. Was he truly her *naseeb*? Making love with Strick was astounding. She was almost embarrassed by how badly she wanted him. But, as much as Raya enjoyed the physical part of her relationship with Strick, it was the emotional closeness that unnerved her the most. She'd never felt as connected to anyone. Not even Naila, her favorite sister. What she experienced with Strick felt honest and true. But was it? She'd been wrong about her brother.

She arrived at Mr. Cuffe's store to find him finishing up with a customer, a woman in her forties with soft brown hair streaked with silver.

"Good day, Mrs. Price," Mr. Cuffe said.

"Thank you," the woman said, nodding politely to Raya as she turned to leave. Mr. Cuffe excused himself momentarily and disappeared into the back of the shop.

"Are you Mrs. Price?" Raya asked the woman. "Mr. Alfred Price's mother?"

Suspicion flickered in the woman's face. "Yes, that is correct."

"I am Miss Darwish, the new owner of Castle Tremayne," she said in a friendly manner.

"I thought that's who you might be."

"Your son is doing a wonderful job painting the new mural at the castle."

"Is he?" she said, her reserve intact.

Alfred and his father were so amiable that Mrs. Price's aloof manner surprised Raya. Although it shouldn't because, of course, members of the same family usually had differing temperaments. "I have also made your husband's acquaintance. He was kind enough to convey my aunt and me from the inn to Castle Tremayne when we first arrived."

"The men in my family are often taken in by a pretty face."

Raya stiffened. Mrs. Price wasn't just standoffish, she was downright rude. "You were on your way out so I will not keep you any longer."

"Good day to you," Mrs. Price answered, stepping past her. But when she reached the door, she paused and faced Raya. "I hope you are not like her."

"I beg your pardon?"

"The duchess."

"If you are referring to my cousin Deena, I am afraid that I never met her. But I am aware that she and your son were friendly."

"They were more than that." Contempt laced her voice. "It was indecent. She took advantage of his good nature."

Surely Mrs. Price wasn't insinuating that Alfred and Deena were lovers. "How do you mean?"

"She seduced him. An older woman like that. It was disgusting. And then she made him do the other things."

Raya swallowed. "What things?"

"She had him secretly sell things for her. Items that rightly belonged to Castle Tremayne. She had no right. If the duke had caught him, my Alfred would be in terrible trouble. One accusation of theft from His Grace would land my Alfred in the gaol."

Raya's stomach tightened. "He secretly sold castle artifacts?"

"I beg of you," Mrs. Price continued, "do not involve my boy in your schemes the way the duchess did."

"I have no intention of selling anything that belongs to the castle. And your son and I are friends. That is all."

"I hope you will keep it that way." She looked Raya up and down. "He doesn't need to become involved with your sort."

Raya's neck heated. "And what sort is that?"

Mrs. Price pursed her lips. "Good day." She pulled the door open, the bell sounding as she marched out and slammed it shut behind her.

"Is it true?" Raya demanded to know.

Alfred dipped his brush in blue and swept it over the part of the mural where he was creating a sky with gray clouds and a dash of sunlight. "Are you going to be more specific? Or am I supposed to guess what you mean by that?"

"Did you and Deena have a liaison? Is that specific enough for you?"

His head swung around. She certainly had his attention now. "Where did you hear that?"

"From your mother. I just made her acquaintance in the village."

He blew out a long breath. "My mother has a loose tongue."

"So it's true."

"Your cousin was a good woman."

"I am asking for the truth, not a character reference."

"Very well. The truth is that Deena Darwish—"

"Deena Carey."

His mouth twisted. "I did not like to think of her by her married name."

"Why? Did it remind you that you were conducting an affair with a married woman?"

"You have it all wrong. Deena and I did not develop a romantic attachment until long after her husband died. Deena liked to have a good time but she was not immoral. She would never have cheated on the old man."

Deena was widowed for two years before her death. "When did your . . . liaison begin?"

"In the last year of her life."

"What about the things you sold? Items that belonged to Castle Tremayne for decades, even centuries, in some cases."

"Deena insisted. She said the estate was losing money and that her stepson wanted nothing more than to see her fail. She was determined to make a success of the castle."

"What exactly did she ask you to do?"

"The duchess selected the items she wanted to sell. I just delivered them. Deena and the buyers agreed on a price before I transferred the pieces to their new owners."

"How did the exchange of money work? Did they pay you?"

He shook his head. "I never saw any money. It was sent directly to Deena."

"How many items are we talking about?"

"I honestly couldn't tell you. She would send crates or packages with me and I would take them wherever she told me to. I never opened them."

"If you never saw what you delivered, how do you know they were pieces from the castle?"

"Because Deena told me as much. I took her at her word." He threw up his hands. "I am an artist, not a fence or a traveling salesman. I did what I did because Deena asked me to."

"The duke will be very unhappy when he hears of this."

He clutched her hand. "Please do not tell him. What if he blames me? I was in love with Deena. I would have done anything she asked. I can't lose my position here."

"I am your employer and the owner of Castle Tremayne. Not Strickland. He can't dismiss you."

He examined her face. "You are determined to tell him."

"I am," she said firmly. "I am not a liar and I don't intend to start being one now. I cannot abide dishonesty."

CHAPTER TWENTY-TWO

"O bviously Alfred Price has to go," Strick said when Raya told what she'd learned during a walk to the ruins. "He was instrumental in the looting perpetrated by Deena."

"You cannot blame him," she protested. "At least not entirely."

"I most certainly can. His actions resulted in the loss of some of Tremayne's most valuable possessions."

"He was just an errand boy." She took Strick's hand as he helped her over a stile. "He didn't want to lose all favor with Deena."

"I cannot believe they were lovers." He kept hold of her when they continued walking. "I would never have guessed. There were no rumors at all. I wonder if it went on when Father was alive."

Raya's hand felt delicate in his large, gentle grip. She liked the sensation. But it would be a mistake to allow herself to fall too deeply into the duke's thrall.

She slid her hand away. Strickland held on briefly, but then let her go. The lines in his forehead deepened, but he said nothing.

"Alfred says the liaison did not start until a year after your father died," Raya said.

"Well, he would say that, wouldn't he?" Strick said irritably. "Price would not want to add bedding a married woman to his list of transgressions. I want him gone. As soon as possible."

Raya halted. "It isn't up to you."

"Why would you fight me on this?" His face darkened. "Is Price that important to you?"

His possessive tone caught her off guard. "You cannot possibly be jealous of him? He means nothing to me."

"He is significant enough that you would defy me."

"Defy you?" Her back went up. "Is this what our marriage will be like? You dictating what you want done and expecting me to scurry about obeying your orders?"

He flushed. "You care so deeply for Alfred Price that you are willing to quarrel with me over him?"

"This is not about Alfred. This is about me running the castle as I see fit."

He pushed his lips together. "I see. You are reminding me that you own the castle and can do whatever you like."

"I would not put it so crassly," she retorted. "However, now that you mention it, I seem to recall your assurance that marriage would not result in me losing control of castle operations, particularly the business enterprises."

He opened his mouth to retort, but then seemed to change his mind. He shut his mouth so tightly that his lips formed a grim line.

"What?" she asked. "What were you about to say?"

His expression twisted into a painful-looking grimace. "Not a thing," he ground out.

"Then why do you look like you are about to burst?"

He straightened his shoulders and smoothed his features, visibly making an effort to calm himself. "I am not." He forced an even tone. "Just tell me why it is so important to you to keep Price on."

"He has a job to finish. The mural is a popular stop on the tour. And several people have already paid handsomely to have their likenesses added to it."

He considered her words. "And once the mural is complete, will you agree not to employ him again?"

She didn't think Alfred should be punished for being honest with her. Even though his mother's revelations hadn't left him much choice. "I promise to seriously consider it."

"This is going to be harder than I thought," he murmured more to himself than to her.

"What is? Marriage to me?" Her neck heated. "Maybe you'd like to reconsider. It's not too late."

"Don't be silly," he said lightly. "I expect to quarrel with you on a regular basis. You are a naturally cantankerous woman. That's part of your charm."

"As long as you understand that I will never be biddable."

He barked a laugh. "You made that plain on the day we met."

"Just so we are clear."

"Crystal."

The ruins came into view. "You never said why we are going to the old abbey."

"To see the sunset. The last time we left in a hurry without properly enjoying the view."

"And whose fault was that?"

He laughed. "Mine. And tonight, I shall make it up to you."

"OH, STRICK." RAYA took in the violet flowers carpeting the entire inside shell of the abbey. "It's beautiful."

"You did say that purple is your favorite color so I had the gardener remove all of the other flowers and replace them with your preferred shade."

"It's so extravagant."

"I'm a duke. We, as a lot, are supposed to be excessive."

No one had ever done anything so whimsically thoughtful to please her. She looked beyond him to the table that was set for supper. "I suppose this time around you will allow me to stay for dessert?"

He pulled her to him. "I intend to be dessert."

Warmth trickled through her. She maneuvered out of his arms. "I am famished," she said, moving toward the table.

He followed. "Excellent. I have a plan for this evening that begins with eating and watching the sunset."

She registered the gleam in his eye. "And then?"

"You shall have to wait to see." He removed the silver domes covering the serving platters.

She surveyed the offerings. Then she saw it. The pieces of baked chicken and caramelized onions, spiced with brick-red sumac, artfully arranged atop Arabic flatbread and sprinkled with pine nuts and parsley. Her mouth watered. "Is that *musakhan*?"

Strick beamed as he took his seat beside her. "It is."

"But when . . . How?"

"You did say this dish is one of your favorites."

"You were listening." Warmth tingled through her. Her eyes stung. No one in her life had ever wanted to please her like Strick. The thoughtful gestures left her speechless. She allowed herself to drop her guard, putting away any reservations and suspicions. At least for now, she wanted to fully enjoy the evening Strick planned for them. "I cannot believe you remembered my favorite meal."

"I confess to forgetting the name of the dish but when I described it to your aunt, she immediately knew to what I was referring. I asked her to instruct Mrs. Cranch on how to make the meal." His eyes twinkled. "As I understand it, your aunt found Mrs. Cranch's technique to be lacking so she took over and prepared it herself."

"Which means it is definitely going to be delicious." She watched him fill her plate. "Auntie Majida makes the best *musakhan*. But how did you get the sumac spice? Do you have it in England?"

"I instructed Philips to get it by any means necessary. I believe he had to send for it from Manchester."

"Manchester?"

"There are a number of Arab cotton mercantile types there so he was able to procure your sumac from one of the local shops."

"I cannot believe you went to so much trouble."

"Nothing is too much effort for my future duchess."

She watched as he served himself a generous helping. "You have to make sure your first bite includes chicken, bread and onions. You eat it with your hands."

"You really are a managing female." He took a bite and rolled the food over in his mouth. "Hmm. That tang is quite tasty."

She smiled happily. "I told you." She proceeded to eat, pleased to find that Auntie's *musakhan* was as delicious as ever, and extraordinarily happy to be able to share her favorite Palestinian dish with Strick. They chatted easily, enjoying the view as they waited for the sun to vanish below the horizon. It unnerved her to think how easily she could become accustomed to being in Strick's company. How easily she might come to depend on him for her happiness.

"Did I see the representative from the railroad at the castle earlier today?" she asked, hoping that business talk would keep the atmosphere from becoming too intimate.

"Yes." Strick reached for a linen to clean sumac-infused olive oil from his hands. "The railroad is ready to discuss the particulars."

"What are they offering?"

"Leave it to you to discuss business during a romantic dinner."

"I find such talk to be very stimulating."

The gold in his eyes flared. "I see you are learning how to titillate me just with your words."

She hadn't meant it like that, but she couldn't resist being drawn to his charisma. "If that is so, it is because I am learning from the best."

"The railway is offering a very generous lump sum for use of my land."

She pondered that. "Perhaps you should consider leasing the land so the payment is ongoing."

"That is definitely something to think about."

"Soon you'll have sufficient funds to buy me out."

He paused. "We don't know that. It appears that the terms they are offering might not be as generous as we expected."

"Truly? How can that be? I understood that cutting through Tremayne land was critical to the new line they are building."

He shrugged, appearing surprisingly unconcerned. "I'm not sure why."

"Are you disappointed?"

"Not at all." He gently tweaked her chin. "I would rather share Tremayne with you than have it all to myself."

She blinked, stunned. "But the castle means everything to you."

"It once did. But that was before. Now, nothing gives me more pleasure than the idea of you and me living here together forever."

"Even though I've invited strangers into your home? You once objected very strenuously to turning Castle Tremayne into a business enterprise."

"I have come around to seeing the value in your approach to taking Tremayne into the next century."

Warmth rippled through her. Strick was dangerously appealing when he was argumentative, but an amenable duke who valued her business sense was all the more so. "Perhaps we should head back," she said. "The sun has set and it's getting dark."

"First, we have some business to attend to." He withdrew something from his pocket. A gold emerald ring. "Will you, Miss Raya Darwish, do me the greatest honor by agreeing to become my wife?"

She inhaled. "Oh, Strick, it's lovely."

"My last proposal was pitiful so I thought to make this one special."

He succeeded. Nothing could be more special than being here with Strick, sharing her favorite foods and watching the marvelous sunset. "The ring is stunning. I've never owned anything like it."

"This emerald has passed from one Duchess of Strickland to the next for generations," he said solemnly. "Will you accept it now to carry this tradition forward?"

Raya stared at the ring, struck by how badly she wanted to accept his proposal, a part of her feeling relieved that she didn't have much choice. To save Tremayne Enterprises, she had to wed. She held out her hand. "Yes, I will marry you."

EVEN AS SHE accepted his mother's ring, Strick sensed that Raya still held part of herself from him. She might be present in body, but her innermost thoughts were like buried treasure yet to be unearthed. He batted his frustration away. Little by little, he would earn her trust.

He lit candles on the table and presented her with another gift. Raya stared at the ruby and gold bracelet, her expressive face glowing in the flickering light.

"But this is one of your precious artifacts," she protested. "It's an important part of your collection."

"You are precious." He slid the bracelet onto

her wrist. "The Saxons believed that a good king was a giver of gold. Rings, weapons embellished with gold. All of it."

"And you view yourself as my king?"

"I view myself as your husband."

"We are not wed yet."

"In my heart, we most certainly are. The world might require the show of a ceremony to make it official, but we know we are bound to each other for life."

"Maybe it really is *naseeb*," she said softly.

"What is that?"

"Destiny. The Arabs believe that people have fated mates. And you are mine." She looked embarrassed. "You probably think that's silly."

"On the contrary, I am delighted." He gently laid her down, half expecting her to protest. "If fate has brought us together, we have no choice but to marry."

She didn't object. Instead Raya quirked a smile as he positioned himself over her. "It *is* out of our hands."

"Precisely." He understood her. For now, she offered her body. Her mind would take more time. He felt under her skirts until he found the slit in her drawers. He used his fingers to stroke and tease her. "And who are we to tempt fate?"

She closed her eyes and they made love again under the stars, cushioned by the soft blanket of violet wildflowers he'd created just for her.

CHAPTER TWENTY-THREE

A lady does not discuss any topic that is too absorbing because it might lead to a discussion," Frances instructed.

"Talking about something interesting is objectionable?" Raya asked. "Why is that?"

"Lengthy or intense discussions are frowned upon in polite conversation."

"I see. So the more boring the better."

Frances laughed. "Exactly."

Raya was beginning to rethink her decision to seek Frances out for duchess lessons. But she didn't want to embarrass Strick, or herself, during the rare times Raya did venture into society. She might as well learn the basic rules, which would also be to her advantage when trying to drum up business for Tremayne. "What else?"

"At a meal, never remove your gloves until you have been seated."

"That, I think I can remember."

"Certainly," Frances said encouragingly. "However, do take care not to be confused when gentlemen remove their gloves before they are seated. There are different rules for men."

"Isn't that always the case?" Raya remarked.

"Yes, indeed," Frances agreed. They were at Trentham House and Frances had invited Raya to stay for luncheon after their lesson.

"Do you actually enjoy moving in society?" Raya asked as they finished eating.

"I do. It is the world into which I have been born. As Strick's duchess, you will be at the very top of the social hierarchy. Many will do your bidding to try and gain your favor."

"Pity it is wasted on me," Raya said before excusing herself to use the washroom.

Trentham House was not as grand as Castle Tremayne but it was still palatial enough to get lost in. She made her way down an upper corridor and opened a door to find it was a small storeroom rather than the lavatory. She was about to shut the door when something caught her eye. She went closer for a better look. Shock sprinkled through her.

It couldn't be.

But there was no mistaking the pair of embellished green drinking glasses ornamented with an anguished man with limbs entwined in the vines. Raya caught her breath. What were Strick's missing artifacts doing in an upstairs closet in the home of the duke's closest friend?

Her mind racing, Raya debated what to do. Should she act as if nothing had happened and tell Strick about her discovery once she got home? What if the glasses were moved in the interim? She'd have no proof. She looked down at her gown. She could try hiding the glasses in her skirts but what if they fell and shattered? The pieces were too precious to take the risk.

"There you are," Frances said from behind her. "I was afraid you'd gotten lost."

Raya spun around, her heart slamming in her chest. "I did get lost." She tried not to sound breathless. "I found a storeroom rather than the washroom."

Frances smiled serenely. "These big old houses are very easy to get lost in, that is for certain." But then her attention darted over to the artifacts and her smile faded. "Oh."

"Yes." Raya's pulse throbbed in her ears. "Oh, indeed."

Frances paled. "It's not what you think."

"How do you know what I am thinking?"

"We can just return them," she said urgently. "There is no need for Strick to know about this."

"Why did you steal them?"

Frances's eyes widened. "Me?"

"Hello?" Strick's voice sounded from down-stairs. "Is anyone at home? I am here to escort my betrothed back to Tremayne."

"We're up here," Raya called out. She and Frances held each other's gaze while listening to the sounds of Strick's boots striking the wood flooring as he bounded up the stairs.

"There you are." He appeared on the threshold. "What are you two doing in here?"

Raya kept her eyes on Frances. "Do you want to tell him or should I?"

Panic flickered in the other woman's face. "Nothing at all," she said smoothly. "Miss Darwish got lost on the way to the washroom. I came to retrieve her."

"I see. Are you two going to stay here all day or shall we go down?"

"Strickland," Raya said, her throat tight.

"What is it?" He sobered once he registered the expression on her face. "What has happened?"

"I found your missing artifacts."

He frowned. "What do you mean?"

She pointed at the goblets. His eyes widened. "Are those my goblets? What are they doing here?"

"That's what I was asking Frances when you arrived."

"If you will excuse me." Frances turned to go. "You can see yourselves out."

"Wait just a moment," Strickland commanded. "Frances, what is going on?"

She backed out the door. "Speak to my brother. This has nothing to do with me."

STRICK STORMED INTO the Trentham House study to find Guy in shirtsleeves, meeting with his steward. "What the devil is going on here?"

Guy looked up, surprised. "Strick? I am meeting with my steward. What does it look like?"

"I need to speak with you," Strick ground out. "Alone."

Guy nodded at Raya, who came in behind Strick. "Miss Darwish."

"Mr. Vaughan," she responded politely.

Guy rose and reached for his jacket to make himself presentable in her presence. "That will be all," he said to his steward. Once he was gone, Guy said, "What has happened?"

"That's what I'd like you to tell me." Strick's neck burned. "What are my goblets doing here?"

Guy looked from Strick to Raya and then back again. "I don't know what you're talking about."

Strick thought he knew his friend inside and out, and Guy's show of incredulity seemed authentic. "My King Lycurgus pieces are in your storeroom."

Guy frowned. "Are you referring to the goblets that Deena sold?"

"I *thought* she sold them. Imagine my surprise when Raya informed me they've taken up residence in your closet."

"Impossible."

"I just saw them for myself."

"There is clearly some mistake. What would your goblets be doing in my house?"

"That's what I'd like to know," Strick said.

Horror dawned on Guy's face. "You can't think that I . . . What? . . . Stole your Saxon objects? You're not serious."

"I'm waiting for an explanation."

"For what?" he said, exasperated. "I don't have

one. I don't know what those objects are doing in Trentham House."

Strick stared at him. "I want to believe you."

"But you don't? What are you suggesting? That I clandestinely entered Castle Tremayne and stole two precious objects?"

"I am not suggesting anything. I am merely looking for answers. Your sister said the goblets had nothing to do with her. That we should talk to you."

"Frances said that? But why would she—" Guy's expression changed. He clamped his mouth shut.

"Well?" Strick demanded. "I am waiting for an explanation."

Guy ran his hand over his mouth and chin. "Frances said you should talk to me?"

"That's right," Strick said impatiently.

Guy was silent for a while. Then he spoke. "What can I say?" He stared at the parquet floor. "I . . . erm . . . didn't intend to cause harm."

Strick felt the blood rush from his face. "Surely you are not . . . You can't be . . . confessing?"

"It was . . . an impulse." Guy grasped for words, his face ashen.

"What kind of impulse?" Strick couldn't believe what he was hearing. Before this moment, he'd have trusted Guy, his oldest friend in the world, with his life.

"I was going to sell them because I am perilously low on funds."

"Since when?" Strick demanded, dubious. "You've always been flush."

Guy paused. "Times are hard. I don't have to tell you that."

"If you were going to sell the goblets, why do you still have them?" Raya asked.

"An. Excellent. Question." Guy drew the words out. "I decided I couldn't go through with it. That I couldn't do something so deceitful and dishonest."

Strick threw up his hands. "I cannot believe this."

Guy locked eyes with him. "I hope you can forgive me."

"GUY STEALING FROM me?" Strick helped Raya into the carriage for the ride home. "How could I have been so wrong about him?"

"He said he has money troubles." Raya wanted to comfort Strick. "Money, or the lack thereof, can make people behave in strange ways."

He stared out the window. "My oldest and dearest friend. I've known him since I was a boy."

Raya hesitated to give voice to her thought but she did so anyway. "It is possible he took other things as well?"

"I suppose anything is possible." He gave her a bleak look. "You are thinking that I wrongfully accused Deena."

"Not entirely. Alfred Price did confirm that Cousin Deena was selling castle treasures."

He resumed staring out the window. "I wonder

if Guy would admit to taking more items. I've always thought of him as truthful but now I feel like I don't know my friend at all."

Something about the encounter didn't sit well with Raya. But she brushed it off. She didn't know Guy well enough to question his reaction—complete confusion and then quiet acceptance—to being accused of thievery. "You had no idea at all that he was low on funds?"

He shook his head. "As far as I knew, his finances were in good order. Far better than mine. He has far fewer expenses. It's difficult for me to fathom that he would steal from me despite knowing I might need to sell the goblets to keep Castle Tremayne afloat."

When they arrived home, Strick had a faraway look in his eyes that made Raya's heart hurt for him. "I think I shall go for a walk," he said.

"Would you like me to go with you?" she asked.

He gave her a half smile. "Thank you, but I think I need to be alone with my thoughts." She felt helpless as she watched him stride away toward the gardens. She could only imagine how betrayed and hurt Strick must feel.

The castle was quiet. Tremayne was only open to visitors Wednesday through Saturday. Today was Monday, a good day to look over the books. She went to the morning room and settled in to work. About an hour later, a rustling noise sounded outside the closed sitting room door. Raya looked up, hoping it was Strick back from his walk. Instead of coming in or knocking, the person on the other side of the door slipped something under the door. It was a note from Strick.

Please join me in the tea shop at your earliest convenience.

Raya rose immediately to go to him. She went through a back door to reach the rear outer courtyard. But when she got to the tea shop it was empty. The chairs were stacked on top of the tables. Someone had recently cleaned the floors.

"Hello?" she called out, her voice echoing in the empty space. "Strick?"

A cracking sound came from above. Raya looked up in time to see the loose wooden beam break away and come crashing toward her.

CHAPTER TWENTY-FOUR

Raya dove under the nearest table.
She landed hard on her hip and tucked herself into a tight ball just as the structural support roared down. A huge crash was followed by the sound of cracking wood. Raya squeezed her eyes shut, fervently hoping the table would hold under the weight of the beam. Then it was silent. Dust dancing in the air.

A man was shouting. "Miss Darwish! Raya?"

"I'm here." It wasn't Strick. But she recognized the voice. "Alfred?"

"Yes," the artist called out. "Are you all right?"

"I think so." Her insides feeling shaky, she peered around. Somehow, the beam had just clipped the table she hid under. The tables that took the full brunt of the weight of the wooden support were flattened. Raya shivered and tried not to imagine what would have happened had she taken refuge under a different table.

"Hold on," Alfred called. "I'll get help."

"I think I can manage." She slid out from under the table and carefully climbed over smashed tables and mangled chairs.

"Have a care," Alfred urged as she stepped over jagged-edged pieces of wood.

By the time Raya reached the tea shop entrance, several people had gathered. She recognized workers from the stables and weave shop, from the brewery, sawmill and dairy. But no Strick.

"Has anyone seen His Grace?" she asked, fearing he might have been in the tea shop waiting for her after all.

No one had.

"Are you certain you are unhurt?" Alfred asked.

Raya took stock of herself. "Nothing seems to be broken or injured." She brushed dust off her sleeves and shook out her skirts, and managed to regain enough composure to assure everyone that she was well. But she needed a bath and a change of clothes.

Alfred offered to walk her back to the castle. "What were you doing in the tea shop?" he asked as they walked.

She told him and then asked a question of her own. "What were you doing in the outer bailey?"

"I needed to consult with you regarding one of the tourists who paid for his likeness to be added to the mural. I hoped you would approve the design and placement."

"I can take care of that now, if you'd like."

"Nonsense. It can wait until later. You've just been through an ordeal." Concern lined his face. "Please have a care."

Raya was worried about Strick. Where was he? "I need to find the duke and make sure he is well."

"His Grace sent a note asking you to join him?"

"Yes, but he hadn't arrived."

"I see." Alfred was ashen-faced. "You could have been killed."

She shivered. "Don't remind me." She studied his face. "You don't believe it was an accident."

"It seems too coincidental, don't you think? You are summoned to the tea shop and as soon as you arrive, a beam falls."

"The beam has been loose. I asked some of the workers to fix it. I suppose they hadn't gotten around to it."

"Or maybe someone told them not to work on it."

"You can't think this is Strickland's doing."

He pressed his lips inward. "First, Deena falls from the ruins that she almost never visited, certainly not alone and at night. And now you—" He shook his head. "I honestly don't know what to think, but I don't like any of it."

"Neither do I."

"Raya!" A voice called from behind her.

She pivoted, relieved to see Strick coming for her. "You're all right. Thank goodness."

"Of course I'm fine. Why wouldn't I be?" He enveloped her in his arms, right there in full view of a shocked Alfred. "Thank God you're safe. I heard what happened."

She fell into his embrace, inhaling his scent,

savoring being in his arms. He was safe! After a few moments, Strick relaxed his hold but kept one arm around Raya's waist as he tucked her against him.

"Your Grace," an obviously stunned Alfred said, greeting the duke.

"Price," he said ebulliently. "Have you heard our good news? Miss Darwish has consented to be my wife."

Alfred blinked but recovered admirably. "May I offer my congratulations?"

"You may," Strick said. "And now I am going to have my betrothed examined by Dr. Michaels to ensure that she is unharmed."

They left Alfred staring after them, Strick's arm still firmly around Raya's waist. "You are making a spectacle," she said as they passed a couple of maids who pretended not to stare at the open display of intimacy.

"You are going to be my duchess and I don't care who knows it. I am proud to have you by my side."

She leaned closer into him. "I was looking for you at the tea shop. Where were you?"

He frowned. "I told you I was going for a walk. This business with Guy is very off-putting. Imagine how alarmed I was when I returned from my walk and came in through the outer bailey. Everyone was talking about how you narrowly escaped being injured by that falling beam."

"But your note said to meet you at the tea shop."

He halted to look her in the face. "What note?"

"You didn't send it." It was a realization rather than a question.

"What note?" he pressed.

"I received a note asking me to meet you at the tea shop. I thought it was from you." She wasn't familiar with Strick's writing. Only his signature, which was on their signed agreement.

"It most certainly was not from me. Where is this note?"

"I left it in my sitting room."

"I want to see it." But by the time they reached the sitting room, the note was nowhere to be found.

"Who would take it?" Raya said, still a bit dazed from the events of a whirlwind afternoon.

Anger flashed in Strick's eyes. "The person who really wrote the note. Who is obviously also the person who tried to harm you."

Raya shivered. And could not help but think of what happened to Deena. "What if it is the same person who hurt my cousin?"

Strick's lips pushed into a grim line. "Then I will find the bastard. And I will make him sorry that he was ever born."

THREE DAYS LATER, Strick signed the railway agreement to allow tracks to be laid across the top corner of his property.

He met with Foley in his private apartments at the castle. After finalizing the documents,

Foley, the railway representative, rose to depart. "Thank you, Your Grace. I believe this agreement will be mutually beneficial."

"Let us hope so." The terms of the deal were very generous, generous enough for Strick to make monthly payments to buy the castle back, if that had been necessary. Generous enough for him to close Tremayne to paying visitors.

But Strick had no interest in shuttering Raya's business enterprises. Tremayne needed more than one revenue stream. It was important to diversify. He'd learned as much from Raya and looked forward to seeing what other moneymaking ventures she'd come up with in the years to come. Together, they would secure Castle Tremayne for their children and grandchildren. The venerable old fortress would not fall into disrepair like so many of the stately homes being sold away or torn down.

"I confess we were surprised that you agreed to make a deal," Foley said. "After Mr. Vaughan turned us down, we worried all of the landowners in the area would follow suit."

That caught Strick's attention. "Guy turned you down?"

Foley nodded. "He has no financial incentive to come to an agreement with the railway. Mr. Vaughan's property is much smaller than yours. He feared that having a railroad come through would cause disruption at the main house."

Guy said he took the goblets because he needed

the funds. Yet he turned down the railway? "Are you saying you made Mr. Vaughan a genuine offer? A lucrative one?"

"We offered very generous terms. But his property is unlike Tremayne. Your acreage is so vast, the railway is miles and miles away from the castle. Nobody at the castle would ever know there was a railroad at the outer edge of the property."

Strick was baffled. "Vaughan told you that he turned you down because he has no need for the money?"

"That is correct."

After Foley departed, Strick scribbled a quick note and had Philips dispatch it at once. Then he went into his bedchamber to tuck the newly signed railway agreement away in his chest of drawers, next to the codicil to his father's will that gave him full ownership of Castle Tremayne.

Afterward, he settled in his sitting room to await his visitor's arrival. Guy appeared an hour later. The two men had not met since Guy admitted stealing Strick's artifacts.

"You summoned?" he asked warily.

"Thank you for coming." The duke held out a hand, inviting his friend to take a seat.

"I must confess to being surprised that you want to see me."

"Why is that?"

Guy looked pained. "Must you force me to

say that I am in deep shame and regret over my betrayal of our friendship?"

"But did you?"

"I beg your pardon?"

"Did you betray our friendship?" Strick asked.

"I do not know how else it could be perceived."

"I just wanted to clarify a few things. It's the least you can do."

Guy took a seat. "Very well."

"Tell me again why you stole from me."

"I need the money. I will regret my actions until my dying day. Do you have any other questions?"

"Just one."

Guy visibly braced himself. "Very well."

"Why are you lying?"

Guy stiffened. "What do you mean?"

"You have plenty of money. So much so that you turned down a generous offer from the railway."

"Where did you learn that?"

"From Foley. He just left. Tell me, if you have plenty of money, why would you steal from me?"

Guy shifted in his chair. "It's complicated."

"I'll bet." Strick relaxed back in his chair. "I thought to myself, 'Why would Guy lie?' Especially to me, his oldest and dearest friend?"

"I have no excuse."

"And then I realized," Strick continued as if Guy hadn't spoken, "that there is at least one person dearer to you than me. And you lied to protect this person."

Guy's face darkened. "You are barking up the wrong tree."

"Judging by your reaction, I don't think I am."

"I will brook no insult to—" he stopped.

"To whom?" Strick prompted. "To your sister? Frances took those goblets, did she not? And you lied to protect her."

"Careful, Strick," Guy warned. "Do not force me to defend my sister's honor."

"Don't be ridiculous. Nobody tolerates duels anymore. Even if you call me out on a field of honor, I will not accept. No one is going to shoot anyone."

"I cannot allow Frances's reputation to be ruined. She wants nothing more than to marry well and move about in society."

"I need to hear the truth from you. It won't leave this room. I give you my word as a gentleman. Did Frances take my goblets?"

"How could it be otherwise?" Guy exhaled and slumped back in his chair. "I didn't take them and Frances did tell you to speak with me when you confronted her."

"Which made you assume that she took them."

"I could see no other answer."

"Did she admit to it when you confronted her?"

"I did not confront her."

"Why not?"

Guy fixed him with a hard stare. "You do realize that Frances is in love with you and has been since she was a girl."

Strick let out a shocked breath. "You cannot be serious."

"She has turned down two very advantageous marriage offers in hopes of one day becoming your duchess."

"I had no idea." Strick was flabbergasted. "I never meant to mislead her."

"And you did not. But she had hopes. Which were dashed once you told us that you intended to wed Miss Darwish."

"But the goblets were stolen well before I decided to wed Miss Darwish."

"I cannot explain it. Perhaps Frances's feelings for you are more intensely troubled than I realized."

Strick thought of his friend's gracious, even-tempered sister. "I cannot imagine it."

"Promise me," Guy said, "promise me that no one will ever hear of this. Frances would be ruined if people knew she'd stolen from you."

"You already have my word. I will tell no one."

"Not even Miss Darwish?"

He hesitated.

Guy pressed him. "You gave me your word."

"I will tell no one." Strick relented. "Not even Raya."

"WHAT SORT OF ring?" Derek asked when Raya visited him at the forge.

Raya showed sketches of Saxon-style rings to the Tremayne blacksmith. "Something like this. I wish to surprise His Grace with it as a wedding gift."

Derek examined the rudimentary drawings that Raya copied from one of Strick's books on Saxon antiquities. She'd chosen the simplest designs.

"Can you make something like it?" she asked.

"I believe so. I'll just need His Grace's ring size."

"Oh. You don't have it?" She hadn't thought of that. "I thought His Grace has made many rings."

"He has but never for himself."

Raya pondered her options. "I shall have to find out his size."

"It would be best if you bring me one of his rings. I could size it perfectly that way."

As luck would have it, Strick was away for the night, at a nearby dig. The timing could not be better. "I shall bring you one of Strickland's rings," she assured the blacksmith.

Normally, she'd feel bad about going through Strick's things without his knowledge. But Strick wouldn't mind, especially if he knew what she was up to.

Mrs. Shaw had to unlock the door to Strick's private apartments for Raya. The housekeeper was the only person on the property with keys for every lock. Ever since Tremayne opened to paying visitors, Strick made a habit of locking his castle quarters. Even though the tours never came close to his living space, he took extra precautions to protect his privacy and the Saxon artifacts he kept in the display case.

Raya entered Strick's private enclave, relishing the scent of books and stale smoke, tinged with a hint of Strick's cologne. Her heart panged. He'd only been gone for a night but she missed him terribly.

She started with the chest of drawers in his bedchamber. His toiletries, including shaving soap, tooth powder and a set of brushes, were neatly laid out on top. The first two drawers contained personal effects but no jewelry.

The third drawer contained some clothing and some papers. The railway logo at the top of one paper caught her attention. She pulled it out. It was an agreement. As she read through it, she saw that Strick had negotiated so well that he'd soon have sufficient funds to buy Tremayne back from her. If that were still necessary. But why hadn't Strick told her the deal was complete? It was a strange oversight considering that he knew how much she enjoyed discussing business.

As she replaced the railway agreement, the document now lying faceup drew her. It was a codicil to a will. To Strick's father's will. She wondered what was in it. Strick had obviously kept his copy for a purpose. Maybe for sentimental reasons.

She shouldn't read it. Doing so would certainly qualify as snooping. But what harm could it do? Strick would probably show it to her if she asked. She began reading.

Her heart dropped as she read the words. The

Duke of Strickland stipulated that after Deena Darwish's death, Castle Tremayne was to pass to his son and heir. She reread the codicil several times before its meaning truly sank in. Deena had never had the power to leave Castle Tremayne to Raya. The castle had only been for Deena to live in during her lifetime. Afterward, it was to pass back into the Carey family. To the heir. *To Strick.*

A hurricane of questions blew through her mind. Could it be true? Was Strick the rightful owner of Castle Tremayne? It made no sense at all. Why would he tolerate Raya's business ventures if he'd had the right to toss her out all along?

He had lied to her.

But why?

She replaced the papers in Strick's drawer. There was another person who knew the truth. She hoped she could trust him to honestly answer her questions.

"YES, IT IS true," the solicitor said. "His Grace is the rightful owner of Castle Tremayne."

The air left Raya's lungs. She'd come into the village to hear the truth from Mr. Combs. "I see."

"The codicil was just discovered a few weeks ago."

"A few weeks ago?" She frowned. "How is that possible? How could such an important document go missing for years?"

Mr. Combs explained that his son, also a solicitor, had drawn up the codicil when Mr. Combs was away and had neglected to inform his father. "When I finally discovered the truth," he said in conclusion, "I immediately told the Duke of Strickland."

"You told His Grace about this weeks ago?"

"I did. And he insisted that I not inform you. He wanted to tell you himself."

"I see." But she didn't. Not at all. None of this made any sense. What was Strick up to? Why would he keep his ownership of the castle from her? And why hide his lucrative railway agreement?

The man was full of secrets.

And that made Raya suspicious.

She thanked the solicitor and walked home. No, not home, she mentally corrected herself. It had taken her months to fully believe that Castle Tremayne belonged to her. And over the last several weeks, she'd grown attached to the fortress. Tremayne might not be in her bones like it was in Strick's, but it was definitely in her heart. Yet the castle didn't belong to her and never had.

Why hadn't Strick told her? What could his motive be? She knew he enjoyed taking her to bed. Did he want to make certain she stayed at Tremayne until he tired of having sex with her? Once he'd had enough, would he tell Raya the truth and send her back to New York? Is that why he hadn't told her about the railway deal? If she knew he had the funds to buy the castle back, then she might expect him to start making payments. And, of course, Strick didn't need to buy back a property that belonged to him.

At least there was one silver lining to be found in this entire confusing mess. Confirmation that Alfred was wrong. Strick wasn't trying to kill her. He had no motive. He already owned the castle.

Anger flared in Raya's belly. Whatever Strick's motives, he'd lied to her for weeks. He'd played her for a fool. Just like Salem, he couldn't be trusted. But now that Raya knew there was a game afoot, she intended to start making moves of her own.

Strick might think he was duping her, but she'd show him who the true fool was.

CHAPTER TWENTY-FIVE

S trick sought Raya out the moment he returned from his dig. He finally found her outdoors with her notebook tucked under her arm, in deep discussion with two men he did not recognize. She was a vision with her dark hair pulled back from her striking face, falling in gentle waves down her back. The sun slanted against luminous eyes and clear skin.

"Thank you, gentlemen," Raya said as Strick strode toward them. "I shall be in contact."

The men nodded at Strick, touching the rims of their hats before taking their leave.

"Finally." He reached for her, feeling like the luckiest man alive to have this woman's attentions. "I've missed you terribly."

She gracefully eluded his grasp. "Behave," she said lightly. "People can see us."

He smiled as he looked into her face. "Maybe we should go somewhere private so I can do some deliciously nasty things to you."

The high arches of her cheeks colored. "As delightful as that sounds, I am busy."

Was it his imagination or was she avoiding looking him directly in the eyes? "Too busy for me to get down on my knees to worship you with my tongue as you deserve?"

She made a show of examining the surrounding landscape. "Sadly, yes."

"What are you so busy with?" If not for the involuntary flush of her face, he'd think her indifferent to his provocations. "What were those men doing here?"

"We were discussing new moneymaking ventures."

"Really?" Her schemes interested him. "Such as?"

"I am contemplating setting up a pen here."

He looked around. "Here?" They stood in an open meadow beyond the gardens that offered some of the castle's best views. "For what?"

"Bear wrestling."

"I beg your pardon?"

"People would pay handsomely to see men try to wrestle a bear."

He barked a laugh. "You cannot be serious."

To his surprise, her face held no trace of mirth. "This meadow is just sitting here when it could be making me money."

"But it provides beautiful views from the castle windows."

"As you know, except for the gardens, this meadow is the only piece of land I own."

"And you intend to desecrate it?"

"I am monetizing the property. Really, Strick, you ought to stop being so backward-looking. My view is toward the future of Castle Tremayne."

"Which includes silly novelties such as bear wrestling?"

"Not just bear wrestling. I have other acts in mind."

"Should I brace myself? Are you adding mud wrestling as well?"

"Don't be silly."

"*I'm* being silly?"

"I intend to host traveling shows in this space."

Alarm rose in him. Was she serious? "What sorts of shows?"

"Human oddities for one. I am told they are all the rage in England."

Strick was beginning to feel the stirrings of rage himself. "You are proposing to host human curiosity exhibits at Castle Tremayne?"

"Possibly." She chewed on the back of her pen. "Perhaps I should build a more permanent exhibition space in addition to the pen."

Strick couldn't believe his ears. "You want to build a venue to showcase human oddities exhibits and a pen for bear wrestling right next to the castle? You do realize that will be the new view for anyone looking out of a south-facing window?"

"Your tower apartments are on the south side, aren't they?" She smiled brightly. "Wouldn't that be great fun?"

"No!" He burst out. "Silly novelty acts at Tremayne are the very opposite of *fun*."

"They might seem silly to you but both activities promise to be quite profitable."

"But making money isn't everything. Part of Castle Tremayne's charm is its unspoiled nature and scenic views."

"Why don't we come to an agreement?" Watching him intently, she patted his arm. "You do whatever you like with *your* land. And I shall do whatever I think best with *my* land."

His skin heated at her touch and his irritation vanished—at least for the moment. He reminded himself that Raya was a savvy woman with better business sense than most men. Her proposed ventures were entirely ridiculous and she'd surely see that in time.

"Are you done here?" he asked.

"For the moment."

He offered his arm. "Allow me to escort you back to the castle."

She paused, a look of consternation flickering across her expressive face. "That's it?"

"Unless you'd prefer to stand out here all day arguing." He couldn't wait until they were in private and he could take her into his arms and hold her. He longed to feel the warm, soft weight of her in his arms. It was extraordinary how he felt about this woman. He craved her company, and not just in bed. Although, of course, he hungered for her there as well.

"No, of course not," she said, taking his arm. As they approached the castle, a familiar-looking carriage pulled up.

"It's Guy," he said.

"Are you expecting him?"

"No. I fully anticipated spending the afternoon with my betrothed. Let's go in the back way and I'll instruct Philips to tell him we are not receiving."

"Nonsense. Go and see your friend." Raya pulled her arm from his. "I have some correspondence to see to. I shall join you later."

Strick couldn't quite interpret Raya's mood. Not cold precisely, or angry, but definitely distant. "Is something wrong?"

She smiled and finally met his gaze. "Whatever could be the matter?"

For a brief moment, it almost seemed as if she expected an answer. But then she smiled, excused herself and drifted off toward one of the castle's back entrances.

To STRICK'S SURPRISE, his visitor wasn't Guy.

Frances emerged from the coach, smartly dressed in a vibrant red gown and matching feathered hat. She'd obviously made an effort with her appearance. Strick greeted her in a friendly but guarded manner. Had an unrequited infatuation really turned Frances into a thief?

"I need to speak with you," she said after greeting him. "In private."

Given the situation, being alone didn't seem like a good idea, but Strick couldn't refuse her.

He directed Frances to an old solar chamber that once served as the private quarters of his ancestors, but was now a formal sitting room.

"I don't believe I have been in this room since I was a girl," she remarked as she entered.

"It is not part of the tour so we'll have some privacy." He took care to leave the door ajar.

Frances noticed. "You needn't worry, I don't intend to throw myself at you."

He cracked a smile, relieved to see she was the same Frances he'd always cared for as a friend. "I feel like I should make my apologies."

"Whatever for?"

"If I misled you—"

"You're a duke and my best friend's older brother." She set down the fringe-tasseled reticule that matched her gown. "Would anyone truly be surprised if I harbored hopes in that direction? After all, every girl dreams of becoming a duchess."

He cocked a brow. "Was it me you wanted? Or the title?"

"I am no fool." One corner of her mouth edged up. "I wanted both of course."

He barked a laugh. "I appreciate your candor."

"I accept that you are betrothed to Miss Darwish and that I must set my sights elsewhere."

Strick relaxed a little. "I confess to being a bit concerned when you appeared dressed in one of your finest day gowns."

"Women use clothing as armor. I chose this gown to boost my confidence, not to impress you."

"Why?" he asked in a gentle tone. "What can I do for you, Frances?"

She faced him square on. "It is imperative that you know I didn't take your goblets. I swear it."

Her choice of topic surprised him. "There was no lasting harm done. The pieces are back in my possession."

"And I am very glad for that. However, it is important to me that you know that I did not take them. Why would I?"

He could not think of a tactful response.

She continued. "I was as shocked as Miss Darwish when I saw them at Trentham House."

"Why did you say I should speak to Guy?"

"Because I had no idea why the goblets were there. I assumed he'd have a perfectly reasonable explanation."

"And Guy made the mistaken assumption that you'd taken them." It was a state of affairs more in keeping of what he knew of Frances and her brother.

"Precisely. I was beside myself when I realized he'd taken the blame to protect me. I don't know how those goblets ended up at our home but I swear on my life that I did not put them there."

"I believe you." But how had the goblets ended up at Trentham House?

"Why would anyone put your artifacts in our storeroom?" she asked. "It makes no sense at all."

"I have no idea. But I am happy we have cleared up the issue between us."

She smiled. "Then we are friends again?"

"Absolutely." He gave her a brief hug. "Always."

RAYA WAS SURPRISED to hear voices coming from the little-used solar that was not part of the tour.

She popped her head in to make sure tourists hadn't strayed into a private part of the castle. Instead of finding lost tourists, she came upon Strick embracing Frances. A sharp pain cut through her stomach, as though she'd swallowed a handful of nails. She tapped down a sudden urge to charge over and tear Strick away from the other woman.

Her violently possessive reaction shocked Raya's senses. She was not a person given to extreme impulses, but Strick clearly triggered her basest instincts. Before she could quietly back out, Strick sighted her.

"Raya, come in."

She reluctantly advanced into the room. "Hello, Frances."

The other woman greeted her with a wary look. "Good afternoon."

"I don't mean to interrupt," Raya said.

"You're not," they both said in unison before Frances added, "I was just leaving."

"Won't you stay for tea?" Strick asked Frances, his voice warm and welcoming. Jealousy sliced through Raya. Not twenty minutes ago, he couldn't wait to be alone with her. Now he urged Frances to linger?

"I cannot stay. I do have some errands to run," Frances said before making her goodbyes and quickly taking her leave.

Raya watched after her. "What was that about?"

"Nothing of importance," Strick said, pulling her into his arms.

"You were embracing her."

He nibbled on her neck. "Are you jealous?"

"Do you make a habit of putting your hands on young unmarried women?"

"I definitely want to make it a habit with you." He kissed her slow and unhurried. Thoroughly enough to make her knees buckle. Raya had intended to pull away but once his lips touched hers, she was lost. She kissed him back. Ardently. Using her tongue to mate with his, but instead of a dance, the play of their tongues was more like a duel. And it heated her body like an inferno.

Damn him for having this power over her. For having the capacity to hurt her with lies and obscuration. She intended to force him to confess by conceiving the most absurd ventures for Castle Tremayne. The more ludicrous the better, until Strick finally snapped and admitted he owned the property and would not allow her to implement her inane ideas. The horrified expression on his face when she mentioned bear wrestling and human oddities had almost made her burst out laughing.

Strick backed her up against the rear of a sofa. "I'm glad we're alone," he said against her mouth, "because I have been having filthy thoughts of you all day."

Their tongues tangled. He grabbed her buttocks, squeezing and massaging. She pulled at his shirt until she could slide her hands underneath to feel his warm skin. She dragged her nails down his back.

He uttered a sound of surprise. "My lioness."

"Why were you embracing Frances?" she demanded to know, nipping his lip.

"What? It's nothing. She's nothing." He turned her to face the sofa and started hiking up her skirts. "I'm going to take you from behind."

She should say no. Strick was a liar. A fraudster. He was obviously fond of Frances. And now he could have both Frances and the castle. He didn't have to wed Raya to keep Tremayne. But she lost her train of thought the moment his fingers reached between her legs. He played with her sensitive flesh, inciting her body to want more. To need more. To need *him*.

"You bastard," she ground out through clenched teeth as she grew wet under his touch.

His fingers stilled. "Do you want me to stop?"

Yes. "No. Hurry." Desperate to feel him inside her, she wiggled her bottom back against the hard iron of his cock.

He exhaled on a long curse. "If you keep that up, I'm going to spill."

She released a sound of frustration and desire. She would have him one last time. "Hurry."

His cock replaced his fingers. Big. Thick. Hard. He filled her, stretched her completely, pushing until he was fully seated. "You feel so good."

Being taken from behind heightened everything. She could feel his solid flesh inside of her with greater sensitivity and intensity. He started to move, pumping into her in long, powerful strokes.

Raya moved with him, bumping back against him. Completely in rhythm. In sync. Tears built in her throat. Why did it have to be so good with someone so duplicitous? A man who deceived her, who continued his lies even as he moved intimately inside of her.

The sounds of their lovemaking, his vigorous movements, the slapping of their bodies coming together, echoed through the chamber. Perspiration slickened her skin. Her muscles started to ache. She relished every second of it.

Strick pounded into Raya, bringing her to the edge, all of her muscles taut. Emotion roiled through her. She felt alive. Crazed. "Don't stop," she half sobbed, desperate for him. Even though he was a phony. A cheat. And who knows what else.

He slammed into her, fast and frantic. "I love being in your pussy." His breath was humid against her neck. His vulgar words were flames licking her skin.

"You like that, don't you?" He stroked her insides, seating himself deep enough to touch her soul. "You like how I feel inside of you. Say it."

Raya did not want to give him the satisfaction. She wanted to deny him. But, unlike Strick, she wasn't a liar. "Yes!" she ground out contemptuously. "I *love* it!

She heard the quick intake of his breath. Felt a surge of power that her words could affect him so. "You want more?" he asked, his voice rough. "Do you want it harder?"

"Yes." She nodded. "Do it."

"Tell me to pound you harder." He gripped her hips, repositioning himself so that she felt him more keenly.

Raya never imagined such coarse words coming out of her mouth. And she couldn't quite say the worst of them. But she tried, because it titillated her as much as it did him. "Harder, Anthony. Please!"

He uttered a sound of satisfaction and quickened his pace, going rougher, deeper. She teetered on the edge as he thrust into her, until it was unbearable, everything in her taut. She scaled the pinnacle and finally reached her breaking point. The tension snapped. She was flying, her muscles in glorious release. Waves of bliss swept over her and pulsed between her legs.

He pulled out just before he came, and she felt him shuddering over her. "I cannot wait until I can release inside of you," he said, holding her gently because she barely had the strength to hold herself up. She turned in time to see him press a white handkerchief against his member, milking himself. She foolishly despaired that he hadn't left that part of him inside of her.

They collapsed onto the sofa, spent and out of breath. Strick pulled her into his lap, stroking her hair, kissing her neck. She nuzzled into his affections like a needy cat. She loved it when he held her. She indulged in his embrace for several minutes before asking the question hovering in her mind.

"Why were you embracing Frances?" She had to know. The housekeeper's words swirled in her head. *His Grace is so very fond of Miss Vaughan. We all assume he will one day make her his duchess.*

Strick nibbled on her ear. "It was nothing."

"It was obviously something."

"There was a minor misunderstanding."

"About what?"

"Nothing." He caressed her breast through her shirt. "It's inconsequential."

He wasn't going to tell her. That much was obvious. The warmth from their coupling cooled. *Think*, Raya, *think*, she castigated herself. How can you protect yourself?

"You were magnificent." He wrapped his arms around her. "I've never bedded a more passionate woman. You get me so hard."

The words he spoke to her weeks ago came back. *I waited to wed until I could secure the castle's finances and assure its financial well-being.* Her stomach dropped. That must be it. The reason why Strick was not already married to Frances. Strick kept the truth from Raya because he obviously enjoyed bedding her and wanted to continue.

Once he tired of the Arab merchant's daughter, Strick would tell Raya the truth and send her back to America. Then he'd marry Frances. A true lady. A woman who clearly had a place in his affections, who would make a perfect duchess.

And where would that leave Raya? Alone. Without a business. Back at the mercy of her brother. She'd built up two businesses and would end up possessing neither.

No. She would not allow that to happen. Not again.

Strick pressed his lips against her temple. "What are you thinking about?"

How to save myself. She didn't own the castle. But she could still stake her claim. "I want to establish my ownership of the castle's business enterprises."

He chuckled. "Here I am having prurient thoughts and your mind is already returned to business matters."

"I think we should draw up an agreement."

"It's not necessary. It's all yours anyway."

They both knew that was a lie. She would never have taken him for a swindler. But here they were. "I still want it in writing. And for both of us to sign."

"Whatever you want," he said, as if it didn't matter to him.

She pulled away and rose.

"Where are you going?" he asked. "Come back here."

"To see Mr. Combs and have him draw up the agreement." She needed to strike fast.

"But I am not done with you yet," he protested.

Oh, they were definitely finished with each other. Raya had had her fun with Strick. But now she must secure her future. She'd been a pawn in other people's games for too long.

It was past time to turn the situation to her advantage.

STRICK KEPT WAITING for Raya to realize just how bad of an idea it was to host bear wrestling and human curiosities at Castle Tremayne.

But instead, her proposals grew more outrageous. In the following couple of days, she talked of hosting magicians, hypnotists and even a traveling circus. As much as he cared for Raya, Strick could never allow anyone to turn his beloved home into a literal circus.

Still, he held out hope that Raya would inevitably come to her senses. That she would refocus on developing profitable ventures that didn't cheapen the castle, such as the house tours, gift shop and tea house, and were in line with her original vision for rescuing Tremayne from financial ruin.

Raya asked Strick to join her for a walk in her meadow two days after their coupling in the solar. He hoped it was to tell him that she'd given up the silly idea of building a venue and pen.

"What do you say?" he asked in a deep, suggestive tone. "We could disappear into the hedgerow and go at each other like animals."

But instead of making her flush, or sparking that heated look in her eyes, his suggestion amused her. She giggled.

Strick tried not to feel insulted. Their last coupling in the solar had been their hottest ever. "How is that amusing?"

"You just made me remember the morning after my sister Nadine's wedding night, when Auntie Majida asked if her new husband was a *saba* or a *daba*."

"Translation?"

"She wanted to know if Nadine's new husband made love with the force and vigor of a *saba*, a lion. Or was he a *daba*? A useless hyena?"

"There's no question that you bring out the lion in me. And I cannot wait to make you roar."

She halted. "Here we are." They stood in the center of her meadow. "Do you think this space is big enough for a racetrack?"

"A what?" By now, Strick knew better than to laugh. "No, most definitely not. The meadow is too small." Thank God.

"But what if it started here and encircled the castle?"

He pressed his lips inward. "You are thinking about building a horse racing track that would cut around the castle? Need I remind you that the land directly beyond the gardens on the north side belongs to me?"

"Are you suggesting you would not approve a racetrack that encircles the castle?"

"I am not merely suggesting it," he clarified. "I am declaring outright that I would never allow you to put a racetrack on my land under any circumstances."

"Hmm." She cupped her chin as she pondered the possibilities. "I suppose the track could cut through the formal gardens."

Strick's temper snapped. "You are proposing to build a racetrack that quite literally runs in the castle's backyard?" His neck burned. "I absolutely forbid any such thing!"

She cocked her head, regarding him intently. "Are you in a position to forbid my building a racetrack around the castle?"

He was about to blurt out the truth before he spotted the triumphant gleam in her dark eyes. "By God!" he exclaimed. "You know."

She fluttered those long thick lashes in an unconvincing show of ignorance. "I know what?"

Strick registered the edge in her voice. And around each word. "You know the truth about who owns Castle Tremayne."

Anger flashed in her eyes. "At long last, you finally admit to being a liar."

"You *do* know," he repeated.

And everything finally made sense. The

emotional distance. Her ridiculous proposals. All designed to get under his skin, to get him to admit that he owned Castle Tremayne. "Why pretend to consider all of these absurd ventures? Why not just ask me?"

"Are you suggesting that I should have been more direct?" She crossed her arms over her chest. "Say, as straightforward as you have been?"

"There was no reason to tell you—"

"No reason?" Her voice rose. "No reason to be truthful with me?"

"Because it doesn't change anything."

"It changes everything and you know it. Which is why you didn't reveal the truth."

"You don't understand. I did it to protect you. To protect us. To safeguard what we have together."

"Meaning you enjoy bedding me and you weren't ready to stop."

"I will never be ready to stop. Once we're married—"

"Married?" she repeated with a contemptuous laugh.

"I didn't tell you because I wanted everything to remain the same."

"And you decided to use lies and obfuscation to keep it so."

"Because the truth is irrelevant. I still intend for you to manage castle operations, for us to marry, for our son to one day inherit all that we've built together. Everything will be as it should."

She shook her head, regarding him as if he

were a stranger, as if she'd never been more disappointed. "The truth is never irrelevant. And that's why you kept it from me." She turned away.

"Where are you going?" The distance he'd felt from her over the last several days now made perfect sense. After discovering the truth, she'd tested him and found him lacking. "We have to talk about this, Raya."

"I have a meeting with Cook about new menus for the tea shop."

And then she uttered the words he'd feared the most. Words that were like a punch to the gut.

"And really, there is nothing to discuss. If I don't own the castle, then I don't belong here."

CHAPTER TWENTY-SIX

Raya quickly approved the tea shop menu and escaped back to the refuge of the morning room. Her thoughts were scattered, her emotions a tight knot lodged in the middle of her chest.

Finally having the truth out in the open made her dispossession feel all too real. She'd have to tell Auntie Majida soon and then book their passage home. She would not hold Strick to any of it. Not the marriage proposal. And not ownership of Castle Tremayne's business enterprises. It was time to stop trying to insinuate herself where she didn't belong.

Strick belonged to Castle Tremayne. Home for Raya was the brownstone on Henry Street in Brooklyn. It was time for a new plan. Her time in England taught Raya that she was capable of excelling in business beyond the linen trade. With her enterprising mind, she'd find a way to start anew in New York.

Her eyes moved over the desk and caught on a new letter Philips must have brought in earlier. It was from New York. From Salem. She tore it open and read it quickly at first, and then more slowly a second time to fully digest its contents. She could hardly believe what she was reading. After reading the missive for the fourth time, Raya set it aside and went to the window, staring out at the tourists who'd gathered in the bailey, and the ones strolling on the parapet walk.

She contemplated her brother's words, and the irony of how the very person who had cast her out was now throwing her a lifeline. She could finally envision a viable way forward. Even if her heart felt like it was being ripped out of place because the future she saw did not include Castle Tremayne. Or the Duke of Strickland.

She closed her eyes and rubbed them, moving her head in circles to release the tightness in her neck that had built for days. Strong, warm hands were suddenly on her nape, kneading gently but firmly. She hadn't heard Strick come in. She started to protest.

"Allow me, please," he said against her neck. "It is the least I can do considering I am the source of your tension."

She relented, dipping her chin to give him access. His strong, capable hands were heaven on her stiff muscles. Now that her course was set, none of this really mattered anymore anyway. "You were wrong to lie to me."

"I am sorry." He pressed and stroked the sore places, working out the tightness. Raya's breathing slowed. She relaxed as he soothed her muscles, coaxing them to slacken.

"Please forgive me," he whispered into her ear. His hands traveled up to cup and massage the back of her head. "I was afraid you would leave me. That without the castle there would be nothing to keep you here. That I would not be enough."

Her heart constricted. "How could you ever think you aren't enough?" She leaned her head back into his hands as he applied pressure to the upper sides of her neck. "Do you think I'd give myself to just anyone?"

"I cannot explain it. I have no excuse." His hands slid down to her shoulders, moving in circular motions. "I felt desperate. Crazed. Afraid. I cannot bear the thought of losing you. I love you, Raya."

She shouldn't say it, because her confession would make their parting that much more difficult. But Raya had to speak the truth at least this once. Strick deserved that. They both did. "I feel the same. You own my heart."

He wrapped his arms around her from behind. "Thank goodness."

She reveled in his warmth. "Our elders used to say that lovers don't somehow finally meet, but that they were in each other all along."

"That makes perfect sense. You do feel like a part of me. Perhaps you truly were always there."

He breathed a sigh of relief. "You'll stay with me then?"

"No," she said sadly, "I cannot."

HE SLACKENED HIS embrace, releasing her. "You are still angry at me for not being honest." Her words were a bomb blowing up his life. "I don't blame you, but please allow me to make it up to you."

"If we had the luxury of time, I would make you grovel for hours on end, but we don't. Besides, my leaving has nothing to do with your being untruthful."

He threw up his hands. "I am lost. Why are we out of time?"

She walked over to her desk and retrieved a letter. "This is from my brother, Salem. He is offering me a thirty percent stake in Darwish and Company. I don't own anything here. Not really."

"I agreed to give you full ownership of Castle Tremayne Enterprises."

"That was in the throes of lovemaking when we were still deceiving each other."

"The offer stands. It's only fair. You *are* Castle Tremayne Enterprises. The business wouldn't exist without you."

"I am very glad I could be of service. It is extraordinarily rewarding to know that I have left my mark here."

"Stop talking as if you are already gone," he demanded. "You are not only contemplating deserting me. You're giving up on Castle Tremayne as well."

"I leave Castle Tremayne in excellent and capable hands," she said gently. "In the full control of its rightful owner, as it should be."

"Am I not reason enough to stay?" he asked, his voice husky with emotion. "Does business always come first with you?"

Her face softened. "It is not just the temptation of truly owning a piece of my family business that compels me to leave. There is more to it."

"How can it possibly be a good enough reason to part us?"

"My father's company is failing. Salem doesn't have the skills to properly run it. He never had any patience for the details. He needs me."

"*I* need you. Castle Tremayne needs you. Your brother deserted you. He only wants you back because he cannot succeed without you. You cannot trust him or his word."

"This is not just about helping Salem. Many members of my family depend on the proceeds from Darwish and Company, including my mother and my sister Naila, who is still unwed. A number of relatives work for the company. If I don't return, I am not only letting Salem down, I risk allowing my mother, sister and other relatives to fall to ruin. I cannot let that happen."

"Why must you be the one to save your entire family?"

"There is no one else."

"But we are betrothed. We are supposed to marry and stay together forever."

A cloud of profound sadness enveloped her. "We have to release each other from our pledge," she said with excruciating gentleness. "I must return to my world and you deserve to take your rightful place in yours. Everyone should know that Castle Tremayne belongs to you."

None of it meant anything if Raya wasn't going to be by his side. "When do you plan to leave?"

"I should begin making arrangements immediately."

"That's too soon." Desperation clawed at him. "You must at least stay for another few months, four at least, to make certain the ventures you've just launched here at Castle Tremayne are running smoothly and successfully."

"Anthony, dragging this out will only make our parting more painful."

"This couldn't possibly be any more agonizing. I understand that you cannot desert your family but neither should you abandon all of the people here at the castle and in the village who look to you to lead us in financially securing Tremayne's future."

"You can do this without me," she assured him.

He didn't want to. "You cannot leave so quickly. It isn't fair to us. Your family will have you forever. Surely you can give us a few months."

She chewed her lip. "Very well. I shall stay for two months to ensure everything here is running smoothly."

Strick exhaled, relief slicing through him. He'd won a reprieve. He had eight weeks to convince Raya to stay. She was far too tenderhearted. The brother couldn't be trusted. He'd already betrayed Raya once. What would stop him from hurting his sister again once he had her home and under his control? Strick couldn't bear to see her deceived again.

Besides, Castle Tremayne was Raya's true home. Strick understood better than anyone what it was like once Tremayne got into a person's blood and he recognized it in Raya. She was already intrinsically linked to this ancient place. It was only a matter of time before she saw it for herself.

"THIS LEDGER IS for the tea house." Raya stacked the books on top of one another on her worktable in the morning room. "This one is for the weaving operation." She held up the final register. "The gift shop." She tossed it on the table. "Are you even paying attention?"

"Isn't this premature?" Strick yawned. "After all, you are staying for at least two more months?"

"Not *at least* two more months. *Exactly* two more months. Which will be over before you know it." She tried to maintain a brisk tone, despite the persistent stomachache since making the decision to leave Castle Tremayne, and Strick, forever. "You need to learn where I keep the records."

He couldn't act less interested. "Have you informed your aunt about your departure plans?"

"Not yet. As soon as she learns we are no longer betrothed, she will insist that we leave immediately." She stood up to organize the ledgers on the sideboard behind the worktable. "The only reason she tolerates us being alone together is because she still believes we are getting married."

A thoughtful expression came over Strick's face. "Does she?" He came up behind Raya and nibbled her neck.

Pleasure shivered through her. "What are you doing? We're supposed to be working."

"That was your plan." His mouth traveled up to her earlobe. "This is mine."

Raya sighed. "This is unwise. You are making it more difficult for us to part."

"That's the idea," he murmured against her ear.

"Behave." She ducked away before things went too far. "We have business to attend to."

"You've shown me where the ledgers are." He reached for her. "All work and no play makes Strick a dull boy."

As if he could ever be boring. "I am not referring to the ledgers, I am talking about the trinkets you make in the forge."

He stopped reaching for her. "What about them?"

"I think we . . . you . . . should sell the metal-work pieces you make in the gift shop."

"I am hardly a skilled craftsman. I make those pieces as a hobby, for my amusement."

"I've seen some of your pieces and I think they are lovely."

"They are very plain." Nothing like the ornate designs in his collection.

"Simple but beautiful," she corrected. "People would happily pay for a trinket made by a real duke who lives in the castle they are visiting."

"Very well," he relented. "If you think it's a worthwhile idea, then it probably is. There are a couple of baskets full of pieces in my apartments."

"Excellent." She smiled. How far they'd come from those earliest days when he thought her proposals were outlandish. "I'll have the servants who work in the shop go through them and sort out the pieces."

"Anything else?" he asked.

"No, I believe that is everything."

"Excellent." He waggled his eyebrows and pulled her to him. "Now it's time for frisky business."

She angled away from him. Every time they made love, she gave him a part of her soul. Once he had too much of her, Raya could never leave. "I think we should refrain from being intimate."

"What?" A horrified expression stamped his face. "Why?"

"Must I state the obvious?"

"The obvious is that making love with each other is one of life's greatest pleasures and we should do it as often as possible."

"We are no longer betrothed," she reminded him.

"Don't remind me."

"Please," she beseeched him, "you have to let me go."

"I AM NEVER letting her go," Strick announced later that evening while out with Hawk. The earl was passing through, just for the night, on his way to visit one of his minor estates. They were spending the evening at a gaming den in a neighboring village.

Strick tilted his chair on its back legs, against a surprisingly well-done wall mural. "She is out of her mind if she thinks I will let her go without a fight."

Hawk's red-tinged eyes widened. "Good lord!" He slammed his tankard down on the wooden table. "You actually love this girl."

"I adore her." Strick saw no reason to deny the truth. He'd happily tell anyone who asked. "I'll do anything to keep her by my side."

"It's useless you know. She'll tear your heart out."

"You haven't even met Raya yet."

"Mark my words," Hawk said dully. "It's best not to involve your heart when it comes to any woman."

"Raya's not just any woman. I intend to take her to wife."

Hawk grimaced. "You are asking for a world of pain."

Strick had never known his friend to be attached to any female. "You sound as if you are speaking from experience."

"I'm no saint. I have been with women."

"I am aware." Hawk was discreet about his affairs. "But have you been serious with any of them?"

"I intended to marry a woman once."

"A woman in America." Strick leaned forward, his chair settling back on four legs. "That's why you came back changed."

"Nonsense. I am still the same man."

Strick saw no point in arguing. Besides, he wanted to know more. "You've never mentioned meeting anyone special when you visited Philadelphia six years ago."

"There was no point. It was all over and in the past by the time I returned home."

"But you were serious about her?"

"Very. It was, of course, long before I inherited the title. I was visiting my mother's cousin who owns a print shop. He has no children and I was a man in need of an occupation. I was going to settle there and take over the shop, build a life for myself in America."

"What was she like?"

"Kind and nurturing, whip-smart with a wry

sense of humor." Hawk sighed. "Yet also very strong and firm in her convictions."

"She sounds perfect. What happened with her?"

"I've no idea. She's probably married with a dozen kids by now."

"No, I meant what went wrong between the two of you?"

"I was a man with no prospects. A foreigner." Hawk's face clouded. "Her family did not approve. I begged her to come away with me. But ultimately, she allowed her family to persuade her to reject my proposal."

"Do you think she would have made a different decision if she'd known you'd become an earl?"

"We shall never know."

"Is this American the reason you've never married?"

"Don't be ridiculous. I never think of her. She's so far in the past that I barely remember what she looks like." He poured more whisky down his throat. "I just have not found the right woman to be my countess."

"Maybe you should go easy on the drink. Aren't you leaving early in the morning to travel on to your estate?"

"You are driving me to drink. I beg you to stop this drivel about affairs of the heart."

The proprietor, thrilled to have both a duke and an earl in the house, came over. "Your Grace, my lord, is there anything else I can get you? Supper perhaps?"

"Nothing." Strick's eye caught on a colorful wall mural again. The technique looked vaguely familiar. "Who did your mural?"

"A young artist from a neighboring village. It was a repayment of sorts. He played too deep and came away with massive gambling debts."

"And this young artist's name?" Strick asked.

"Alfred Price." He studied Strick's surprised expression. "Do you know the young man?"

"I certainly do. Price's father is one of my tenants and Alfred himself is currently painting a mural at Castle Tremayne."

"Then I'd advise you to lock up the silver," the proprietor said. "That boy owes money to many people."

Strick blinked. "How many?"

"No one in the village will extend credit to the younger Price. Not the shopkeeper or tavern owner."

"How very interesting," Strick said. "We shall have to keep a much closer eye on young Mr. Price."

CHAPTER TWENTY-SEVEN

I t's beautiful." Raya stood back to admire the mural. "Well done."

Alfred looked on proudly. "The landscape is finally complete." He wiped his brushes with a stained cloth. "Next, I begin to add the faces of the guests who've paid for the honor."

"Wrong." Strick's strident voice boomed over them. He strode in with a hard expression on his face. "Next, you pack up your paints and brushes and leave Castle Tremayne."

Alfred's brows knitted. "Excuse me?"

"I will not excuse you. Leave and never return."

"What has happened?" Raya asked.

Alfred puffed his chest out. "With all due respect, Your Grace, Miss Darwish is my employer. Not you."

"She might be your employer but I own this castle and I am kicking you out on your arse."

Alfred's mouth dropped open. "Miss Darwish owns Castle Tremayne."

"Actually," Raya explained, "I do not. There was a codicil to the old duke's will that gave the castle to Strickland after Deena's demise. We are also no longer betrothed, by the way, although we haven't told anybody yet."

"You don't owe this man any explanation," Strickland told her. "It is *he* who owes you an accounting."

"Do you?" Raya said to Alfred. "For what?"

Uncertainty glittered in Alfred's eyes. "I have no idea."

"Hawk and I visited Deerfield and saw a very familiar-looking mural on the wall of a gaming hell there."

"I can explain," Alfred sputtered.

"What is Deerfield?" Raya asked.

"It's a neighboring village." Strick shot a speaking glance at Alfred. "Can you explain why you owe upwards of fifty pounds to a gaming hell in Deerfield?"

Raya did a quick calculation. She gasped. "That's a small fortune!" Especially for a man of modest means.

"How is that of consequence?" Alfred's pleading eyes turned on Raya. "You said my work is excellent. I am laboring to pay off my debts. I made a mistake and got in too deep but I plan to make it right."

Strick made a derisive sound. "Did you pay off some of your debts with artifacts you stole from Castle Tremayne?"

"No! I told you that the duchess asked me to deliver the items. I never saw a shilling from the sale of any of those artifacts. I swear it!"

Strick's mouth twisted with derision. "Your pledges have little value here."

Hate filled Alfred's face as he stared at the duke. "You killed Deena, didn't you? You'd stop at nothing to have your castle back."

"That's it," Raya snapped, surprising herself with her virulent reaction. "Please pack up your supplies and go."

"*You* are turning on me?" Disbelief lit the artist's face. "I thought we were friends."

"You have accused His Grace of murder. Any insult to the duke is an insult to me."

His lips flapped. "But you are no longer betrothed."

"Perhaps not, but Strickland will always be my friend," she said staunchly, feeling the truth of it deep in her bones. "And I will not stand by and allow anyone to insult my dearest friend."

"Have a care," Alfred warned. "You are not safe with him."

"Have you not heard?" Raya fought to keep ahold of her temper. "I don't own Castle Tremayne. I never did. I don't own anything. Strick has nothing to gain by hurting me."

Strick leveled a cold stare at Alfred. "This discussion is concluded. Leave before I toss you out the window."

They both watched the man quickly pack his supplies and depart.

Strick advanced on Raya, his golden-brown

eyes wonderfully warm. "An insult to me is an insult to you?"

Raya backed away, her cheeks heating. "He cast doubt on my judgment. How dare he imply that I am a silly girl who doesn't know any better than to align myself with a murderer?"

Strick took a step closer. "One could never think you silly. Prickly, perhaps, but never silly."

"We still don't know for certain that Alfred is a thief."

"I won't take the chance. Price is very deeply in debt. He owes far more money than he could ever pay back using honest means. I refuse to allow him access to the castle and all of its contents."

"I understand that." He stood so close that she felt his body heat. The scent of shaving soap on his skin wafted into her nostrils. "But it would not be fair to label him a thief in the village if we have no proof."

He inched closer. "If you think Price is innocent, why didn't you fight me on his dismissal?"

Raya backed up and found herself up against the hard, cool wall. "I do not know whether he is guilty or not. But once he insulted you, there was no question that he had to go."

"How fortunate I am to have my magnificent Arab queen as my champion." He reached out to feather a loose tendril of hair away from Raya's face. "I thought asserting my ownership of Castle Tremayne would anger you."

She licked her lips. "It had the opposite effect."

His brows went up. "It excited you."

Watching Strick take command of his castle did arouse her. "Hardly," she lied. "No one likes a bossy man."

A knowing smile curved his lips. "I think you do."

"Must you always be so annoying?"

His lips brushed the curve of her ear. "If you allow me to take you up against this wall, I promise you will be anything but annoyed."

Raya's throat was dry. "We cannot."

His tongue dipped into her ear, sending rivulets of pleasure. "Oh, we most certainly can."

"We are no longer betrothed." She forced the words out even though her body ached to succumb. "It isn't right."

"You told Price that I am your best friend." His mouth moved to the side of her neck. "It could be a friendly fuck."

"I don't engage in sexual relations with my friends."

"But I am not just any friend." He nipped the delicate flesh at her nape. "I am your very best friend."

Her knees almost gave way. She'd never wanted anything so badly. He clasped her leg behind the knee and lifted, giving himself room to press his hardness against her.

Sensation quivered through her. "Is this what you do with your best friends?" she asked.

"It depends." His fingers were suddenly under

her skirts, searching for the slit of her drawers. "I've never had a best friend like you. Your quim wants to be friends." He stroked her intimate flesh. "See that? You're very, very wet."

"If only my body would align with my mind," she panted.

"It does, of course." The tip of his finger circled the sensitive nub at the apex of her thighs. "We both know you have dirty thoughts about me."

That was the problem. Strick dominated all of her thoughts, dirty or otherwise. The memory of him, of them together, would haunt her forever. The enormity of how much she was giving up waved over Raya. Grief trembled through her. She stifled a sob.

Strick's fingers stilled. "Raya?" Concern etched his face. "Please don't cry. I will stop if this upsets you."

She couldn't control her emotions. "I'm sorry."

"For what?" he asked gently.

Tears leaked from her eyes. "For everything." For leaving him. For deserting Tremayne. For being wrong about fate meaning for them to be together forever.

A stricken look came over him. "Shhh. Don't cry." He pulled her into his embrace and together they slid down the wall until they were seated with Raya snug in his lap. He kissed her temple. "I did not mean to upset you."

"I truly thought you were my *naseeb*." She couldn't contain her tears. "If I hadn't been convinced, I wouldn't have let things between us progress so far."

He stroked her back. "You've done nothing wrong. Don't apologize for being an honorable woman," he said huskily. "Nor for being a dutiful daughter and a good sister, a far better one, I might add, than your brother deserves."

"I shall miss you so, so much."

"And I, you. More than you'll ever know."

Tears blurred her sight, but she still registered the pain in his eyes. And, to her shock, the wetness against his cheeks. She raised her hand to brush it away. "Oh no." Anguish ripped through her. "Don't. Please don't."

He shook his head, burying his face in her neck. She hugged him tightly, absorbing his torment, trying to will his agony away. Even though it was impossible.

THEY AVOIDED EACH other in the weeks that followed.

They nodded politely if they ran into each other and kept any necessary discussions short and focused on business matters. Strick couldn't bear to be near Raya without wanting to touch her, but their last physical encounter upset her so profoundly that it tore his heart out. He would do anything in his power to avoid causing her any distress.

Instead, he spent hours at a time in the forge, engaging in grueling work in punishing heat.

The hammering and pounding required all of his strength, and he twisted and stretched the metal until his muscles burned and sweat poured off him. His creations would end up for sale in the gift shop, but the real reason Strick spent so much time in the smithy was to expend his restless energy and distract himself from thoughts of Raya.

Not that it worked. No matter how many rings, bracelets or letter openers he made, Strick couldn't stop thinking of her. Where was she at that very moment? What was she doing? What was she thinking? How was she feeling?

On one Thursday, Strick quit the forge well before the midday meal, much earlier than he liked. Castle Tremayne opened to the public on Thursday afternoons and Strick stayed away when tourists were on the grounds. The forge was part of the tour and he did not care to be put on display.

Walking through the outer bailey, he heard a high-pitched female voice. Alfred Price's mother stood by the tea shop, speaking sharply and motioning with her hands. As Strick drew nearer, he realized Raya was the recipient of the woman's ire.

"The duchess used him, but you are worse," the older woman said. "You used him and cast him aside."

"Alfred's work here is concluded." Standing with perfect posture, Raya spoke in a calm voice. She wore a dark skirt and a crisp white shirt that gave her olive complexion a radiant glow. Her midnight hair, pinned back from her face, tumbled down her back in lustrous waves. "He was well compensated for his time."

"You wanted him the way she wanted him," Mrs. Price said. "It's shameful."

"I do not appreciate what you are implying," Raya said evenly. "I assure you that nothing could be further from the truth. I employed your son to paint a mural, which is now completed."

Strick admired Raya's aplomb, even though members of the staff paused to listen while pretending to go about their business. Some workers, women from the village, stood in the doorway of the weaving house, taking in the scene.

"Look at you, acting all high and mighty." Mrs. Price raised her voice. "When we've all heard the rumors about you and the duke."

A stranger might not see the almost imperceptible stiffening of Raya's muscles. "His Grace and I are no longer betrothed."

"We've all heard," Mrs. Price said with a contemptuous laugh. "He got tired of you, did he?"

Strick resisted the urge to intervene, but that would cause more of a scene and launch a whole new round of gossip. Mrs. Price was fortunate because Strick would never be as restrained as Raya.

"Family matters require that I return to America," Raya said.

"Isn't that grand? You came here just long enough to ruin my poor Alfred and now you think you can just sail back to America?"

"We are done here." Raya turned to the nearest servant. "Please see Mrs. Price out."

"You think to dismiss me? You? A foreign nobody?"

"Yes," Raya said, the words matter-of-fact, "I am dismissing you. Good day to you, madam." A couple of workers from the sawmill approached. They nodded politely to Raya before showing the old lady out. As she turned away, Raya spotted Strick. Her face lit up before she quickly shuttered her expression. He hated that she felt the need to conceal her emotions from him.

Strick strode toward her. "I believe you all have duties to attend to," he said to the servants and staff who pretended not to watch. They all quickly vanished.

"Being tiresome obviously runs in the family. That woman is as unpalatable as her son," he said to Raya once he reached her. "In your place, I would have kicked the old lady out on her arse the moment she opened her mouth."

"Yes, well, I am not a duke." Her lips curled into a slight smile. "I am just a girl from New York."

"Is that an attempt at modesty, Miss Darwish? It doesn't become the shrewd businesswoman who set Castle Tremayne on the road to profitability."

"Miss Darwish, is it?" she murmured.

"I am trying to keep my distance. Although it is killing me. Whether you're in my bed or out of it, you cannot help being a nuisance, can you?"

Her eyes sparkled. "Apparently not."

His heart glowed to see the light in her eyes. "Although why I would miss a bossy termagant is beyond me."

One corner of her lips curved up. "There really is no explaining it."

They strolled back to the castle, neither of them in any hurry. Strick was keenly aware that leisurely walks with Raya would soon be in the past. "It won't be long now."

She nodded. "It is time. Auntie knows about us. I have booked our passage for the fourth of next month."

Three weeks. Pain lanced Strick's heart, even though he'd known it was coming. "You were trouble from the first." He rubbed his chest. "You are literally going to give me a broken heart."

"I think we should have one last farewell dinner."

"Is that wise?"

"Of course not. Will that stop you?"

"Hell no. But I thought you wanted me to keep my distance."

She sighed. "I did. Because I thought it would be easier."

"Is it?"

"No, not at all. Nothing makes parting less painful."

"I've tried to forget about you. I've been working in the forge as much as possible."

"Did it help?"

"No, but I do have an excellent stockpile of trinkets for the gift shop."

"I'm pleased your labors weren't wasted." She paused. "So, we agree? Tomorrow, we share one last private dinner together?"

He grinned. "I shall ask Cook to make a feast."

"I'd rather take a picnic basket to the ruins."

"We will be very alone there."

Mischief gleamed in her eyes. "That is the idea."

He narrowed his eyes at her. "Just to be clear. If I get you alone at the abbey, I will want to take you long and hard. And slow and soft."

She bit her bottom lip. "I am counting on it."

His cock stiffened. "You are treading on very dangerous territory."

"I think our last time together in that way should be memorable, not maudlin like our last meeting."

"Are you suggesting that clutching one another and crying like babies isn't an ideal way to remember our liaison?"

"And I think it's past time that I conquer my fears." She drew a breath. "I'd like to see the view of Castle Tremayne from the lantern tower."

"Truly?" He blinked. "But what of your dislike of heights?"

"You will be with me. I cannot think of a more

fitting way to say goodbye to this place than to make love one last time at the ruins and then to see the splendor of Tremayne from the best vantage point on the estate."

He could think of nothing he wanted more. "And you still expect me to let you return to America afterward?"

Her eyes glistened. "I expect you to exert yourself to make memories that will last a lifetime."

CHAPTER TWENTY-EIGHT

Raya spent much of the following day going through all of her papers and organizing the ledgers for Strick for after she was gone. She did so with a dragging sensation in her chest. Parting with Strick was the hardest part about returning to New York, but leaving her business behind also stung. Running Castle Tremayne Enterprises energized Raya and she took immense satisfaction in knowing she'd built the business from nothing. Because of her efforts, Castle Tremayne was going to thrive well into the next century. She took pride in knowing she'd left her stamp on the place.

At least she and Strick would have this evening. One final night together at the old ruins. It might ravage her heart but she couldn't wait to spend time alone with him. However, until then, she had work to do.

Raya went through the walnut sideboard, where Deena kept castle papers. The three center drawers were flanked by cupboards on each side. She had examined them quickly when she first arrived hoping to find something that revealed more about Deena, but found nothing. Now, an old wrinkled paper caught her attention because she recognized Deena's writing.

It was a list of items with no obvious connection. If Raya came across it when she first arrived at Castle Tremayne, it would have meant nothing to her. She went through the itemization: a vase, a porcelain figure, a painting and then, at the bottom:

drinking goblets (Strickland)—Ask AP?

Why had Deena listed Strick's goblets? Was this a list of the items she'd sold off? And AP had to be Alfred Price, didn't it? A knock on the door cut into her thoughts and Otis came in.

"Mr. Cuffe down at the gift shop asked me to bring you the sales figures for last month."

Raya briefly looked up. "Yes, leave it on the table, please."

"Very good, miss." He set the papers down and turned to depart.

Then she had a thought. "Otis."

"Yes, miss?"

"Was Mr. Alfred Price often here at the castle visiting the late duchess?"

He stared at his shoes. "We aren't supposed to tell tales about our employer, miss."

"The duchess is no longer with us and I have no desire to gossip about her. I became very fond of her through our letters and just want to find the truth."

He looked up. "About what, miss?"

"About the friendship between the duchess and Alfred."

He frowned. "I don't think they were friends, miss."

"But he was here often after the late duke died, was he not?"

"He came by now and again. Her Grace had small jobs for him around the estate. Mostly Mr. Price came to see Mrs. Shaw."

"Mrs. Shaw?" The housekeeper? "Whatever for?"

"She has a soft spot for Alfred, says he reminds her of her son."

"Mrs. Shaw has a son?" There certainly was a lot about the staff that she didn't know.

Otis nodded. "But her boy lives in London and she doesn't see him much. Alfred would come by now and again. He was probably here for the biscuits and cakes Mrs. Shaw served whenever he came to have tea with her."

"Alfred and Mrs. Shaw?" Raya was so engrossed in the duke and in developing business ventures at Castle Tremayne that she hadn't noticed much else. "I had no idea."

"About two weeks before she died, Her Grace told Mrs. Shaw she didn't want Alfred to come around as much."

"Deena did? Why?"

He bit his lip.

"Please speak frankly," she urged.

"I overheard something that I've never told anyone."

"What was it?"

"I was bringing in Her Grace's post when I heard her arguing with Alfred."

"Could you tell what the disagreement was about?"

"She accused him of taking some goblets that belong to His Grace."

Raya sucked in a breath. "Deena thought Alfred stole Strick's missing Saxon goblets?" The pair that had somehow ended up in the Vaughans' upstairs closet?

He nodded. "Alfred told Her Grace that he would never steal from her on account of the fact that they were in love. And the duchess laughed at that. But then she saw that he was serious."

"They weren't in love?"

Otis scoffed. "As if the duchess would involve herself with someone like Alfred! He must be touched in the head. Her Grace explained to Alfred that he'd mistaken her amiability for something else. That Americans were naturally less reserved and more friendly."

"How did Alfred react?"

"He was very upset. After he went away Her Grace asked me not to tell anyone what I'd overheard. She said people would gossip even if Alfred's claims were all lies."

"Did you believe her? Was there truly nothing between them?"

"I did believe her. Her Grace was so unsettled that she asked me to summon Mrs. Shaw."

"What did she say to the housekeeper?"

"I didn't hear for myself but later Mrs. Shaw told us that Alfred made the duchess uncomfortable and Her Grace preferred Alfred not visit Mrs. Shaw at the castle."

Raya was beginning to realize how much she'd erred in not paying more attention to staff interactions. "Was Mrs. Shaw upset that Alfred couldn't visit as much?"

Otis shrugged. "She didn't seem too bothered. She said the staff should be sure to follow the duchess's direction, that Alfred was not welcome to visit too often or wander too freely."

"I see." How surprising that Mrs. Shaw had so willingly bowed to Deena's wishes. It was like pulling teeth to get the housekeeper to listen to anything that Raya had to say. "Thank you, Otis. Could you ask Mrs. Shaw to come and see me?"

Surprise stamped the footman's face. "But why?" He blushed. "Forgive me, miss. A servant should never question his employer. I'll tell her straightaway."

Raya's thoughts swirled while she waited for Mrs. Shaw. Returning Strick's family heirlooms to him was the finest farewell present she could give him.

"You asked to see me, Miss Darwish?" The housekeeper stood by the door.

"Yes, please come in."

"What may I do for you, Miss Darwish?"

"As you know," she began, "I shall be leaving soon."

Mrs. Shaw did not bother to hide her pleasure at the prospect of being rid of her.

"But before I go," Raya continued, "I should like to retrieve the heirlooms that were taken from Castle Tremayne."

The housekeeper pursed her lips. "I am sure that has nothing to do with me."

"Not directly, no. But you are fond of Alfred, as he is of you." She paused, knowing her proposal was a gamble. "I was hoping perhaps you could speak to him, convince him that it would be in his best interests to return anything he might have taken—if any of it is still in his possession."

Mrs. Shaw's face blanked. "I don't know anything about Alfred taking things from Castle Tremayne."

"If they were returned," Raya rushed on, "I would see to it that no questions were asked. If the items were to reappear, then there would be no theft and Alfred would not be in any trouble."

Mrs. Shaw looked conflicted, as if she wanted to say something but then thought better of it.

"What is it, Mrs. Shaw? Please speak frankly. I am leaving soon and I am no longer your employer. You have nothing to fear from me. You have my word that if Alfred returns the stolen items, I will never tell His Grace anything about this conversation."

"I suppose it is only right for those items to be returned to Castle Tremayne." The housekeeper spoke hesitantly.

"Precisely. You would be doing Alfred a favor if you could convince him to return the items. He would be getting himself out of trouble."

"He'll never return them. He's too afraid. We would have to go and retrieve them."

"Is that possible?" Raya's heart beat faster. "Do you know where he's hidden the heirlooms?"

Mrs. Shaw looked pained and uncertain. "Alfred is not a bad boy. He is just misguided. He told me he took the objects in a fit of desperation and wanted to return them but didn't know how without implicating himself."

"Alfred told you that? When?"

"Just the other day, when His Grace dismissed Alfred and told him never to return." She twisted her hands in her skirts. "I was shocked when Alfred confessed and I begged him to bring back what he took."

"And what did he say?"

"He refused." She paused and drew a long breath. "But I know where he's hidden them."

"Where? How do you know?"

"If I tell you, I must have your word that you will tell no one. You and I will go and retrieve the heirlooms and Alfred will not be accused of stealing."

"You have my word," Raya assured her.

"He hid them at the ruins. Few people went near the abbey after Her Grace died. The villagers think the ruins are cursed. But now Alfred is worried that your tourists will find them."

"Where at the ruins?" She imagined them buried under the purple wildflowers that Strick had planted for her.

"In the lantern tower. There's a hidden cupboard there. Alfred said he was going to move the heirlooms as soon as he could and take them to a fence."

"We cannot let that happen." Raya stepped toward the housekeeper. "We must go and retrieve the objects before he moves them."

She looked taken aback. "You wish to go now?"

"Absolutely."

She paused, obviously conflicted. "Very well." It was the first time Raya and the housekeeper had ever been in accord about anything but they finally had a common purpose. The two women departed the castle without telling anyone. Raya was practically giddy at the prospect of being able to return Strick's family heirlooms to him at this evening's picnic.

It would make for a perfect night.

ONCE THEY REACHED the ruins, Raya faltered. Her heart slammed in her chest as she stared up at the lantern tower. It seemed impossibly high. But Raya took several deep calming breaths. After all she'd accomplished at Castle Tremayne, surely she could conquer her childish fear of heights.

"Is something amiss?" Mrs. Shaw asked.

"No." Raya squared her shoulders. "Nothing." She wasn't the same person who'd arrived at Castle Tremayne months ago. Being the mistress of a grand house, and a successful businesswoman in her own right, bolstered Raya's confidence. There was nothing she couldn't do. It was past time to lay this last barrier to rest. "Let's go."

The housekeeper led the way up the winding stairs. The stone steps were worn and uneven. Raya didn't look up as they progressed. Instead, she kept her focus on her feet moving methodically, climbing higher and higher.

They reached the tower, a circular room with immense windows that used to be filled with stained glass, but now were just gaping holes. Raya's legs were leaden, heavy and hard to move. Trying to avoid the view, which would show how high up they were, Raya looked around the circular space. "I don't see any cupboards."

"Have you taken note of the view?" Mrs. Shaw asked. "It is the finest vista of Castle Tremayne. Come and see."

Raya refused to show any trepidation in front of the housekeeper. Strick and Auntie Majida were the only people in England aware of her aversion to heights and Raya intended to keep it that way. She forced herself to edge closer.

"Come along." Mrs. Shaw grabbed her elbow

and abruptly pulled her to the gaping window. "Isn't it a sight to behold?"

Raya's neck tingled. A strange energy emanated from the housekeeper. "Where are the heirlooms?"

Mrs. Shaw stood uncomfortably close. "If you look far out enough, you can see the property lines."

Gulping air into her lungs, Raya forced herself to look up. They were a million miles from the ground. Tension tightened her muscles, a knot forming in her stomach.

And yet, the view took her breath away, and filled her with awe.

The green landscape, the rolling hills, Castle Tremayne rising proudly in the distance. The magnificence of this place assaulted all of her senses. The light breeze on her cheeks, the musty scent of the tower, the majesty of the centuries-old fortress and the natural splendor that surrounded it.

Raya waited for full-fledged panic to take over. Or dire distress. Yes, she felt nervous and hypervigilant, but beneath the tight muscles and shortness of breath, lay a steely confidence. Raya had never felt as sure of herself.

Castle Tremayne had made a woman out of her.

"She was the same as you." Mrs. Shaw stood to the side and slightly behind Raya, effectively boxing her in against the window. She retained a firm grip on Raya's arm. "The duchess also thought she could outsmart me."

Raya realized she'd fallen into the housekeeper's trap. "The artifacts are not here."

Mrs. Shaw gave a harsh laugh. "Who would hide heirlooms here? The weather would ruin them, erasing their value."

"You and Alfred were in it together. You both stole from Castle Tremayne."

"We helped ourselves to a few things. It's hardly stealing. Neither you nor your late cousin had any right to the castle or any of its possessions."

"Did you lock me in the cellar?"

"I did. You and your sort don't belong here. I hoped to frighten you but you don't scare easily. Even the beam didn't deter you."

"That was you as well?"

"Alfred had to help with that. I'm too old to climb."

"Alfred dropped the beam on me?" That explained why he was the first person to arrive on the scene.

"He missed on purpose. The boy is weak-hearted. He kept caterwauling that even though he might be a thief, he's not a killer, too."

"Unlike you."

"Putting it all together, are you? I told your cousin the same story I told you. That poor Alfred wasn't truly a thief. She also came with me to retrieve the stolen items."

Raya shivered. "You pushed Deena." It wasn't a question.

The housekeeper didn't bother to deny it. "She got too close to the truth. Just like you. She never saw it coming. I hit her over the head with a rock from behind. She was senseless before I pushed her. She didn't realize what was happening."

Grief lodged in Raya's throat. Poor Deena.

"I should have taken care of Otis long ago," Mrs. Shaw continued. "I didn't realize he knew so much."

"You overheard us talking."

"The walls have ears. There is a servant's passage that goes past the morning room. There isn't much that goes on in the castle that I don't see or hear about."

"That's how you know I have a fear of heights."

"Bravo! Very good."

"How did your little operation work? I presume you stole the items and had Alfred take them to a fence."

"As an artist, Alfred understood their value and I had access to every room in the castle. It was no hardship to take what we wanted."

"Why were the duke's goblets at Trentham House?"

"That was Alfred's doing." Mrs. Shaw rolled her eyes. "He worried about being caught and wanted to implicate someone else. It was a fool's errand."

"He kept telling me that the duke pushed Deena."

She chuckled. "That is what the silly boy believes. There was no need for me to enlighten him."

Guilt assailed Raya. How could she have ever contemplated, even for a minute, that Strick was capable of harming Deena? She refocused on Mrs. Shaw. Flattering the older woman might buy a little time. "It makes perfect sense that you are the brains of the operation."

"I had as much right to those objects as some Arab charlatan from America. Why should a foreigner have more rights to Castle Tremayne's treasures than me? I have worked here for thirty years. There was no money left. I was never going to get the pension I deserve."

"But the castle is making money now and is back in the duke's hands." Raya assessed the situation as she spoke. One wrong move on her part and she would stumble out of the window. Mrs. Shaw would barely have to exert any energy to push her.

"Yes, it would have all worked out perfectly if you had just sailed back to America. Strickland would have continued to blame his late stepmother for the missing heirlooms and artifacts and all would be well."

"And, ultimately, he would settle a healthy pension on you, to go along with the tidy sum you collected from the items you stole."

"His Grace *will* give me a healthy pension. Because he will be none the wiser."

Mrs. Shaw didn't have to spell out her intentions. Raya wasn't supposed to live long enough to tell Strick the truth. She pretended to sway on her feet. "I'm a little dizzy."

She heard the smile in Mrs. Shaw's voice. "How unfortunate for you that you have a fear of heights."

Raya put the back of her hand against her mouth. "I think I am going to be sick." She forced herself to gag.

Mrs. Shaw reflexively stepped back, giving Raya enough room to maneuver. She whirled and used all of her strength to shove the older woman away from her. The housekeeper fell back against the wall between two window openings.

Fury glittered in her eyes. "Why, you—"

Raya planted her feet and braced herself. "Just try it, old lady." Her hands curled into fists at her sides. "I'll toss you out the window so fast you won't know what you're about."

Steps sounded on the stairs. Someone was coming. Strick appeared on the top step with an armful of purple wildflowers. His eyes widened when he spotted Raya. "What in the world?"

Seizing the opportunity, Mrs. Shaw bolted toward the duke. He didn't see the housekeeper coming until just before she rammed into him. The jolt took him by surprise and he stumbled backward, the blooms flying out of his arms in a purple haze.

"Strick!" Raya screamed as he tumbled down the stairs.

The housekeeper kept going, dashing down the stairs in an uneven clatter of footsteps. Raya darted to the landing. She found Strick a few steps down, halfway sprawled against the wall, his long legs askew. A folded piece of paper lay a few steps down from him.

"Are you all right?" she called down.

He struggled to sit up. "Aside from the assault on my ducal dignity, I appear to be intact."

Relief flowed through her. She went to him and helped him get upright and retrieved the paper that had fallen from his jacket. Stuffing it in her pocket, she settled on the stair next to him, drained and relieved, adrenaline still zipping through her.

He rubbed his head. "What was that all about?"

"Your housekeeper is not only humorless and unlikable, she's also a murderer."

His head swung toward Raya. "WHAT?"

"Deena didn't fall. She was pushed."

His eyes widened. "By Mrs. Shaw?"

"And Deena wasn't stealing from Tremayne—your housekeeper was. With Alfred's help." She proceeded to tell him everything, about the list and Otis's revelations, Mrs. Shaw's confession and how she'd lured Raya to the tower.

"Mrs. Shaw? I would never have guessed." He shook his head. "At least I was right about Alfred."

"You were."

"I cannot believe you were willing to come up to the tower in order to return my family's things."

"I thought it would be the perfect farewell gift."

He grimaced. "Don't remind me of your departure."

"The heirlooms are precious objects that belong at Tremayne."

"*You* are precious to me. I would never want you to risk yourself."

"To be fair, when I agreed to accompany Mrs. Shaw to the tower, I had no idea she intended to push me out the window. You were right, by the way, the view is spectacular."

"You weren't afraid?" he asked.

She shook her head in wonder. All these years, a false fear had lived in her. "I was nervous, to be sure, but looking out over the estate, I realized that my fear of heights is more of a child's memory rather than an adult's reality."

"Thank goodness you weren't hurt. When I think of what could have happened . . ." His voice trailed off.

She squeezed his hand. "The only advantage Mrs. Shaw had over me was the element of surprise, which she gave away almost the moment we entered the tower," she reassured him. "I wasn't truly in danger after that. She underestimated me."

"Which we all do to our peril," he said with a smile. "I remember being beyond aggravated that a young beautiful Arab girl from America thought she could run my estate better than me. And then you went and saved my castle from financial ruin."

"You are exaggerating. Your agreement with the railroad helped you become a great deal more solvent."

"But you made Castle Tremayne into an independent self-supporting business, as well as a home." He brought her hand to his lips. "I am forever grateful."

"Oh, I almost forgot." She withdrew the paper from her pocket. "You dropped this when you fell."

He took it from her, a secret smile on his lips. "I wouldn't want to lose this."

"Why?" She watched him slide the paper into his pocket. "What's in it?"

"It's a parting gift."

"For me?"

"I was going to give it to you this evening when we met. But it looks as if our date will have to be postponed." His eyes twinkled as he withdrew the document from his jacket and placed it in her hand. "I might as well give it to you now."

"You seem awfully pleased with yourself." She unfolded the paper to read its contents. It was a legal document. "What is this?"

"You might not own the castle but you are now the legal owner of Castle Tremayne Enterprises."

Raya's mouth dropped open. "This paper gives me all rights to the castle's business operations?" She stared at him. "But why?"

"Because you deserve it. You are the rightful owner of the enterprise. Without you, the business would not exist."

She regarded him with suspicion. "Is this a ploy to keep me here?"

"I agreed to give you ownership of Castle Tremayne Enterprises. Your brother hasn't given you much reason to trust men, but I am a man of my word."

"But I'm leaving soon."

"I am prepared to oversee the business in your absence. But it is yours and always will be."

"I can't take this." She handed the paper over. "It makes no sense."

"I want you to have the security you deserve." He gently pushed the document back on her. "No one will ever be able to take Tremayne Enterprises from you. Whatever happens with your brother, you will always be financially independent. I know how important that is to you."

It was a gift beyond her wildest imaginings. The words on the document blurred as Raya blinked back tears. "But why would you risk your castle's future?" Her throat felt sore. "What if I sold the enterprise to someone awful?"

"You won't. I trust you completely. You might not realize it yet, but Castle Tremayne is in your blood. You will always do right by it."

Raya suddenly remembered something. She shot to her feet. "Oh no! The housekeeper threatened to hurt Otis. We have to find her."

"She won't get far once the word is out that I want her found." He stood up. "Which we should do immediately. Thank goodness I appeared in the tower when I did."

"What are you doing here so early?" Raya asked as they walked down the stairs with her hand in his. "Our picnic isn't until this evening."

"I wanted to create a bed of flowers for us."

"That's very romantic."

"Once we apprehend Alfred and Mrs. Shaw, I intend to demonstrate just how romantic I can be."

She slipped the ownership agreement into her pocket and tightened her hold on his hand. "I cannot wait."

CHAPTER TWENTY-NINE

A re you certain you are all right with coming up here?" Strick asked three days later. "Yes." Raya followed him up the stairs to the lantern tower. They'd finally been able to enjoy their planned picnic at the ruins. Both Mrs. Shaw and Alfred were apprehended shortly after Mrs. Shaw escaped the tower and would soon face justice.

"I worry after what Mrs. Shaw put you through—"

"I've spent half of my life being afraid of heights. I refuse to allow that woman to dictate my behavior."

"You've nothing to prove," Strick told her.

Perhaps not, but Raya wanted to show herself that she could return to the lantern tower. That she wasn't afraid. Nervous, perhaps, but not crippled by paralyzing fear. Plus, the lantern tower was the perfect place to tell Strick her news and present him with his gift.

When they reached the tower, the sweet scent of wildflowers filled the air. Raya's eyes widened. "Oh, Strick, how beautiful." Hundreds of blooms covered the tower floor. He'd made the bed of flowers that he hadn't completed the last time.

He reached for her hand and kissed it. "I want to make love with you one last time amid your wildflowers."

She smiled to herself.

He dropped her hand. "What is that?"

She straightened her lips. "What?"

"That secret smile."

"I'm just thinking about what's to come."

He scowled. "You seem entirely too happy for someone who is abandoning her lover and returning to America." He paused and then asked hesitantly, "Are you looking forward to it?"

"I have missed my family."

"Dare I hope that you will pine for me just a little once you leave?" he asked grumpily.

"I have a gift for you."

"What sort of gift?"

She held out a velvet pouch. "See for yourself."

He loosened the drawstring and spilled its contents into his open palm. He stared down at the ring.

"Do you like it?" she asked eagerly.

"It has Saxon markings."

"I drew the design based on some of your pieces."

He slipped it onto his finger. "It's perfect."

"Are you sure it's not too simple? I asked Derek, the blacksmith in the forge, to make it."

"I shall treasure it always."

"Oh," she said, "and there's something I forgot to mention."

"Hurry up and enlighten me so we can make good use of this bed of flowers."

"When I was up here with Mrs. Shaw, I started to realize something when I looked at the view."

"What?" he asked impatiently

"That you are correct. Tremayne is in my blood." She faced him. "And so are you."

"I was wondering when you'd finally realize that."

"So, I'm not leaving."

His face blanked. "I beg your pardon?"

"You are stuck with me."

"But what of your family? The business?"

"I think we should take an extended marriage trip to New York. While I am there, I can set the business on a profitable course and find the right person to work alongside Salem."

Delight sparkled in his eyes. "I am thrilled, but couldn't you have thought of this solution before now? Or did you prefer to torture me first?"

"Duty compelled me to feel I had no choice but to return home. But when I looked out upon Castle Tremayne from up here, it struck me that the house on Henry Street is no longer home. You, and Tremayne, are my home now."

He pulled her toward him and gave her a long, leisurely kiss that made her legs feel like butter. "Are you certain?"

She nodded. "When Mrs. Shaw threatened to

push me, the idea that I might never see you or this place again was too painful to contemplate. And then, you gave me Tremayne Enterprises. Outright. You attached no conditions to your gift. You placed so much faith in me. How could I *not* trust you with my future?"

"Thank God." He exhaled. "My first command as your husband—"

She lifted a brow. "Command?"

He continued talking despite the interruption. "—will be to put you in charge of all finances."

"All of the finances?"

He nodded. "Household and otherwise. Including the railroad deal. You love money. I prefer to focus on my study of antiquities. It's the perfect arrangement. If you agree, that is."

"As if I would turn down a chance to handle all of our money."

"Precisely." He tugged her toward the closest wall. "Dare I hope all of this money talk has gotten you nice and wet?"

She batted her eyelashes at him. "I do find such talk to be very stimulating."

"I am counting on that." He slid back against the wall and pulled her down onto his lap, his fingers seeking out the slit in her drawers, delighting in the moisture he found there. "Mmm. You're very wet." He stroked her. "Delicious."

He hardened beneath her bottom. She wiggled a little. "I see the future is rising up to meet me." She worked eagerly to unbutton his fly.

"Minx." His cock sprang out, hard and ready. She adjusted her skirts and eased down onto him. He filled her completely. Lust rolled through her. She started to move, taking control.

"That's right, my duchess. Take it." He grunted as he thrust up into her. "Take all of me."

She moved with abandon, for the first time as a woman at liberty to take everything she wanted in life. At the moment, she needed more of Strick. To feel him everywhere. And she wasn't afraid to ask. "Suck my tits."

Fire burned in his eyes. "Look who has acquired a filthy mouth."

"I thought you liked it," she responded, moving urgently over him, the pressure rising in her.

"Oh, I do." He ripped her bodice open, working through the layers of clothing until her breasts were bare. "More than you know." He flicked her nipple with his tongue before sucking the erect tip into his mouth. "I'm going to enjoy these sweet tits of yours every day until we're old and gray."

"And after that?" Raya asked breathlessly.

"I'm going to keep burying myself inside your luscious pussy until I'm too old to move. At which time, you shall have to do all of the work while I recline and enjoy the very spectacular view."

"Demanding to the end, I see." She leaned back, bracing her hands behind her on his muscular thighs. He sucked hard on her breast, teasing one nipple with his tongue before moving to feast on the other. As she rode him, his fingers slid to her quim, stroking slow and steady at first and then faster with increasing intensity. The perfect pace and pressure driving her to the edge.

She was so close. Her legs started to tremble. She squeezed her eyes shut and cried out, the tension in her body finally shattering. She hugged Strick tight as he came inside of her for the first time, pumping his seed into her womb. They remained with their arms wrapped around each other, their heavy breathing in sync.

With waves of pleasure still rolling over her, Raya opened her eyes to gaze out at Castle Tremayne. In the distance, the fortress shone in the late afternoon light, the setting sun casting it in a warm glow, beckoning her like an old friend. Raya smiled.

She was home at last.

ACKNOWLEDGMENTS

My deepest gratitude to my editor, Carrie Feron, and my agent, Kevan Lyon, whose compassion, patience and guidance were needed more than ever during the year I wrote this manuscript.

Thanks also to Asanté Simons, Amy Halperin and the entire team at Avon for all you do to deliver the best version of my books to the world; to the social media bloggers who enthusiastically share my novels with their followers; and to all of you who take the time to read them. I know your time is precious.

To the Fluffy Sloths: Noelle Britte, Diane Sloan and Mary Lofald, there's no one I'd rather share trauma with. What an honor it is to know you.

To Joanna Shupe, Sadia Kullane, Megann Yaqub and Margaret Besheer, I appreciate each of you beyond measure. To Mom, Amy, Eddie and Sameer, I know how lucky I am to have you in my life.

My boys, Zach and Laith, are now young men who lift me up and fill my life with joy. I am in awe of your perseverance. I love you both so much.

And to my husband, Taoufiq, for teaching me that love endures, no matter what.